THE NINE

C.G. HARRIS

Hot
Chocolate
Press

The Judas Files *a 5-book action-packed, supernatural series filled with snarky characters & dark humor.*

The Judas Files Completed Series:

Book 1-THE NINE

Book 2-NEW DOMINION

Book 3-ARTFUL EVIL

Book 4 - WAR ORIGIN

Book 5 - FINAL RUIN

————————

Download the FREE SHORT STORY, Exiled

Join the C.G. Harris Legion

Join the C.G. Harris Legion to receive book intel, useless trivia, special giveaways, plus you'll learn about Hula Harry and get his Drink of the Week.
https://www.cgharris.net/legion-sign-up-page

————————

Printed in the United States of America: First Printing, 2019
Hot Chocolate Press, Fort Collins, Colorado
Cover design by: Karri Klawiter
Print ISBN: 978-1-7333341-1-2

————————

WWW.CGHARRIS.NET

CHAPTER ONE

C old. It's the worst thing about Hell. You could wrap yourself in miles of spare rags and old salvaged clothes then light them on fire, but it never made a difference. When the cold came from inside, nothing could make you warm again.

Hell's been called a lot of different things—Doom Town, The Asylum, Hades, Gahanna, The Rotten Apple. But when Dante wrote The Inferno, he got the story right. Part of it anyway. He talked about the nine circles of Hell and how each one was worse than the last. Subtract levels one through eight, and he had it. Everything is like level nine, where the real baddies went to endure subzero climates and have their nether-regions cradled in cryogenic underwear.

My part of The Nine, as we locals refer to the place, is a cozy little armpit known as Scrapyard City. It's a dry, frigid maze of high-rise shanties, catwalks, and junk metal barely fit to stand, much less protect the Woebegone souls who inhabit them. My black-market shop is grounded right in the middle of it all, giving me a great view of the drum-fires and fellow Woebegone who still believe they can absorb some warmth off the flames. If it's heat they wanted, they were about to get all they could handle.

I glanced out through the open window of my shop and stared at the reddening sky. A firestorm was coming. A twisted reprieve to the humdrum of arctic life.

The crowds of Woebegone going about their business on the catwalks and pathways outside hadn't noticed the impending catastrophe. Most wrapped themselves up like Tusken Raiders, so their clothes obscured their view. I stuck to my t-shirt and button-fly 501s. They kept me just as warm, and I was comfortable.

I pulled a brace out of my shop window and let one of the heavy overhead shutters come down. My little store happened to be one of the only shielded structures in Scrapyard City. If I didn't close up before the impending storm, my tiny slice of paradise would be overrun with every killer, thief, and rapist within two-hundred yards. The bolt for the shutter slid in place with a grinding thunk. I was about to reach for the brace holding up the other, but something caught my eye on the corrugated walkway outside my window.

A young girl, a Woebegone no more than nineteen, staggered along looking less than oriented. I squinted, thinking she looked familiar, and shied back when I remembered from where. A girl from my past life. The resemblance was uncanny. The moment I made the connection, I knew it couldn't be her, but she made my arm hair prickle anyway.

I watched the girl for a few moments, her wide, erratic eyes shifting from place to place, body language and movement aimless. She was a fresh born out of the Gnashing Fields— the endless pools of burning sulfur where Woebegone suffer an eternity of torture and rebirth when they die in The Nine—no doubt about it. She would have no memory—no clue about where she was or what happened. At least not until she regained her memories in a few weeks, but the firestorm was coming now.

I squeezed my eyes shut. It wasn't my problem. There were hundreds—thousands—of other fresh born out there, just like her. The storm would have them all. Tough luck, but that's the way it was. I wouldn't run out and risk my neck for some strange girl, even if she did remind me of someone from my past life. Someone I owed an enormous debt to. Someone who suffered because I didn't have the guts to help her sooner.

I pulled the brace to the second shutter and let the heavy steel slam before ramming the last bolt home. Then I ran out the door, risking my stupid neck for a girl I didn't know.

The other Woebegone had noticed the sky by now. It was hard to miss. A rolling cloud of thick, black smoke full of lightning and swirling flame. The girl stood there, barefoot in jeans and a thin plaid shirt. The crowd tossed her around like an old dodge ball. Her hands were up, protecting either side of her face, as if she could box herself in against the insanity. I sighed as the first drop of molten fire hit the ground.

I wound through the frantic crowd, feeling hot wind swirl and gust through the twisted pathways. The Woebegone ran every-where, and I lost sight of the girl several times as the mass of bodies bounced me back and forth. She had her hands over her ears now, squinting her eyes shut and shaking her head. I sprinted forward, shouldering the Woebegone aside. One hit me hard enough to spin me backward, but I kept going, making my way to the girl.

"Miss," I called out to her. "Miss, if you come with me, I can help you."

My hand touched her shoulder, and she spun to look at me. The innocence in her deep blue eyes was so plain; I could not imagine how she ended up in a place like this. They were the color of robin's eggs, and her blond hair was a tangled mess around her fingers.

"Miss," I said again, ducking a little to match her height. "You need help." I reached out to take her hand. The young woman met my eyes, and in one smooth motion, she slapped me so hard my cheek felt like it had caved in.

She screamed, "Leave me alone," and scurried off like a frightened rabbit.

I stood there rubbing my face and took inventory of my teeth with my tongue.

The girl didn't run far. She sprinted up two flights of rusty stairs, only to find herself cornered between a corrugated steel wall and a dead-end rail—the one thing standing between her and a 30-foot drop to the frozen ground.

Her gaze darted to every dark corner or ledge big enough to squeeze a toe onto. She seemed desperate for an escape, but she wouldn't find one. Scrapyard City had collapsed and been put back together so many times the entire place looked more like a loose pile of junk than a collection of structures. The city was a virtual labyrinth of ladders, stairs, and catwalks that led nowhere. And if the firestorm turned out to be half as bad as it appeared, the resident Woebegone would be rebuilding their ramshackle structures yet again.

I tried not to come off as creepy or threatening as I grinned and crept toward the frightened girl's cornered position.

Nope. Not creepy or threatening at all.

"What's happening? Where am I? Leave me alone." She shook her head in little panicked jerks.

My hands were out in front of me to show I meant no harm when a hot stream of molten fire grazed my forearm. I winced and ground my teeth. The storm was ready to break. I didn't know how much longer I could risk standing out in the open and still make it back to my shop in one, less than overdone, piece.

The girl screamed again. A wordless shriek born of pure hysteria.

"I'm getting fried trying to help you. Stop wailing and come here."

The girl answered with another scream, only this time she punctuated the sonic gesture with a turn and climbed onto the rail.

"Whoa." I froze, and my stomach dropped into my boots. She wasn't even going to wait for the storm. "Calm down." My hand found its way into my pocket, and I laced my fingers through a familiar metallic object. "You are not going to make it if you jump. Let me help you."

I took a step forward, and the girl threw her legs over the rail. The wind picked up, and the ever-increasing hailstorm of Satan's molten spit became harder and harder to avoid. If this girl didn't come down in the next few seconds, we were both going to take a long soak in the Gnashing Field sulfur pools.

The girl tilted her head and leaned forward, but she had her hands wrapped around the rail, not quite committed to her suicidal insanity. I lunged, drawing the Knuckle Stunner out of my pocket as I went. She never heard me coming.

I caught her wrist and jerked her back just as her fingers loosened on the rusty metal railing.

"Sorry about this, Miss, but we're out of time. We have to go." I tapped her with the Knuckle Stunner wrapped in my fist, a defense weapon made right here in The Nine. The high-tech set of brass knuckles short circuited the brain—temporarily. How long the effect lasted and how much the blow hurt depended on how hard you punched. The girl fell into my arms, and I managed to pull her back over the rail and heft her onto my shoulder.

A loose piece of tin rattled against a nearby wall, so I tore the panel off the rusty screw that held it in place. The razor-sharp hunk of metal wasn't perfect, but it made a decent makeshift fire umbrella. The flimsy sheet of metal might prevent us from gaining a few red-hot piercings on our way back to my shop.

Scorching wind assaulted my face and threatened to steal my garden shed umbrella as we crossed the open catwalk. The girl still didn't move. Definitely a good thing. If she woke up now, I'd have to leave her. Woebegone began to fall. They sprawled down the stairs, sometimes two and three deep, making it all but impossible to navigate with the girl's dead weight on one shoulder and my shield clutched in my other hand.

I lost my balance, and my heel came down hard on someone's fingers. They made an audible crunch. A Woebegone screamed, and I glanced down to see a man lying below me, a three-inch hole burned through his bicep.

"If you don't move, you're going to have a lot worse things to worry about." I gave him a nudge with my sneaker, but he just looked at me with a pathetic expression. "Sorry, Bud. Only one rider per storm. If you don't care enough to help yourself, I can't help you either."

I trudged forward, hearing the hollow ting of molten fire hit my shield. The Woebegone had thinned, many finding shelter, more finding death and a return to the Gnashing Fields. My legs felt like they were ready to fold like cheap plastic. I really needed to think about jogging or maybe check out that new CrossFit torture craze.

My shop came into view, and I groaned, coming to a momentary halt. A goon had taken up squatter's rights in my doorway. He stood there with an ear-to-ear grin, watching as the Woebegone fell to the increasing storm. I had left without locking my door. Not a smart move. Lucky for me, the goon seemed too preoccupied with the show to go in and lock the place down.

His face hardened as I made my way toward him. "Shove off, this is my place."

The guy had a good eight inches on me and at least fifty pounds. Marred, poorly done tattoos covered his shaved head and shirtless body. My favorite artistic catastrophe was the pelican stenciled across his fat belly. The bird wore a sailor's hat and bore one scrawny leg half the length of the other.

"Afraid I can't do that," I said. "This is my place, so if you could step aside ..."

Pelican Belly made his move. I tossed my shield in his direction as a distraction and drew the Knuckle Stunner. With the girl on my shoulder, I couldn't dodge his hay-maker completely, but I managed to sneak my own shot in. This time the Knuckle Stunner went off with an audible crack, and Pelican Belly went flying. He hit the wall and staggered, then he straightened and shot me a smile, inviting me in with a wave of his grimy hand.

CHAPTER TWO

My face ached from the girl's slap, and now Pelican Belly's glancing ham-hock blow. All in all, I was beginning to feel a little under appreciated. I wasn't sure if Pelican Belly had noticed the Knuckle Stunner. My first shot barely connected. He had managed his own maneuver to avoid the full force of my punch. He was more agile than I gave him credit for. That, and I hauling a hundred and twenty-pound girl on one shoulder. I didn't have time to fool around, so I gambled he was as ignorant as he looked. A clear shot at my face should be enough to do the trick.

"Nice of you to deliver a girl." He met my step and drew back, thinking he could end the whole thing with one punch. "I'll have some fun with her during the storm."

Dumb as dumb could get. He was right about one thing. One punch was enough. I surged forward, ducking his blow, and lanced him square in the chest with the Knuckle Stunner. He never had a chance. It wasn't pretty, but Pelican Belly went out like a birthday candle—fat rolls, bad breath, and all. I stepped over the pile of tattooed blubber, set my more tender cargo down inside the shop, and then headed out to see to my unwanted guest.

When I got back in, I slammed the door closed with a heavy thunk. The sound always reminded me of the door on an old Cadillac. I threw all three bolts and leaned my forehead against the pitted steel to catch my breath. Pelican Belly had been heavy, but I had managed to drag him to a spot under an overhang. At least he was safer than lying in the open. He should wake up in plenty of time to find real shelter, provided his ego didn't send him running back to my shop. Much as he may have deserved it, I couldn't let him die. I didn't want his blood on my hands. Pelican Belly wouldn't be the first Woebegone I had sent to the Gnashing Fields, but I didn't enjoy killing the way most lowlifes in The Nine did.

A weak groan rose from the floor behind me, and I looked to see the girl stir in the hazy light. Her eyes fluttered open, and she skittered backward into the wall as she scanned our cramped interior. The front of my shop was about the size of a walk-in closet, but reinforced I-beams and rusty steel walls made the place about as bomb proof as it could get.

I reached to the counter on my left and retrieved a shabby box of matches and a homemade lantern I had fabricated from an old canteen and some scrounged motor oil. My cramped metal room got coal mine dark with all the doors and windows secured. It didn't bother me, but I figured a little light might go a long way toward calming my guest's anxiety. The match flared to life with a flash of eye-watering sulfur. When I touched the greasy wick, a small flame illuminated the shop with an oily yellow glow. An ominous tendril of thick, black smoke rose from the lamp, and long shadows flickered along the walls, dancing with the howling wind outside. I realized I had achieved an atmosphere even more creepy than the dark.

The girl's gaze fell to a sliding metal door on the back wall. I stepped forward to head her off before she could move.

"Hold on. Don't get worked up again." I held out my hands and tried to appear calm, but I made sure to stay out of swinging distance. "You're safe. I promise. If you want to go out and kill yourself, I'll open the doors and send you on your suicidal way after the firestorm. For now, sit tight and relax. This is the safest place in Scrapyard City. My shop has stood through hundreds of storms. It's not going to fall during this one."

The girl peered at me, drew her knees to her chest, and hugged them in her arms.

I took that as an expression of agreement. At least for now. "Good."

I released a thick thermal blanket attached to the ceiling and let the weighted fabric cover the door like a grungy grey curtain. "So, what should I call you? Do you remember anything? Your name?"

The girl's face went pale, and tears welled into her eyes. She shook her head.

"Wow, you are a fresh one." I moved over to the shop's big front window and released another thermal blanket above the counter. "Don't worry, it'll all come back after a while. Waking out of the fields is no fun, but we've all been through it. For now, why don't I call you, Stray?"

I smiled and tried to seem reassuring, but Stray just stared up at me.

I raised an eyebrow. "Try to contain your excitement."

She still didn't move.

"Look, if you just sit there, this is going to be a long few hours. I saved your life, the least you could do is offer a little conversation."

"Do you know what happened to me?" Her voice came out stronger than I expected, high and youthful, but confident.

"Not specifically, no. There's a lot of ways to die in The Nine. My guess is some jerk knocked you off for fun, or you offed yourself. Doesn't really matter. Every death lands in the Gnashing Fields. I don't understand the suicide angle though. Woebegone do it all the time, but killing yourself to be tortured and reborn right back where you started? Doesn't make any sense."

Stray shuddered. "I remember that. The burning. The pain never seemed to end."

I sighed and nodded. "Another one of their cute tricks. You might only be out of the action here for a few days, but your perception of time in the Gnashing Fields is different. Your stay can feel like an eternity when you're in the pools."

Stray stood and brushed herself off, looking a little more steady. "So, what is this place? What do you do here?"

Stray reached for the sliding door at the back of the tiny room.

"Hold on." I put out a hand to stop her, but it was too late.

The door slid to the side to reveal my secret warehouse stash. A gutted school bus that had somehow made its way beneath piles of rubble and building collapses. Dozens of beams and girders criss-crossed the area above and around the old yellow husk. The thing could take a direct hit from an atom bomb without getting a scratch. A subway train had crashed through the far wall and smashed the front end of the bus at some point in ancient history, although I couldn't imagine when. I had never seen a school bus or subway train since I'd been here, and I'd been here for a very long time.

The bus's side door opened up to the rear wall of my shop, giving me a convenient little staircase to ascend into my hideaway. Stray bounded up the tall steps like a pixie made of super balls. I hit the first step, missed the second, and did my best impression of a bobsled racing down a rock quarry. By the time I recovered, she had already made a beeline for the most valuable item in my stores. Almost a quarter case of unexpired, individually wrapped Hostess Twinkie cakes.

She reached for them, and my hand shot into my pocket to draw out the Knuckle Stunner as I sprinted toward her. "I don't want to hurt you," I growled. "Don't touch the Twinkies."

Stray turned to look at me and noticed the Knuckle Stunner in my hand. "Are you serious? I can't even remember my name. I was just hungry."

"You may not understand the whole picture here, but the items in this store are priceless to a lot of Hellions out there. They are beyond difficult to come by."

Stray surveyed the mishmash merchandise around her. Two cans of Dr. Pepper, a few photos, a locket, and a box of old cigars.

"Not many have seen this room, and less have seen what's stored inside. I saved your life, but I can make you this promise." I leaned in close and narrowed my eyes. "If you ever speak a word about what you saw here, you won't live to see another day. I know enough secrets about the Hellions down here to guarantee your stay in the Gnashing Fields will be long and recurring."

"Over Twinkies?" Stray raised an unfazed eyebrow. "Seriously."

She tilted her head as if she replayed a part of our conversation in her mind. "You trade goods for secrets, don't you? You said you know lots of secrets about the Hellions. You trade this stuff for information and then what? Trade information for more stuff? That's pretty smart. You stay in business with a built-in insurance plan. What do you do with the information? Blackmail or something?"

I stood there dumbfounded for a second. "What? No—not blackmail. People ask me to find information. I have the means to do it, that's all."

"So, you trade them the information, and they use it for blackmail."

I smacked my face and shook my head. "No—I don't know. Look, for someone who just crawled out of the soup, you're a little too smart for your own good."

Stray shrugged. "Sorry. Don't worry. I'm not going to tell anyone about your shop, I promise. You saved my life, and at the moment, you're my only friend."

She smiled and glanced at the locket laid over the back of a lonely torn-up green passenger seat. "Can I touch this without you zapping me?"

I rolled my eyes and threw my hands out, "Why not?"

She picked up the locket and popped the tiny latch open, revealing the picture inside.

"Who wanted this?"

"No one," I said. "That's mine. The piece has sentimental value."

"Is this your mom or something? She looks young."

"All right, you saw the locket. Now put it down."

Stray laid the old silver piece across the seat with tender care and glanced back at me again. "What's in your hand? Is that what you knocked me out with earlier?"

"Yes. If you keep asking me questions, I'm going to show you how it works."

Stray smiled and kept talking. "Are you allowed to own something like that? Seems like the big baddies would be awfully uptight about anyone having weapons."

"Woebegone are not allowed to own anything, much less weapons, but I'm different. I know people."

A gust of wind whipped against the side of the shop causing a stream of dust to fall from the ceiling. Stray looked at me, and I smiled, gratified that something had the ability to make her stop chattering, at least for the moment.

"We'll ride out the storm, and then you can be on your way. If you keep your promise, I will help you settle in somewhere until you regain your memory and figure out where you belong, deal?"

Stray held her fist out. I stared at it.

"Fist bump," she said. "I think it's a thing."

I reached out and rapped her fist with mine. A huge bang came from the door at the same time, making me jump and drawing a little squeak from Stray.

"I know you're in there. Let me in, or I will put my fist through the wall and pull your scrawny ass out through the hole."

Pelican Belly. Apparently, his ego had brought him back after all.

CHAPTER THREE

This guy just didn't quit. What he lacked in brains, he made up for in tenacity, and he lacked a whole lot in the noodle department.

"That's a steel reinforced door." My voice rang off the tiny metal space, but with all the wind, lava rain, and general screaming going on outside, I figured he would have a hard time hearing me. "You would need more firepower to blast through that door than any Woebegone could get their hands on—at least not without my help," I added the last part under my breath. "Your size twelves won't make a dent. Don't be stupid. Go find a safe place to ride out the storm. You can beat my brains in later."

I walked over to open a false panel in the wall above Stray's head. She had retreated to the far corner and slid to the floor, hugging her knees to her chest again. I pulled out my Whip-Crack—another Hell-born weapon, and by far my favorite—an unholy offspring of a twelve-foot bullwhip and a chainsaw. The trajectory could be controlled remotely through the grip, and the blades worked through some ultra-complicated centrifugal gearing I didn't begin to understand. All I knew was, move the whip and the blades spun. Move the whip fast, and deforestation laws began to tremble.

The whip played out on the floor, sounding like a thousand chainmail snakes slithering in a writhing mass of evil death. The raspy noise sent goosebumps over my skin.

"Go back to your hole and ride out the storm," I cried again. No response. I glanced at Stray. She shrugged, looking as surprised as I was.

"You still out there, Pelican Belly?" I listened again, but no answer.

"Maybe he has more brains than we thought." I gave Stray a sideways grin. "We might as well make ourselves comfortable ..."

A huge thunk shook the shop in the way only three-hundred pounds of man-mush could. Pelican Belly must have thrown his whole body at the door. The storm picked up speed outside. At this point, there was no way he could avoid the rain of fire plummeting out of the sky. Molten rock would be coming down in big chunks now, hammering everything they hit. The wind would be strong enough to whisk the lava into a sandstorm of fiery glass. I didn't understand how Pelican Belly survived. Maybe he had come up with some sort of makeshift corrugated steel cocoon. Whatever he did, it wouldn't last long.

His shouts became screams. Stray pressed herself further into the corner with her hands over her ears. Another thump hit the door, then another. I took a step forward, my humanity driving me to let him in and save him from his own arrogant stupidity. But I willed myself to stop. My reward for such an action would be death—and not just mine, but Stray's as well. The blows came faster, weaker now. More desperate than sure. A lump rose up in my throat, and I redoubled my will. Something metal ricocheted off the outside of the shop. Pelican Belly let out one last shriek, and then there was silence.

I stood for a moment, half expecting another thump at the door. Stray looked up, pulling her hands away from her ears to check for a noise. I glanced down at her and wanted to say everything would okay. Instead, I white knuckled the handle of my Whip-Crack. I doubted the sound of my stretched voice would be all that soothing. Her eyes brimmed with tears, but she made no move to wipe them away. I opened my mouth to say something despite my strain. My words were interrupted by another, much more civilized knock.

My head twisted back toward the door, and I felt the blood drain from my face. Impossible. The storm hammered the outside of my shop like a freight train. No Woebegone could survive being out in those conditions. The walls of my store shook so bad I worried we might not make it through.

Another polite knock.

"Gabriel Gantry. I know you are in there. Come out. You have been summoned to The Judas Agency."

The low graveled voice echoed off the walls, seeming to drag a thousand screaming voices in behind it. A Hellion. Not just any Hellion; only a high-level demon could withstand the kind of storm that raged outside. What would a hellion like that want with me? The thought made my skin want to crawl away and hide.

I searched my mind for any reason for him to be there. My little black-market business wasn't legal, but the Judas Agency didn't trouble itself with this sort of small-time stuff. They were known as the Disaster Factory for a reason. They went Topside to wreak havoc among the living. To come after someone down here, it would have to be big ... or personal.

"That harpy never mentioned her gluten intolerance problem," I shouted at the door. "She asked for a Twinkie. It's not my fault." I tried to sound indignant, but fear made my voice crack like a prepubescent 13-year-old's. "Are you the uncle she talked about? I told her I would find her a whole case of gluten free cupcakes, but I need time. I can't pull cupcakes out of my butt. Even if I could, she wouldn't want them."

"This is not about a harpy," came the voice again. "Though I may look into your black-market dealings when my benefactor is through with you. Come out. You have been summoned. If you do not come out, I am coming in."

I sucked in a breath. A bozo with a size twelve boot was one thing, a high-level Hellion was another. This guy could peel the shop door like the outside of an onion and never shed a tear. If he saw my stores in the back, I would be done for. A couple of Twinkies might buy me some trouble, but my whole stock along with my little weapons stash might be enough to put me in the Gnashing Fields for a very long time.

"Alright, I'll come out as soon as the storm's over." I stalled, trying to think of a way to escape. "I don't want to die out there."

The exasperation in the Hellion's voice became almost palpable. "If I were charged with bringing back your corpse, you would be dead. You will be under my protection from the storm. This is your last opportunity to come in peace."

I stood still, staring at my feet. My mind raced: stall, escape, brute force. All failed or suicidal. I couldn't see a way out of this one. I sighed and hit the retract button on the Whip-Crack. The serpentine weapon coiled to a manageable size. I placed it and the Knuckle Stunner back in the wall and closed the false panel.

Stray bolted to her feet and grabbed my arm. "What are you doing?"

"I'm coming out," I shouted. "Give me one second." I gave Stray a crooked smile and did my best to look sure of my decision.

"Stay in the shop until I get back. Don't go out or open the doors, and you'll be safe. If I don't come back at all, I guess the place is yours. But I'm coming back, so don't get any ideas." I rubbed the spiky buzzed hair on my head and stared at the door again. "Just take care of my shop. Don't let anyone rob me blind, and I'll set you up like a queen. Can you manage that?"

Stray nodded. "I'll keep everything safe while you're gone. Thanks for helping me and for letting me stay. I know you didn't have to."

I nodded without looking at her and walked toward the door. The heat shield still hung in place, so I stepped around it to throw back the bolts. I didn't know how much good it would do, but if the Hellion couldn't follow through on his promise, I wanted to be sure I was the only barbecued Woebegone in the shop today.

CHAPTER FOUR

I opened the door and got a real look at a full-on firestorm for the first time—something few if any Woebegone had ever seen without facing a gruesome demise. The air itself seemed to be on fire. Wind whipped dust devils into self-sustaining heat vortexes, and fire fell from the sky in every conceivable form. Collapsing metal creaked, moaned, and shrieked out a symphony of ear shattering noise, and the smell of charred earth and burnt flesh made my eyes water. I slapped both hands over my nose and mouth but even that didn't block out the stench. Huge solid chunks of flaming brimstone pummeled rooftops, walkways, and walls, exploding like fracture grenades, sending hot stone shards in every direction. Molten raindrops and flaming hail the size of golf balls pelted everything in sight. Seeing this storm was like having a ringside seat to the end of the world.

I steadied myself against the door, trying to take in the sheer brutality of it all. My toe hit something hard on the ground. A new brimstone addition to the rocky landscape. When I glanced down, I wished I hadn't. My foot had connected with Pelican Belly's knee, or at least the mangled lump had resembled his knee. His body had been charred and stripped by the fiery wind and falling rock. He was nothing more than a broken, burning pile of blackened blubber. Even that would be gone soon. I was glad I still held a hand over my face to cover the gagging heaves that followed as I turned away.

I forced myself to shove the information overload to the side and regain my composure. When I did, a small underlying detail stood out. I had opened the door on a firestorm and hadn't fried like an over-nuked 7-Eleven burrito. The thought made me glance toward the burning lump of bad tattoos, but I managed to jerk my head around before my eyes betrayed me. The temperate atmosphere made my skin tingle with unease, unused to performing in an environment between arctic and inferno. Even my door, which should have fried my hand like a spam omelet, felt cool to the touch. An object hurled out of the sky. A white-hot comet constructed of stone and death streaked toward me. I let out a shriek and crossed my arms over my head, as if that would help. Given a little more time to react, I might have ducked, or at least peed, but the falling mini-mountain impacted with a muffled thud and deflected away before I had time to do either. I opened one eye and checked on all my appendages—everything present and accounted for. Then I gazed upon a sight almost as imposing as the storm.

An eight-foot, almost human looking Hellion emerged from around the corner of my tiny shop. He had albino skin, snow white hair and blood red eyes. Long, linen-white horns swept out of his forehead and reached toward the sky. Yeah, other than that, dead ringer for human.

I closed the door behind me, checking to see if any heat from the firestorm had penetrated the barrier. The fire blanket didn't even seem singed. If I knew how to pull off a trick like that, I'd be set for life ... death, whatever.

"So, what's this all about?" I crossed my arms, uncrossed them, then tried to lean back on the door, but I lost my balance and had to catch myself. I opted to stand like an awkward idiot instead. "Is there any way I can just pay a fine or something? You and I could come to some sort of agreement. I'd be glad to throw in a little something to show my thanks, if you know what I mean."

The Hellion stared down at me. "Did you offer me a bribe?"

"A bribe?" I laughed and waved my arms around like a drunk marionette. "No, I think you should show appreciation when someone does something nice, that's all. Is it a bribe when you receive a thank you card? No, it's good manners."

I didn't know a Hellion had the ability to roll his eyes, but this one did. He turned his gigantic bulk away and started walking. Huge feathered wings hung close to his back and fluttered along with his many layers of flowing white robes. The image painted a picture that appeared both filthy and regal at the same time. Like a majestic grey eagle who'd weathered a terrific storm. His wings were somehow soiled and lusterless, and at the same time prepared to soar. I didn't want to follow him, but every step he took raised the temperature around me. Whatever trick he used to keep me safe didn't have much of a range.

I sprinted to catch up to my escort, and the air around me went cool again. The Hellion held some sort of device in his hand. The little silver orb glowed blue and pulsed every time a stone or flame came close enough to threaten us, which was pretty much always.

"Is that a shield?" I asked. "What would it take to get something like that?"

"More pain than your soul could provide in an eternity."

"What about a low interest credit plan instead?"

The Hellion peered down at me and rolled his thumb over a knob on the side of the shield generator. Sweat began to pour out of my head, and my eyeballs threatened to dehydrate and turn to sand.

"I was sent to bring you alive. They said nothing about uninjured."

"Alright, alright," I held out my hands and squinted my eyes shut. "Turn the A/C back on. I was kidding. I kid when I get nervous. It's how I cope."

"You must be nervous a great deal of the time."

I looked up at the Hellion, trying to read his face, but he never cracked so much as a grin. "A demon with jokes, now I've seen everything." My comedic companion rolled the knob again, and the temperature made a return trip from the surface of the sun.

"So, seriously, are you going to tell me what this is all about? This isn't about Celia? I swear I didn't know she had a twin sister."

My eyes were glued to the Hellion and his little shield gadget, so when he stopped and opened the door to a beat-up VW Bug, he caught me by surprise. Most of the car's top, along with the two front seats, had been removed, allowing the huge demon to sit in the back and drive with his head and horns sticking out the roof. The body appeared to be intact, but saying the car had an abundance of patina would be an understatement. The chrome bumpers seemed to be the only pristine part of the car.

I stood on the driver's side and gawked at the rusted monstrosity.

"1955 Oval Window VW Bug," The Hellion exclaimed. "The only true classic of the twentieth century." He started the car and black smoke emanated from the exhaust pipe, the hood vents, the undercarriage, the tail lights—pretty much everywhere.

"Is this thing safe?" I asked. "And why didn't the storm destroy your car?"

The Hellion rummaged around the passenger side floor for a moment and came up with a seat belt. He tossed it to me and said, "If it will make you feel better, you can put this on. I wouldn't leave a prize like this unprotected. This vehicle has its own shield generator. Now get in before I turn the A/C off again."

I carried the seatbelt around to the passenger side of the car and got in. "All the demons they could have sent, and I got Jay Leno."

The old Bug revved up and pulled away, sounding like a three-quarter ton truck slogging through the La Brea Tar Pits. A veritable fog of black exhaust plumed out behind us. I looked over at my horned chauffeur. The barest hint of a smile touched his lips as the wind parted his snowy white hair.

We raced through the narrow streets at breakneck speeds. The Woebegone were clear, thanks to the firestorm, so there was no need to worry about the usual crowds and wandering pedestrians. Molten rain, wind, and gravel-sized brimstone still streaked out of the rolling fire clouds above, but the storm had slowed. My companion's little device made short work of everything, allowing us to fly through the dwindling inferno like a Teflon-coated snowball.

Shanty high-rises had collapsed into heaps of steel and mortar. The Gnashing Fields would be overflowing tonight. It would take time for the Woebegone to return and rebuild, but that's what we did. Rebuilding was all we could to do. We built hope, watched hope be destroyed, died, suffered, got reborn and started over. Afterlife in The Nine.

A few more erratic turns, and we arrived at a high-rise complex I had hoped to never see. All mirrored glass and rusted steel, the building stood as six separate structures, ringed to face one another and connected with a bridge at every sixth floor. The first building stood at six stories, and every building after that stood six stories taller, giving the whole structure an ascending, or descending appearance, depending on your perspective.

My escort pulled up to the front of the tallest building and yanked the emergency brake. "Go to the top floor and tell the receptionist who you are. They are expecting you."

"You're not going to walk me up? How do you know I won't run?"

This time, the Hellion did smile. The sight terrified me. He hadn't seen a dentist in at least a century.

"Running would be—unwise."

I stepped out of the car, and the Bug tore away before I could answer—or close the door. Must be late to pick up his next victim.

I glanced up at the sky, and to my astonishment the rolling black clouds parted over the structure as if it were an island in a stream, leaving the building untouched by the storm. I shook my head and considered running anyway, but the Hellion's fetid smile stuck in my head. *Running would be unwise.* Something told me he was right. I had a feeling the Judas Agency would find me no matter where I ran. I had become a goldfish in a bowl, and the Judas cat stared in, ready for a snack. There was no other choice. I had to go in and straighten out whatever misunderstanding had gotten me into this mess. The junior agent assigned to my case better have a good sense of humor—better than my ghost-face chauffeur, at least.

My feet required more persuasion than my brain, but they shuffled forward several moments later, and I made my way inside. The elevator to the top floor oozed more posh and luxury than anything found on earth with the Topside crowds. I wondered why the Hellion allowed me to enter the place on my own. Criminals did not head into prison through the grand ballroom. They came in through the back door, with guards, handcuffs, and the occasional nightstick-shaped contusion.

The elevator dinged, and the doors opened, revealing an office area full of brass, dark wood, and marble. The floor tiles spelled out *Judas Agency*, in flourished intricate detail, and led to a pair of tall, double glass doors several yards away.

I crossed the entry and made my way through the doors to the desk, where a Woebegone woman wearing a dark dress and glasses sat waiting. She peered up at me, squinting a pair of wary brown eyes.

"I'm Gabriel Gantry. I think I have an appointment." I did my best to come off as confident, or at least not like a puddle of quivering Jell-O. My trembling legs did not cooperate.

The Woebegone woman picked up a phone and said a few words I couldn't hear, then she hung up. "Mr. Iscariot is waiting for you. You may go in.

CHAPTER FIVE

"I'm sorry," I said with a nervous laugh. "You said I am seeing who?"

"Mr. Iscariot. I suggest you do not keep him waiting."

I held out a hand to interrupt her. It shook like an epileptic flounder, so I jerked my arm back to my side. "Is there more than one Mr. Iscariot? Like John or Bob?" My voice went up about three octaves, and the lower half of my body went full on wiggling toddler, ready to make a graceless sprint toward the elevator.

"Geez, I hope there's not more than one of them," she whispered. "One's about all I can handle. Do you know how many times he's sent me back to the Gnashing Fields?"

I stopped breathing.

"I'm kidding about the Gnashing Fields. He likes me." She looked me up and down for a second. "I would get in there if I were you, though."

Then, as if she read my mind, I heard an audible clunk come from the elevator doors.

"Just so you're aware, that was the sound of a timed lock. It helps to deter a quick exit. Mr. Iscariot's name has an ... effect on some people." She wrinkled her nose as if she were sharing some dirty bit of gossip that had nothing to do with me.

I nodded like a clueless zombie and stared at the huge double doors to the left of the receptionist's desk. Intricate scenes were carved into the dark wood, starting at the top with a depiction of the Last Supper and what appeared to be the betrayal of Christ, then a gruesome suicide. After that, the scenes degraded into every sort of torture and torment imaginable. A graphic biography to remind all ye who enter here, this place meant business.

I knocked so softly I'm not sure my knuckles even touched the wood. On the third timid tap, both doors swung wide with an ominous groan.

"Come in, Mr. Gantry." The voice came from inside and to the right of the open doors.

I glanced down at my pants to make sure I hadn't wet myself, then I walked inside.

Judas Iscariot's cavernous office did not disappoint any more than his door had. The huge room practically radiated dark wood and blood red marble. The walls were a museum quality display of masterful paintings depicting graphic views of the plague, Jewish concentration camps, great famines, and every sort of war fought with sticks, swords, or suicide bombers. Scattered among the horror show, glass cases held creative tools, torture devices, and statues depicting savage atrocities that almost defied imagination. The whole scene made me want to bolt out the door and try my luck with the elevator—or perhaps an open window.

Judas sat at the far end of the cavernous office behind his desk, another acre of rare dark wood. He wore the piece as one more accessory to his power and intimidation. I forced my feet to move toward him as he stared me down with dark eyes.

Behind him stood two Hellions. One I recognized. The red-eyed albino giant who had brought me here. I hadn't rushed up after he had dropped me off, but he must have taken the back-door Bat-Elevator to beat me to Judas's office.

The other I did not know, but she intimidated me more than the Albino. She crouched like a raptor atop a platform in her corner of the room, looking ready to pounce. Her black leathery wings had spikes along the ridges, and her thick, frayed hair shot out like a dark mane cut off at her shoulders. The tight black leather armor she wore revealed more skin than it covered. The outfit served no function, at least not for a fight, but somehow, I doubted she needed it. The loose blindfold over her eyes disturbed me most of all. As if she had to be sightless in order to remain under control. Despite the blindfold, she tracked my every move with a very disheartening grin.

"Thank you for coming," Judas said. "My associate, Procel, said you came quietly. Not many do."

"I can't imagine why. This is such a nice place. Maybe a little dark, but nothing a few lamps couldn't fix. Have you ever considered skylights?"

The Hellion on the perch lost her grin and leaned forward. I leaned back and lost a little of the bladder control I had worried about earlier.

Judas held up a hand to stop her from moving. "Mastema and Procel are my most trusted and faithful associates. Neither will abide a flippant attitude."

I nodded, taking a step back to regain my balance. For the moment, my body wouldn't be persuaded to lean forward again.

Judas stood and orbited his desk to approach me. He had long brown hair, an unkempt beard and angular features. His suit was impeccably tailored, black silk piled upon more black silk. He eyed me up and down as he circled, sizing me up like a used car.

"I've been watching you, Gabe," Judas said. "Your friends call you Gabe?"

I nodded again.

He smiled and nodded as well. "I hope we can be friends, Gabe. I want to make you a proposition. Not many can survive as long as you have without being recycled through the Gnashing

Fields. You manage to run a successful black-market business. I understand you have amassed quite a stockpile."

This time I nodded in furious little jerks. "If there's something I can get for you ... Anything at all, let me know."

Judas laughed. "I am not interested in the items you keep in that husk of a school bus."

I managed to control most of my shock, but my eyebrows went up enough for Judas to pick up on.

"I am aware of your little enterprise and how you work. The Woebegone come to you with secrets. Those learned by accident or secrets you send them out to obtain. In return, you provide the goods stockpiled in your little store. The secrets go to low level Hellions possessing enough power to travel to the surface and steal your trinkets as payment for the information. Hellions who may need leverage against a competitor or a jilted lover looking for revenge. A nice operation, but what benefits do you receive?"

"Nothing, I swear," I stammered. "Sometimes I eat a Twinkie or read a book before I give it out, but that's all."

Judas smiled and nodded. "Admirable, but I think a talent like yours should be rewarded, don't you?"

For the first time I found myself a little confused. I thought I had bought a one-way ticket to a torture tunnel, but had Judas Iscariot just offered me, what—a job?

"I need people like you on my staff. Those skilled at gathering secrets and manipulating the Woebegone. If you can handle them, manipulating people Topside should be easy."

He paused a moment to allow his words to sink in.

"You want me to work as a Topside agent?" My astonishment won out, and my eyebrows broke loose and tried to crawl up my forehead.

"Look around you, the things you see are always the end result of careful planning and manipulation. People such as yourself can bring such harm and suffering to the world. Hitler, Stalin, Hussein; all pawns to my agents. Whispers and secrets are more powerful than any bomb, gun, or sword. That sort of power can't be manu-factured; you must be born with the talent. You possess that talent, Gabe."

I did not find myself at a loss for words often, but this was one of those times. The most influential betrayer in history just told me I had the talent to sway nations. The fact that he wanted me to sway them into killing one another made me feel sick.

"You should be aware that a position like this isn't like your black-market operation in Scrapyard City. With it, you will earn all the perks an agent of the Judas Agency deserves. In addition to the protection of the Agency itself, you will be allowed full access to our stores and armory. You will be provided a place to live, a clothing stipend, and enjoy about every indulgence you ever savored on earth. I'll bet you were you a lady's man back in the day, weren't you, Gabe?"

Mastema regained her grin and let out a little growl that made me squirm. Not in a good way, more like an earthworm under the knife of a junior high science student sort of squirm.

"Best of all," Judas touched my arm and a wash of relief passed from my head all the way to my toes. A sensation I could hardly remember. Warmth. Not the temperature of the air or room, but blessed warmth coursing through my bones. The soul freezing chill of The Nine had disappeared. Tears flooded into my eyes like a childish dolt. I didn't say anything for a moment. I wanted to revel in the sensation a moment longer. Then I lifted my head and choked out the words my lips didn't want to utter.

"I'm sorry, sir. But I must respectfully decline your offer."

I hung my head and tried to stop the sob that escaped my lips. Refusing Judas Iscariot meant torture and endless rebirth in the burning sulfur, but I could never be a part of his Agency. I was not perfect. Lord knows my reasons for being in The Nine were many, but I did my best to atone for those sins. I would never go back to the person I was when the world owned me.

I waited for Mastema to remove her blindfold and come

swooping down like some vulturous sex raptor. Procel had brought me, she would drag me away. But she never moved, and the frost never returned to my bones.

I looked up at Judas and saw him ... smiling.

"Excellent. That was precisely what I hoped to hear."

CHAPTER SIX

I stood in the middle of the room looking brilliant with my mouth hanging open. "Wait … what?"

"Yes." Judas motioned to the bone frame chair behind me. "Why don't you sit down? You look like you need to rest a moment."

I shook my head, flopped down on the seat, and said, "No, thanks. I'll stand."

That drew a chuckle out of Judas.

"I have watched you for some time, Gabe, but not because I want another agent, at least not one to put in the field like the rest." Judas picked up a small oval-shaped box from his desk and rolled the silver curio around in his palm. "As head of the Judas Agency, I am witness to horrible things under my watch. I see to the things that must be done. I always have, no matter what those things might be." Judas clenched the little silver box in his palm and gave me a hard stare. For once I didn't say a word.

He waited a moment then resumed his absent toying. "To that effect, I organized a small contingent of double agents. They undertake tasks my superiors may not fully agree with or know about. Tasks which must be carried out, nonetheless, for the good of us all. Thirty Woebegone, handpicked by me to infiltrate the Judas Agency, report on current operations and disrupt them when necessary. Influence equals power, and you know how to wield the sort of influence I am looking for and for the right reasons. You want to do what's right for others, not for yourself."

I put my hands to my face and tried to wrap my head around the words coming out of Judas's mouth.

"Hold on. You want to stop bad things from happening? Is this a joke? You run the Judas Agency—The Disaster Factory. You are the most ruthless and feared Woebegone who ever was—no offense. If you want to shut something off, why can't you throw the switch?"

Judas stood and paced back and forth in front of the desk. "I would not be in charge for very long if I halted every operation I was ordered to carry out. I run the Judas Agency, but I do not rule the underworld. One overzealous operation can unbalance a structure more delicate than most can comprehend. Sometimes restraint, or even damage control, is necessary. Other reasons I may have for halting operations are my own."

Judas stopped rolling the box in his hand and began thumbing the latch open and closed with repetitive clicks.

"As for gathering information, The Judas Agency operates under a cell structure. No one department is fully aware of what another is doing. That way, no one entity possesses enough information to disrupt the entire Agency. Even I am not apprised of all operations and dealings. I merely keep the organization together and ensure operations run smoothly. Cell or department leaders come to me if problems arise, but the Hellions in charge of each faction are equipped and capable. I am not often consulted. Which is why I need you. I need agents to infiltrate, discover, and disrupt operations where I cannot."

I sat back in my chair and took in a deep breath. "This is not what I expected."

"If it were, I would not be doing my job very well."

I nodded. "Can I just think for a second?"

"Of course." Judas stopped in front of me and flipped his little box open. "Take this, perhaps it will help you make up your mind."

I held out a hand, and Judas dropped a silver coin into my palm. I felt a jolt and the floor beneath me seemed to rumble. Mastema let out another chuckle.

"What is this?" I threw the coin to the ground. The rough-cut piece of silver hit with the weight of a bowling ball. My chair flipped over backward as I sprang to my feet and backed away. When I glanced at where I'd dropped the coin, it was gone. Something small and weighty existed in my palm again. I looked. The coin had somehow returned to my hand. I wound up to throw the thing across the room, but Judas held out a hand to stop me.

"Throw the coin as far as you like later, but that denarius belongs to you now. The coin marks you as my agent, and no one can remove it from your person, not even you."

"What if I don't want the job?" Panic bubbled into my legs, making my knees wobble again. I stumbled and tripped over the fallen chair. "I didn't accept yet."

"You accepted the moment you heard my story and touched the coin." Judas shot me a tight-lipped smile. "That coin is one of thirty special silver denarii. It will give you power, among other things. I could never allow you to leave here with the knowledge I imparted to you. Not without some assurance you would keep my secret."

Things were happening way too fast. I felt trapped—I was trapped. I had nowhere to go, and Judas Iscariot had just shackled me with a magic boomeranging denarius. What was next? Ear tags and an anal tracker?

"Try to relax," Judas said. "Everyone reacts this way at first, but you must understand, you have been entrusted with what may be one of the most important and volatile secrets in the known universe. We cannot take that lightly. There is no way to tell you about the

Agency, and then un-tell you if you decide you are not interested. All I can do is trust my judgement is sound and that I selected someone who will serve in this position. Have I made a wise choice, Gabe? Have I chosen the right man to do this job for me?"

I looked at the two imposing Hellions standing at the back of the huge office and tried not to hyperventilate.

"Tell me about this power the denarius is going to give me." I shifted my gaze back to Judas.

He smiled and clapped his hands together. "Excellent." He stepped forward and put a hand on my shoulder to walk me back to my chair. I bent to pick up the bone framed monstrosity, but Judas insisted I wait while he righted it and scooted the chair back toward his desk. He even held it while I sat down. "You made the right decision."

"Thanks, although I don't think much choice was involved."

"I am sorry, but rest assured you will find this calling a rewarding, if not challenging one."

I nodded. "You were going to tell me about the power. So far that sounds like the best thing in this whole deal."

Judas nodded. "I have seen the denarii do many things. Over time they can enhance strength, or intelligence, or aid your senses in some way. Mind you, there is no guarantee the coin will do those things for you. Only time will tell. The denarius will, however, grant you a single power, tailored to your need for each mission. You will find, whatever your power is, it will be the precise thing you require at the time of your greatest need."

"So, the coin might grant me the power to fly, have super strength, or laser vision?"

Judas gave me a knowing smile. One I wasn't sure I liked. "The power in the denarius is bestowed from—let's just call it upper management. No one knows what the power will be until you have occasion to use it. I like to say it is best to keep the phrase, *the lord works in mysterious ways*, in mind."

"Okaaaaay." I drew out the word, trying to decipher what he meant by that last bit. "Is there any other good news?"

He paused, seeming to consider his words. "The denarii are a direct conduit to unfathomable power. Do not forget that. Most of the time they appear to be nothing more than a worthless marker, a vulnerability to your status, but do not betray your calling. You may be granted access to power, most likely you will not, but these denarii are special."

"Why do I get the feeling you mean more Charles Manson kind of special than Santa Claus special?"

"Mr. Manson heads a team of false prophets. He has nothing to do with a two-thousand-year-old denarius."

I dipped my head and nodded. Sarcasm is lost on Judas Iscariot —check.

"So, what's to stop me from blabbing your secret all over the factory floor as soon as I walk out this door? I'm not saying I would, but ..."

"If you try to reveal this secret, your spirit will be absorbed into the coin, or rather an alternate domain where you will be entombed and tormented in darkness for all eternity."

I blinked. "And how many spirits are entombed in these coins?"

"The ghost halls of the denarii are vast. Let's just say two thousand years is a long time to collect the souls of betrayers."

CHAPTER SEVEN

I crushed my head between my hands, half hoping someone had crept up behind me and smashed my skull with a 2x4. If this were all a bad dream, I could wake up with a headache and move on with my dull ordinary afterlife. No such luck.

"Take this thing back." I held out the denarius in the palm of my hand, but Judas just stared at me, making no move to retrieve the coin.

"I didn't ask for this. I don't want your stupid suicide missions, and I sure don't want to keep your secrets. Take your down payment back." My voice grew louder and ended in a growl.

Judas still didn't react. I closed my hand and lunged for him. But he sidestepped, and I flailed past in a graceless ark. Mastema moved.

Without taking off her blindfold, she snapped her leathery wings once and hit me like a freight train. I didn't even remember landing on the cold red marble. In less than a second, I was laid flat on my back with a half-naked leather-winged demon perched on my chest. I might have been turned on, but her opposable toes and long black claws weren't exactly a page out of a teenage boy's sex fantasies. She tapped the outside of my t-shirt with razor sharp talons and threatened to introduce them to the tender flesh underneath.

Judas crouched by my side. "You need to calm yourself and listen to me."

I squirmed and twitched, but Mastema planted her hands on my wrists, pinning them to the ground next to my head as she let out a warning hiss. The sight of her sharpened teeth and spiked leather-clad breasts, now in a perfect position to suffocate me or rake the skin on my face, was enough to petrify me into submission.

"Much better," Judas said. "The sooner you accept your appointment as my agent, the less distressing it will be to you. This is a large responsibility, but not one beyond your abilities. Hold to your principals, and the denarius will never seek vengeance."

I nodded and looked up at Mastema. She tilted her head and seemed to peer down at me, despite her discolored blindfold, looking like a bird of prey ready to pluck out my innards.

"Mastema," Judas held out a hand. "If you would be so kind."

Mastema jerked her head toward Judas, took his hand without having to search for it, and stepped off my chest. I sat up, sucked in a breath, and tried to remain calm. You could have heard a pin drop in the office. Everyone watched me struggle to my feet and take in another breath to try and relax.

"Fine." I glared at Judas. "I'll live with your ghost hall of creepy souls ... for now."

Judas smiled, but his grin appeared more sympathetic than jovial. "This is a great deal to accept, and your position will become more challenging before it gets better, I'm afraid. But I assure you, this is an appointment someone such as yourself will come to appreciate. You earned an eternity here, but you may find some atonement within your soul. For some that is enough."

I thought about my old life and why I had put my shop together in the first place. "Yeah, alright. But I still don't like the thought of a ticking time bomb in my pocket."

"The denarius may seem like a bomb, but only you can light its fuse. Keep your secret, and the coin will work to your advantage. I maintain several denarius agents who have served for a millennium and continue to do so."

I threw out my arms and let them fall back to my side in frustration. "What am I supposed to do now?"

"You will report to Sabnack. He runs a cell division in the third tower. He will assign you a partner, and you will go from there."

"Wait. No training? No super double agent spy gadgets? You're just going to send me out there on my own with nothing?"

"All Judas agents are trained in the field, and you possess the coin."

"Great. I own a denarius that grants me a mystery superpower, but if anyone finds out, it will suck my soul like a four-hundred-horsepower shop vac. This is how I'm supposed to derail the Judas Agency? Oh, and you were about to tell me how I don't get any training ..." I clasped my hands in mock excitement.

Judas ignored my little tirade and grinned. "Your partner will be charged with bringing you up to speed. You will be assigned easier missions at first, until you're ready to dirty your hands. Make your usual reports to Sabnack. Your partner will train you how and when to do that, but your real responsibility is here. You will report to me once a week. More often if you believe additional communication is necessary."

Judas handed me a sheet of paper with a series of numbers and a map. "That is the code and directions to a rear entrance to this office. None but my people are aware of it. Memorize everything and destroy the paper. The denarius would know the moment even that information fell into the wrong hands."

I sighed and started to recite the numbers in my head. "Of course, it would."

Judas rounded his desk and pulled out another form. What would the underworld be without red tape and bureaucracy? He filled out the document and signed the bottom with a flourish of an old fountain pen.

"Give this to Sabnack. This certifies you as an agent and will give you authority to work in his department."

I took the sheet of paper, folded it twice, and shoved it into the back pocket of my jeans, still holding the code and directions in my other hand.

"Remember," Judas said. "Your priority is to gather information without arousing suspicion. Act when and if you must, but above all report to me, and I will do my best guide your actions in the field."

I nodded.

Procel broke out of his sentry position and ushered me toward the door.

"God speed," Judas said. "And good luck to you."

Procel got to the door before me but did not open it. After a second, Judas sighed without looking up. "The code."

I looked down at the small paper in my hand, remembering that I was supposed to destroy it. "Right." I glanced around, wondering what I should do, then shoved the wad into my mouth and chewed.

Procel squinted in disgust. "You could have torn it up."

I shrugged and slurred, "To-ma-to, to-mah-to."

Procel shook his giant horned head and opened the door to let me leave before I swallowed.

CHAPTER EIGHT

I made my way to tower three and headed for the 22nd floor as my paper instructed. The walk was uneventful, save a few wary stares from well-dressed agents and Hellions who could see I did not belong anywhere near the building.

The elevator door opened, and I stepped out, retrieving the paper out of my back pocket. It had the words, *diamond section, room 2278*, scrawled across the top. A brass plaque guided me to the left, down a wide hallway full of bustling Woebegone. They wore all manner of dress, from suits and skirts to leather nightclub freak-wear, and walked as if they might miss the last train out of whack-town on riot weekend. Almost none of them bothered to glance up at me. If they did, it was only to give me a dirty look for being in their way.

As I maneuvered through the mass of moving bodies, I heard someone having an argument at the end of the hall. A female's voice reverberated off the slick white walls, and the high ceiling, designed to accommodate eight-foot plus Hellions, seemed to amplify the sound. Her voice was soon followed by another I could only describe as a loud growl. I followed more of the shiny brass arrows toward my reporting office, and the voices grew louder. It soon became evident that the two places were one and the same.

A huge lion-headed demon loomed behind a desk wearing what looked like military style armor. His eyes flicked toward me, and the woman standing before him turned to peer back through the glass window that separated us. She was covered from the shoulders down in patchwork, old-school tattoos. Her hair was long, thick and Tidy-Bowl blue. She wore a vest and jeans torn in strategic places to show more of her body art. She also wore an expression of disgust on her face.

"You have got to be kidding me. This is the guy?"

I took that as my invitation to walk in. "Hi, I'm—"

"He can't even finish a coherent sentence," she interrupted. "You want me to train this loser?"

"Excuse me." I held out a hand. "My name is Gabe. I was told to report to this office."

The woman glanced at my hand and then back to the lion-headed demon I assumed was Sabnack, since he happened to be the only Hellion in the room.

"I'm not doing it." She crossed her arms and stared straight into Sabnack's black eyes.

"Not a hand shaker, huh?" I let my arm fall to my side. "Got it. Nothing but high fives from here on out."

Sabnack held out a furry paw-hand, and I put the assignment paperwork in his...pad. "This is Alexandrea Neveu." He growled through his lion mug. "She's your new partner and trainer. She'll grow on you—if you live long enough."

"My name is Alex. If you ever call me Alexandrea, I'll kill you where you stand, find your sulfur pool, wait for you to drag your pathetic soul out, and then I'll kill you again."

"Okay. Hard to work with, check. Seems to be a lot of that going around today."

"Look at this guy," Alex said to Sabnack and continued as if I weren't there. "I'll have to teach him everything. He looks like an eighties reject. He probably smokes and wears nothing but concert t-shirts."

"I'm sorry, could you shut up a second?"

Alex and Sabnack stared at me with equal bewilderment.

I pressed on before they had a chance to recover. "I'm not a child. I'll be fine. I know how to blend, and I'm a quick learner. I'll be doing the job better than her in no time."

Alex took a step in my direction. "You wouldn't last ten seconds Topside without my help. Where'd you steal those Puma high-tops, 1984? And those button-fly jeans were considered historic about fifteen years ago. You're not a child. You're an infant. You couldn't take two steps without getting squashed."

"So blue hair and tattoos are the best way to blend up top now? I doubt it."

I waited a moment, then laughed. "Holy crap, that was lame. Let me try again."

I cleared my throat and furrowed my brow, locking eyes with the woman before me again. "So which tattoo represents the loser boyfriend who got you killed? I assume you have one. All girls like you do."

Standing up straight, I smiled, feeling self-satisfied. "Yeah, much better. Don't you think?"

Alex made a fist and pointed to a tattoo across the front of her fingers. A unicorn with a rainbow coming out of its butt. "It's this one right here. Let me show you."

Sabnack spread his huge feathered wings and let loose a roar loud enough to make my lips tingle. Alex and I stumbled into the glass wall. The entire floor shook with the sound.

"Enough. You will work together. This is not a request. It is not a favor. It is an order. Now, get out of my office before I throw you both out of my window."

CHAPTER NINE

A lex wound her way through the halls on the 22nd floor at the speed of a raging comet. She made her pace look like a walk while I half-jogged just to keep up. The thick sea of Woebegone parted like munchkins in the Wizard of OZ, revealing the white marble road for us to follow.

"Your job will be to shut up and do everything I say," Alex shouted over the rumble of the crowd. "If you have any questions for me, refer back to that job description."

Alex rounded another corridor, running head-long into a poor clerk with a hand full of files. Paper exploded into a fluttering cloud, and I skidded to a stop to avoid colliding with both women.

"I'm so sorry, Hannah." Alex crouched to the floor and began gathering the aftermath with the other young woman.

"Geez, Alex. If you wanted to talk to me all you had to do was ask." Both of them let out a little laugh, and I leaned down to make sure Alex hadn't switched bodies while I wasn't looking. Her face melted into a mask of indigent anger the moment she noticed me peering at her.

Alex handed Hannah her wad of papers. "I'm really sorry. I

have to go. I have to take care of this ... thing." Her eyes flicked to me for half a second, then she stood and was off again. Hannah watched her go and glanced at me.

We stared at each other in bewilderment.

"Weird first day." I shrugged.

Hannah let out an uncomfortable laugh in response and headed off in the other direction without another word. My eyes stayed on Alex. Part of me wanted to plant my feet and refuse to move, but I suspected losing Alex would mean I'd never see her again.

It took a short sprint to catch up, but I matched her breakneck pace. "We need to get one thing straight. You can be pissed about this whole situation, but I'm assigned as your partner, not your employee, your peon, or your slave."

Alex stopped so fast it took me a couple of steps to react. I ground to a halt and turned to face her. We were several feet apart, but she closed the gap between us with slow purposeful strides.

"You can believe that—if you want to come back as a hot pile of goo," she said, "because that's what will happen to you without my help."

She stared into my eyes for a moment, then whizzed past me again.

I shook my head and spun in time to see Alex push her way through a set of ordinary looking double doors. I scrambled to follow her, pushing on the opaque glass instead of the dirty brass plate. The door swung open to reveal a bright room of black lockers. Some appeared to be the type you might find in any gym, but farther into the room they increased in size until they grew big enough to accommodate the Incredible Hulk after a year of ice-cream binges. The height of the ceiling increased too, making the huge room appear like an upside-down swimming pool with the monster section at the deep end. The larger lockers were equipped with gigantic handles and locks that might be operated by anything from a gorilla to a giant-hoofed elephant beast. The Judas Agency was definitely diversity friendly. It would explain why Alex and I wound up in the same locker room.

Something flew at my head as I passed the second aisle. I managed to raise a hand in time to bat a yellow galosh-style rain boot out of the air. The banana colored projectile rebounded off the locker next to me with a loud crash. I glimpsed Alex throw the second one—this one olive green.

"You are going to need these." Alex searched an open rack of coats, checking each of the tags. "Those stupid high-tops will soak up anything you step in, and I'll have to carry you home whining and crying about your feet. What size coat do you wear?"

I opened my mouth to answer, but I never got close.

"Forget it, here's an extra-large. It'll work for now." She tore a stained orange-ish colored coat off a hanger and tossed it to me as well. A knee length overcoat fit for any formal homeless occasion. Streaks of grease and dirt adorned every side, and it bore the distinct human odor of someone oblivious to the words soap, shampoo, or deodorant.

"I am not putting this on." I ground my teeth and held the coat out at arm's length. "I'd be better off wearing a rabies-infected raccoon."

"Pile—of—hot—goo." Alex stretched out and enunciated each word as if this was all she should have to say.

We stared each other down for a moment. I was not losing this one. She broke first.

"I knew it." She shrugged and shook her head. "Do whatever you want. You'll come back either way. I just wanted to save myself a trip to the fields."

Alex crossed the aisle, pressed her palm to a scanner and a locker popped open. This one seemed to be more stout than some of the others, and I soon saw why. Alex drew out a Ruger LC9 pistol and tucked it into the back of her pants, pocketed two spring-assisted knives, and slid an old-time single barrel derringer into her boot.

I tried to act nonchalant as I dropped my bio-culture jacket on the floor and walked over to the coat rack. The first three were mediums. There was a yellow slicker in my size, but it appeared to be in even worse shape than the one I dumped. Didn't anyone around here know about dry cleaners?

I finally ran across a brown overcoat that seemed halfway clean and didn't smell like someone died in it. I pulled it off the hanger and looked at Alex. She stared at me with her arms crossed, wearing the expression of an impatient grade school teacher.

"All set?" Alex shot me a cynical smile and turned to walk away before I could answer.

"Hold on. Don't I need some sort of weapon?"

"Nope." Alex kept walking.

"How about some matching boots." I held up my yellow and green galoshes. "Is that too much to ask?"

"Put them on. Or don't. I don't care."

"This is ridiculous." I ran down the aisle and chased her out a set of double swinging doors doing my best to shrug on the brown lice factory I had scored from the coat rack. "Can you at least tell me where we're going? What's our mission?"

A vision of Judas rushed into my head, and my voice cracked. All of a sudden I felt less like I was trying to survive my first day on the job and more like a preschooler conducting a mafia interrogation.

I cleared my throat and crossed my arms, trying to look relaxed and casual, holding a galosh in each hand so they hung out of my armpits. "I think I have a right to know where we're going and stuff. Not that I care. I just want to know about our mission, so I can do it better. Work with you and all, I mean. It would help if I knew the mission, that's all."

She blinked and kept walking. I shut my mouth before she did us both a favor and shot me.

"Your mission is to get down the hall and onto a nice elevator."

She pointed straight ahead. "If you're good, I'll let you push the button."

The new area felt like backstage to the insanity show we'd been in earlier. The hall was quiet and barren, with unfinished rafters and conduit lining the bare grey walls. Alex's boots clacked along the cheap tiles and echoed off the tall cavernous ceiling. I kicked my white high-tops off ahead of me, so I could pick them up on the way by, and hopped on one foot so I could pull on the green rain boot.

My maneuver stunted my pace, and Alex pulled ahead. I ran a few steps to catch up, smack-swishing between my sock foot and the boot, then jumped along behind her for a few more seconds to pull on the second boot.

Alex rounded a corner and disappeared. I hopped after her, only to find she had stopped. I tried to stop as well but couldn't get my foot down in time. I fell flat on my face instead, then looked up. Alex glanced down at me, shook her head, and pressed a button next to an ornate elevator.

I hauled myself to my feet and gave Alex a serious look. "You said I could press the button." I tried to appear indignant as I finished pulling on my boot and stood next to her.

"I said if you were good."

I harrumphed and looked at the doors. Like other areas in the Agency, they had scenes carved into their shiny brass surface. They depicted different versions of the same place in rows that ran the door's length. The first was a normal city street. Something you might see in downtown Chicago or New York. The next showed the same place, war torn and broken. The one below that showed the buildings intact, but the people lay dead in the streets, apparently from some sort of disease or plague. A third painted a colorful scene of horrific poverty and crime. There were several others, portraying every way a peaceful happy place could be destroyed. A real conversation starter for anyone contemplating suicide.

The elevator doors opened, sparing me from seeing any more, and I followed Alex inside. We both turned to face the front. I peered down at my mismatched boots. Not only were they two different sizes, they were both left feet. Alex grinned. This was going to be the beginning of a long and painful relationship.

CHAPTER TEN

I t had been a long time since I had walked the Earth, but I remembered lots of things from when I was alive. The sound of a V8-engine, the way the summer sun warmed my face, and the fact that elevators weren't supposed to accelerate like the Apollo 11 spacecraft. I didn't recall passing out or landing on terra firma, but I would, for the rest of my long and tortured eternity in Hell, remember the smell that immersed my face when I woke up. If odor possessed a corporeal presence, this one would invade your nostrils like a gallon of liquefied whale guts and swim out your eyes through ammonia tears.

I lifted my face out of a wet paste and opened my eyes. A thin layer of sawdust clung to my fingers as I tried to wipe the goo away. My vision cleared enough for me to make out Alex sitting on a broken-down split rail fence several yards away. She winked and gave me a wiggly fingered wave.

"Good morning, sunshine." Her grin stretched ear to ear in the moonlight. It was all she could do to contain herself. I lay on some sort of mound, putting me eye level with her. When a 500 lb. hog wondered by and shot me a disparaging glare, everything became clear. I had landed face down in a huge pile of pig crap.

It was all I could stand. I got to my feet and shook off my coat, showering my boots in a cloud of dried hog hunks. If Alex had given me a gun, I wouldn't have bothered to get up.

My mismatched lefty galoshes sunk into the manure, starting a mini crap-alanche as I stomped down the hill. Alex let out a laugh. "Cool off there, stud. It takes a little practice to make those landings. At least you hit something soft."

"That's not the only thing I'm going to hit." I clenched my teeth and fists and continued toward her. She did have a gun, and I couldn't really punch a woman. So I wasn't sure what would happen when I got to the fence, but it didn't matter. For a little payback, I would chance getting shot. Even the Gnashing Fields couldn't compete with the maliciousness of Alexandrea Neveu.

Alex glanced toward the ground, and her smile disappeared. A moment later she was off her fence perch and scrambling in my direction, "Wait, don't come any farther."

I thought she had threatened me at first, but then I noticed the panic in her eyes.

"I'm not kidding." She held out a hand. "This is one of those lessons I warned you about earlier. You know, about coming back as a pile of smelly goo?"

I stopped, breathing hard and ready to pounce if she tried some sort of trick. The games would end now, one way or another.

"See that?" Alex pointed at the ground in front of me. I let my gaze flick down for a quick moment, careful not to tip my head and give her a free shot.

"It's a puddle," I said. "So what?"

"Look around. There are puddles all over the place. It rained recently, and rain is one thing we avoid up here. You sink a foot into a rain puddle or get caught out in a storm unprotected, and the rain water will melt you like butter in a microwave. Remember the witch in the Wizard of Oz. Someone got that one right. Our best kept secret, loose in a children's book."

Alex pointed at my open coat and mismatched boots. "I didn't dress you in that getup for kicks—well, not completely. Rain water to us is like sunshine to vampires. Only thing worse is holy water. That's like swallowing a hand grenade and jumping into a fuel truck. Not pretty at all."

I did my best to keep that visual from being added to my library of nightmares, but it had already been cataloged and stored for later. I possessed an all new appreciation for my mismatched boots and homeless slicker.

"If we can't get wet, how do we function up here? Water is in almost everything, even people."

Alex let out an exhausted sigh. "I said raaaainnnnnn waaaaaterrrrrrrr. Clean the pig crap out of your ears. If it is processed for drinking, in food or—well, poop." She laughed a little bit at that. "Or anything else, the water doesn't affect us. Only the wet stuff that comes straight out of the sky. Something about The Nine and the way the Woebegone are put together, I guess. All I know is stay away from it unless you like bathing in battery acid."

Alex turned and began walking up the dirt drive toward a dark farmhouse, making sure to steer clear of any more puddles. I assumed her tall combat boots were waterproof, but even a splash would be bad if rainwater was as horrible as she said. Even drying things off could be a problem.

The full moon cast plenty of light for us to see, so I fell in step behind her, making sure to sidestep the little death pools as well. "So, is there anything else I should know?" I asked. "Do kittens cause herpes, or should I stay away from face-eating ice cream cones?"

"I don't know what you did with kittens when you were alive but stay away from them." Alex curled her upper lip in disgust. "Other than rainwater, we are all but impervious to things up here. It would take nothing short of a C4-throw blanket to make you to say ouch. We heal almost instantly, as long as we're here among the living, and we don't need to eat or sleep. Provided we don't run into a spring shower, we're golden."

"Amazing."

"Do me a favor," Alex stopped and poked a finger in my chest. "When you decide to test your invulnerability later, and I know you will, do it when I'm not around. I don't want to watch you slamming creative appendages in car doors or anything."

I cringed. "Why would you think of a thing like that—never mind, I don't want to know."

We made our way to a Jeep sitting next to the house. Alex opened the door and slid into the driver's seat.

"What are you doing?" I lowered my voice in case someone lurked inside the house.

"Getting us a ride. You didn't think we would walk every-where, did you?"

"What if the people inside wake up?"

"What if the people inside wake up?" Alex mocked in a high over-theatrical voice. "You are an invincible agent sent from the depths of Hell, remember? Demon up a little bit and stop embar-rassing yourself."

"Fine." I stood up straight, walked around to the other side of the jeep and got in.

Alex scrutinized me with a brow raised. "You aren't going to start pouting and talking to yourself, are you?"

I stared out the windshield and deadpanned, "If I don't answer the voices in my head, who else will?"

Alex peered at me a moment longer, then dropped the conver-sation and pulled a flat black box no bigger than her hand out of her pocket.

"What's that?"

She touched the shiny surface and a screen came to life in a color display that seemed almost three-dimensional. I probably looked like a kid who had just watched Santa rattle down his chimney and land in his living room. I couldn't help myself. I had never seen anything so incredible.

"It's a smart phone," she said, looking exasperated. "You know, like an Android."

My eyes got wider. "Android? Like a robot? You've got to be kidding me."

Alex rolled her eyes and turned toward the wheel. "Yes, this is a miniature robot, and he is going to climb under the hood and start the engine with a magic key it produces out of its butt."

I didn't say anything. I couldn't tell if she was joking.

She waited a second then touched the screen again. The Jeep came to life in a startling display of lights, moving pictures, and more color screens.

"No, this is not a robot, it's a phone. It has a computer inside though. Everyone from a prepubescent teenager to a geriatric mouth breather has one. Mine just has a few bells and whistles the Topsider's don't. Like a hack that will start almost any keyless ignition."

I blinked.

"This is going to be a very long night." Alex put the Jeep in gear and rolled out of the driveway. I tried to relax and pretend the UFO array on the dash was something I saw every day.

"Look, I haven't been up here since 1988. Things may have changed a little, but I'll be fine. The world can't be that different."

Alex nodded. "Really? I suppose all the cars had beverage dispensers back in your day." She pointed to a button in the middle of the dash labeled with a big red triangle.

"Some," I lied. "I'm sure they weren't as advanced as the ones you have now." I tried to sound bored to cover the amazement pounding the inside of my head.

Alex nodded, looking impressed. "Where did the drinks come out back in your time?"

I looked around and saw two circular sections behind the gearshift. "Same as yours." I made a general motion toward the area in case I happened to be wrong.

"Well, I stand corrected. You are far more worldly than I

54

thought." She gestured to the bright television screen showing some sort of moving map with a tiny picture of a vehicle in the middle and a bunch of figures and numbers along the edges I didn't understand. "Can you program the flight computer for me? I have a tough time with it while I'm driving."

I tried not to squeal like a six-year-old getting her first Barbie. Of course cars could fly. Alex owned a hand-held computer phone. Maybe an android, I still wasn't sure about that. Flying back and forth to work was probably no more unusual than camping out for concert tickets.

"I thought you were some sort of expert," I said, visions of the Back to The Future movies dancing in my head. "You can't even fly a simple car? Pull over, and I'll fly."

Alex held out for about three seconds before she broke out laughing.

"The car doesn't fly, does it." The words came out as a statement more than a question.

Alex shook her head and tried to control her laughter.

"No drinks, either?" I said.

She lost control again, tears streaming from her eyes. "Not as advanced as the ones you have now," she mocked, and cackled again.

"All right, all right, I deserved that one." I stared out the passenger window to hide the heat rushing into my cheeks. "So, I need to catch up a little. I'll figure it out."

Alex took a deep breath and blew it out with a whistle. "Listen." She let out a few more chuckles that threatened to reignite her laughter again, but she managed to keep them under control. "I will make you a deal. I will try," she drew out the word try for emphasis, "to be more patient when explaining our modern advances, and you stop pretending to know about things like flying cars and drink makers."

Alex stayed quiet for a moment, and I turned to look at her. As soon as our eyes met, we burst out laughing. After a moment, we quieted down, and I stared out at the road. There wasn't much to see in the dark. Trees, boulders, and hillsides blurred past us as Alex navigated the serpentine dirt road. There were no streetlights or buildings. Just an eerie expanse of shadows.

I leaned forward, opened the glove box and rummaged through. At least they still worked the same. When I didn't find what I searched for, I lifted the center console in the armrest. Jackpot. A pack of Marlboro Reds. I shook one out and looked for the lighter and ashtray.

"There isn't one," Alex said.

I glanced over at her.

"An ashtray," she continued. "Cars don't come with them anymore—hardly ever, anyway."

My mouth fell open. "So, what do people do with their cigarettes?"

"May want to brace yourself for this one too," Alex said. "Smoking is a bit of a taboo now. You can't smoke in restaurants or offices, pretty much any public building. Cigarettes gave lots of people cancer, so a big push came through to make everyone want to quit. You would not believe what they charge per pack now."

My shoulders slumped. I felt utterly defeated, but I refused to take the cigarette out of my mouth. "Well, at least I don't have to worry about getting cancer."

CHAPTER ELEVEN

Alex left the road and wheeled the Jeep through heavy brush, uprooting bushes and crawling over rocks and downed trees.

"Are we headed for the South American jungle?" I reached up and grabbed hold of the roll bar on my right, so I didn't slam my head into the side window—again. "My kidneys won't take much more of this. Why didn't we just zap straight to wherever we're going instead of driving this giant cinder-block?"

A grin that stretched from ear to ear had grown on Alex's face. She jerked the wheel—or the wheel jerked her, I wasn't sure which—and the Jeep dropped into a cavernous hole, then rocketed out again on its oversized tires and springs. "Stop complaining. This is fun. We can't transport anywhere we want to go. We have to use a Splice. An Envisage Splice is a place that's been set up as drop point for Judas agents. It's the only way a Woebegone can get here. Not exactly a well-publicized bit of trivia either, for obvious reasons."

"Are you telling me someone added an en-div-ez ... one of those travel things in the middle of a pig farm on purpose?"

Alex shrugged and squeezed the wheel, making a bright tattoo of Animal, from the Muppets, ripple over the muscles in her arm. "Don't hurt yourself. Just call them Splices. All the Splices are set in places where we are less likely to be spotted making an entry Topside."

"Are all the Splices at pig farms?"

"Only the nicer ones."

We broke through another stand of trees, and Alex slammed on the brakes so hard my seatbelt threatened to cut me into triangular pieces.

"We're here." She sang the words in an excited high-pitched jingle.

The Jeep's headlights played along a sheer rock face that stretched so high it blocked the moon, causing anything farther than the Jeep's lights to blend into a black mass of nothing.

Alex shut off the engine—and our headlights—plunging even the area in front of us into darkness. When we opened the doors, the ignition ding seemed almost deafening in the relative stillness of the outdoors. As soon as the doors were closed, I felt like I had to whisper.

Alex had no such compulsion. "Hurry up. I'm not waiting all day." She, and her ear shattering voice, hiked along the rock face, her hand playing along the jagged wall. She seemed to be searching for something, although I didn't know what.

"Do you need some help?" I whispered, unable to help myself. "If we both look, maybe we can find whatever you're looking for a little faster."

Alex peered at me in the dark. "Why are you whispering?" Her voice came out as a loud hiss that could in no way be considered a whisper. "There's no one around for thirty miles."

I forced a normal voice but still couldn't bring it up to full volume. "I said, if you're looking for something, four eyes are better than two."

Alex smiled. "Thanks, but I found what we're looking for."

She jerked at a bush, making the thin branches groan and snap. The narrow root gave way, and the whole thing pulled free.

"Voila!" Alex held out her hands to display a small opening at the base of the wall.

"A cave?"

"A cave. And you're going first. I hate spiders, and bats, and snakes, and centipedes, and earwigs, and roaches, and pretty much anything you are going to find inside of a cave."

I let out a little chuckle and got down on all fours. "So, the fearless wonder isn't so fearless after all."

"Don't let it go to your head. If we spot a bat in there, I may run, and I'll climb right through you to get away if I need too. Now hurry up. It is going to get light soon, and I don't want to be stuck out here when the sun comes up. We need to be back to the farm before anyone wakes up."

"What happened to being a big, bad Judas agent?"

Alex glared at me. "There's a difference between being scared of Mr. Johnson's shotgun and being smart enough to want an uncomplicated exit. Now move."

I crouched and peered into the darkness before she noticed the smirk on my face. The opening was just big enough to squeeze my shoulders through if I worked my way in with my arms above my head. I wasn't claustrophobic, per se, but the idea of being stuffed into a tiny hole underneath a million tons of rock turned out to be discomforting, even for a Woebegone.

I stretched out my arms and dove into the darkness before I thought about it anymore. That's when I learned how dark, dark could be. The limited amount of light emanating from the opening disappeared the moment my body filled the hole. My hands fumbled and scraped across the jagged rock, searching for any sort of purchase. I used my toes to push myself along, as I wiggled my shoulders through the ever-tightening space. I pushed forward again and took a breath. My chest wouldn't expand to breathe. The area was too tight. I tried to back out, but something got stuck. My pants caught on a jagged piece of rock. There was nowhere to go. I tried to take in a breath again, but cold stone crushed my ribs and would not give. Panic crept in and tightened its grip. I wiggled and shook, flexing my muscles, making the opening feel even tighter. Something pushed at my feet, and I tried to relax. Alex was still behind me. The reminder grounded me to reality. I couldn't back out, so I used her as leverage to move forward, blowing out what remained of my air in a last-ditch effort to push through. My hands found an opening, so I pulled with everything I had. If there had been a drop off waiting for me inside, I would have summersaulted right into the abyss.

I emerged into more pitch darkness. The sense that I stood in the midst of a thousand teeming cave monsters became almost palpable. I extended a tentative hand and probed my surroundings. Nothing. No walls, no rocks, no monsters. Now my feet felt like they were perched on a three-foot precipice overlooking a bottom-less black pit. Vertigo set in making me want to crouch to keep my balance.

I concentrated on my breathing. The cool air was stale and damp, and smelled of minerals, moss, and rich soil. It felt almost like being on another planet. I didn't know how Alex planned to see in here, but if she came in behind me and switched on a flashlight after sending me into the dark, it would serve her right to come through that tunnel with her silky blue hair full of over-friendly cockroaches and stinkbugs.

"Wow, it's dark in here." Alex bumped into me, and I realized I still hadn't moved more than two feet from the cave entrance.

"Wait for a few minutes," I said. "Your eyes won't adjust—at all."

Something flared to life in front of my face and threatened to burn out my retinas. The brightness did not come from flashlight, but my eyes were too busy screaming to make out the source. A few seconds later, something yellow flickered and began to take shape. Fire. Alex's tattooed hand held a molten softball-sized sphere of fire. Not a torch or a flair. Just ... fire revolved in her palm.

"Better?" she asked.

My eyes continued to adjust, but I had a hard time believing what I saw.

"How are you doing that?"

"Lesson number three hundred and forty-six." She hefted the fiery ball into the air over her head. "Woebegone can develop a power when we spend enough time Topside. That's part of the reason these little trips are so rare. Management doesn't want a bunch of super-Woebegone running amok in The Nine. It'd be messy. Mine is the ability to manifest fire. It's not something you get to pick, it just happens. And no, I have no idea what yours will be, so don't ask."

"That is incredible." I bit my tongue and tried not to look over eager, but then couldn't help myself. "So, you have no way of knowing what I might manifest?"

Alex sighed and turned away. "No, but I'm sure your power will be annoying. They usually have something to do with your past life. That's all I can tell you." She kept her flaming hand in the air and lit the cavern around us as we walked. Most of the time, the cave had more than enough room to move around and stand up in. We passed several box-like formations on the walls and ceilings and saw beautiful sparkling caverns I knew nothing about. I wagered any spelunker would give his left gas light to discover this place.

We descended through the maze for what felt like an hour, then Alex stopped and peered through a small opening. Unlike the rest of the cave, this area looked loose and somewhat disturbed. As if the rocks had caved in or been uncovered.

"We need to go in there." Alex pointed into the tight dark expanse beyond the opening.

"How do you know all of this?"

"I just know, okay? The lessons are getting a little tiring today. Let's leave it at that for now."

Alex tried to clear some of the loose debris from around the opening with one hand while holding the flame up in the air with the other.

"Here," I said. "Let me do it."

Alex moved back, and I made short work of the rest. The hole was small, but the opening looked like a gaping gorge compared to the pinhole we had wiggled through at the beginning.

Alex's torch hand put off enough light for me to peer inside. A ledge hung about six feet below the opening, and after that, nothing. A sheer drop all the way to Wonderland.

"I'm not sure what we're supposed to do," I said. "But unless I manifest the power of flight in the next few seconds, we're in the wrong place."

Alex leaned in and looked through the opening as well. "What we need is just inside. Lower yourself down to the ledge and collect a sample of the guano."

"Guano?" I arched an eyebrow. "Like poop? We're Agency pooper scoopers?"

"Just get in there. I'll hold the light."

Alex drew out a sample tube from her pocket and handed it to me. "Here. Collect the guano in this."

I took the little ampule and shoved it into the pocket of my slicker. "Why are we doing this? Who wants a bunch a poop from a cave?"

"Don't worry about who wants it or for what. Worry about the fact that we're here to do a job. You may also want to think about the fact that an annoying person might be left to wander these caves in the dark forever."

"Not forever," I said. "Sooner or later I would die and crawl out of the Gnashing Fields. When I got my memories back, I'd show up on your doorstep with a whole new batch of annoying questions."

Alex sighed. "Don't remind me. Now get in there and do your job."

I managed to shimmy through the opening feet first and lower myself without much problem. I tried not to think about what I stepped in, not that it mattered. I was covered head to toe in pig crap. The ledge was much narrower than it had looked from above. I barely had enough room to crouch and still keep my balance. Alex shoved her hand through the hole, but my body blocked most of the light and a view of everything I did.

"Are you about done?" Alex said. "I want to get out of here."

"One moment, princess. There are thousands of bats above your arm so don't make any noise or move around too much. I heard light really freaks them out."

Everything went dark, and I snorted out a laugh. "I am kidding. There are no bats. Can I please have the light back?"

The darkness remained, and I started to worry that Alex may have followed through on her threat to sprint out the door.

"That is not funny." A small flicker grew in the cavern. Alex was trying to scope out the ceiling for herself. "For a comedian, you have quite a death wish. Hurry up and collect the sample, so we can go."

The light grew a little more, but the yellow glow was nowhere near as bright as before.

"Much better, thank you." I resisted the urge to squeak out my best bat impression. Sometimes there was a fine line between hilarity and survival.

I pulled out the sample tube and scooped a bit of what I assumed was bat poop into the little ampule. I was about to close the lid when something occurred to me. Maybe I shouldn't be doing this. Maybe this is what Judas hired me to stop. Should I sabotage the ampule or try to stop Alex somehow? I didn't expect to make such a decision this early in the game. If this were some sort of pivotal moment in a large chain of events, this might be my only chance to stop them. It was the proverbial question about meeting Hitler as a young boy. If you knew what he could become, but weren't sure, would you kill him to avoid all the atrocities he may commit as an adult? Yes, this was only a poop sample, but the principal was the same.

"What is the holdup down there?"

My mind raced, trying to decide what to do. Should I act now and risk exposure, or was I overreacting? I could put myself in jeopardy for nothing.

"Uh, I have a little problem down here." I shoved the ampule into the inner pocket of my jacket. "I lost my balance and dropped the sample over the side."

"Amateur." The light disappeared for a moment, then Alex's hand popped through with another ampule. So much for hoping she only had one.

I reached up to grab it. "Thanks."

"Don't let it happen again."

I crouched and scrubbed the ground with my feet. If I had to give her something, maybe the dirt would pass for what she wanted. The poop looked almost identical. Hopefully, the soil wouldn't contain what they were looking for. I scooped some of the dirt into the container and closed the lid. "All set."

Alex reached through the hole and tried to help me through, but I still had the ampule in my hand. My foot lost traction, and I began to fall backward. Alex clamped down on the hand that clutched to the rocks while I shoved the ampule into my pocket. As soon as my hand was free, I reached for another handhold and pulled myself through. If I slipped, I might have landed on the ledge, but the alternative was enough to make me break out in a cold sweat.

Alex stood with her hand out the moment I emerged. "Hand it over. I don't want any more mistakes."

"I'm fine, thanks." I smiled and reached for the dummy ampule and froze. In my haste, I put them both in the same pocket.

"What? Don't tell me you lost the sample again." Alex began

to reach for me, so I grabbed the first ampule my fingers landed on and pulled it out.

"Of course not. It's right here."

Alex snatched the ampule out of my hand and examined it in the fire light. "Well, you weren't perfect, but you got the job done. Nice work. Let's get out of here. But don't think I am going to forget that crack about the bats."

Alex walked back the way we came. I was pretty sure I could tell the difference between the two samples if I compared them side by side, but I had no idea how to do that. It wasn't like I could ask Alex to hand them over and turn her back for a second. *No, don't worry, everything's fine. I'm just making sure you got the dummy sample, that's all.* Why didn't I throw the stupid thing over the edge? Now I had to steal the ampule back before Alex turned it in and hope I could keep the bad one out of Agency hands.

CHAPTER TWELVE

I stepped out to the elevator/transport/vomit inducer and swallowed hard, willing my face to turn less green. We had made it back to the farm with time to spare and rode the hog crap express all the way back to the Agency. We skipped the locker room and headed straight toward the main corridor—homeless slicker, mismatched boots and all. Alex didn't want to waste any time turning in our sample. She offered to do it on her own, but I still hadn't found a way to compare the two ampules to be sure she had the right one.

A huge metal door reminded me this place had been designed for the demons, and the humans were nothing but an afterthought. I had to use both hands and all my weight to push the behemoth open. I felt like a toddler opening the glass door in the front of a department store. Alex slipped through the door behind me, never offering to lend a hand.

"So, what now?" I fell into step next to her and shoved my hands into the pockets of my jeans. I caught a whiff of myself as we walked and considered dropping my slicker right there in the hall. My high-tops might not be high class, but at least they were comfortable and didn't smell like a bacon outhouse.

"I," Alex drew out the singular to sound like it had about seven beats. "Will take this sample down to the lab. Then I'm going up to my apartment to enjoy some peace. You are going to go home to... wherever home is for you, and to think about whether you want to come back tomorrow."

"Hold on." I held out a hand. "I thought agents got a place to stay here in the Factory."

Alex leaned in toward me and lowered her voice, eyeing me under her manicured eyebrows. "First, these guys do not appreciate the name Disaster Factory—although I don't know why. Watch where you say that and who you say it to, or you may be picking yourself up off the floor."

"Second," Alex leaned back and resumed her usual standoffish demeanor. "I earned my place here. Just because you got that hire slip, doesn't mean someone hands you every perk and privilege of a senior agent."

I nodded. "Fair enough."

My response must have caught her off guard. She seemed ready to say more but didn't.

"How about if I start earning my keep by taking that sample down to the lab so you can get a jump on the peace and quiet."

Alex pulled the little vial out of her pocket and looked down, considering. "I don't think so. You dropped one already. I don't want to start over because you splattered the second sample all over the marble floor."

I threw my head back and tried to look exasperated. "I apologized several times. What do you want me to do? Drop to my knees and beg? It was an accident. I sat on a two-foot ledge above a bottomless pit and everything was slippery." It wasn't really all that slippery, but it made the story sound more dramatic. "It's not like I'm going to run down the hall using the sample as a football. I will treat the precious little tube like a newborn baby, I promise."

I cradled my arms and rocked them back and forth. Alex actually smiled. It was a nice smile when her face wasn't full off all that murdery, pissed off anger.

She stared at me for a minute. I cooed and pretended to tap my imaginary baby on the nose with my finger. "You're a good poop sample aren't you—yes you are ..."

This was enough to draw out a laugh. Alex sighed and almost handed me the vial, then someone at the other end of the cavernous hall caught her attention.

"Alex." A mousey looking young girl bounded toward us. Alex's smile became broader and warmer than I had thought was possible.

I ground my teeth and cursed under my breath.

"I'm glad I found you." Mousey girl came to a stop, a little breathless and looking less than together. She carried a disheveled stack of papers and envelopes that rivaled the state of her hair, glasses, and clothing. More bureaucratic paperwork. I was beginning to believe red tape made up the foundation upon which all things were made.

"Sabnack wants to see you right away."

Alex lost a little of her smile, but she still beamed at the girl standing next to her. "Figures. I'll head over in a minute."

"I don't know. He acted pretty anxious." Mousy girl smiled and raised an eyebrow. "Remember what happened last time you didn't hop to? He's probably still washing that coffee out of his luxurious mane."

The two of them broke out in laughter, and I began to feel like the salad at an all dessert buffet.

Their laughter died down, and they both seemed to notice me standing there at the same time.

"So, is this him?" Mousy girl winked at me. "He's cute."

Alex laughed. "If you go for that sort of thing, I guess. Give him a shot if you want to."

"No. He looks too sweet. I would use him up and break his heart." Mousy girl pushed her glasses up on her nose and tried to push the hair out of her face, but the unruly strands fell right back down.

"You know I can hear you right?" I said. "I'm standing right here."

Mousy Girl looked back to Alex. "Not too smart though. I like that."

Alex laughed again, and Mousy Girl turned to leave. "Don't forget about Sabnack, Alex. He is waiting for you." She threw up a hand and waved back over her shoulder without looking back. "Nice to meet you, cute boy. Watch your back. Alex bites, and I mean it."

"She's interesting." I raised an eyebrow.

"You have no idea." The smile on Alex's lips faded, but it still showed in her eyes. "Looks like you get your wish."

She held the sample out, and I took the vial, trying not to look too eager.

"I will protect this with my life. Point me in the right direction, and I'll be on my way."

"Turn here and head straight. You can't miss it."

My eyebrows shot up. "Seriously. You didn't even trust me to take this around the corner?"

Alex wiggled her finger in front of her face. "They're made of butter, remember? Just try to get it there in one piece."

I felt Alex's eyes on me the whole way. When I got to the corner, I looked back. Sure enough, Alex still stood with her arms crossed looking like a tattooed supermodel hall monitor. I held up the vial to show her it was still safe before I disappeared out of sight.

My mouth still hung open in a toothy grin when my face hit Sabnack's hairy chest. It felt like hitting a brick wall upholstered in smelly fur and armor. My bared teeth found fur, not leather. All the floss in the world wouldn't be enough to rid me of that hairy-chested nightmare.

More importantly, thanks to Sabnack's locomotive style

appearance, the vial I held like a careless child tumbled end over end toward the shattering demise Alex predicted moments ago.

Without thinking, I spun around Sabnack, ducked, and launched myself under his grasp. My face slapped the bottom of his dusky wings as I sailed past, reaching out just in time to snatch the vial before it hit the floor.

My ribs paid the price though. I hit the dark marble hard, stretched out and on my side. Too bad getting hurt down here didn't work the same way as getting hurt Topside. My ribs bent and shifted in ways they were never meant to when I hit the floor, but I didn't hear anything break. The pain receptors in my chest disagreed.

I groaned and rolled onto my back in time to see Alex appear under the canopy of Sabnack's outstretched wings. The expression on the Hellion's face was unreadable, but the purple/red shade of Alex's face told me all I needed to know.

"You had to travel twenty feet, and you couldn't even do that."

I held up the vial in triumph but didn't pull myself off the floor. "Saved it!" I did my best to swallow my internal organs.

Alex reached out and snatched the vial out of my hand.

I reciprocated by backhanding a bare section of her calf where a frayed hole in her jeans showed a tattoo of a chainsaw-juggling clown. I guess impulse control might need to go on the old to do list.

Alex turned back and put her boot in the middle of my chest, leaning in until my ribs sounded all new alarms of pain. "Do you have something you want to say to me?"

"Yes." I groaned, feeling like my head might pop.

Alex leaned in lower, "Well, go on. I'm listening."

I took in about a teaspoon of air and managed to bellow out, "You're welcome."

Sabnack straightened, and his lips twisted into a grin that showed his huge canines.

Alex huffed and pushed away, allowing me to take a breath.

"I assume this is the sample I sent you to retrieve?" Sabnack held a hand out to Alex.

Alex nodded and set the vial into Sabnack's hand. All hope drained away with my dignity.

"Good," Sabnack said. "I'm glad the two of you are getting along. I received word that your assignment together is permanent."

"Oh good," I said. "That penny I threw into the wishing well did the trick."

Alex barely managed to keep her composure. "Will there be anything else today?"

"No," Sabnack shook his head, and his mane swayed in smooth black waves. "I will make sure this gets to the lab. You can help your new partner off the floor and take off for the night."

Alex looked down at me. I put a hand out, wiggling my fingers with mock impatience.

Alex spun and walked away. Sabnack let out a huff that sounded like a laugh, then he snapped his wings and moved on in the opposite direction.

"So, I guess I'll just get up on my own then." I raised my voice and waved the hand I still held in the air. "That's okay. I don't need any help."

I pulled myself off the floor with a groan and reached into my pocket to pull out the second vial. Cradling my ribs in one hand and holding the second vial in the other, I felt small standing in the gigantic hall alone. I had to get to Judas's office before he left for the day—if he left for the day—and tell him what happened. There was still a fifty percent chance they had right stuff. Too bad Judas didn't seem like a glass half full kind of guy.

CHAPTER THIRTEEN

"So, you retrieved two samples." Judas stroked his rough and wild beard, staring me down as he leaned on the obsidian quarry he called a desk.

I nodded like a kid claiming he lost his mom when he got caught peeking into the ladies dressing room. "I thought you might want something to test—so you would know what they were up to."

Judas nodded back still stroking his beard. "And you thought offering them a sample to test would be a good idea as well."

I nodded again, gripping the arms of my bone chair, trying not to look like I was ready to run out of the room screaming like the victim of an atomic wedgie. Judas took the news with calm reservation. So calm that it made the skin on my neck want to crawl over my scalp and say hello to my forehead. I almost wished he would yell, stomp, and scream. Even his crazy bird-lady-sex-demon, Mastema, still eyeing me from behind her blindfold in the corner, would be better than having Judas loom over me, smoothing his beard in slow, considerate strokes.

"At what point did you decide it would be prudent to mix the samples and give them one without knowing which was the decoy?" Judas began to raise his voice. "In the cave, when you were collecting a sample you should have never retrieved in the first place? Or was it when you handed the sample over to your partner a few moments later?" Judas stopped preening his facial hair, balled his fist, and drove it into the stony top of his desk. The impact made the floor shudder beneath my feet. I was wrong. This was much worse than the beard smoothing thing.

"Perhaps the idea came to you when you had a second chance to compare the samples but decided to bobble the opportunity to smash it on the ground instead. Thank goodness you prevented the sample from being damaged there. What a tragedy it would have been if the sample were destroyed. What would the lab have done if they had nothing to test?"

I shrank into my chair, realizing I had screwed up yet another chance to fix my colossal string of poor decisions.

Judas gripped the edge of his desk and leaned toward me, looking like his eyeballs and every vein in his forehead were about to explode.

"Well?" he barked.

The noise made me want to vault over the back of my chair. "Oh—you want me to answer? I uh. Not the last one ... I mean never ... None of the—examples, times you were saying ..."

Judas shot to his feet, and I braced for ... I wasn't really sure what, but it had to be horrible. Judas turned to the side instead, snatched the sample tube off the desk, and handed the ampule to Procel. He still looked relaxed in his usual corner at the rear of the room. "We may as well test this, since our new agent brought enough back for everyone to play with. Maybe he got lucky and gave them the benign sample."

Procel dipped his head, then his gaze shot toward me. His expression was one of concern, almost warning. The look didn't fit the fiery-eyed albino demon, but it was there and gone, then he made his silent retreat out the rear door.

Judas spun back to me, and his stare pinned me to my seat like a physical presence. "Next time you set out to impede an operation, your best course of action would be to avoid bringing any trace of a suspicious and potentially deadly contagion back with you." Judas folded his fingers and made a visible effort to calm his voice. The veins in his head still looked like over-pressured garden hoses. "Perhaps a better course of action might be to retrieve a benign sample or fail to bring anything at all. I hope this is a lesson we might all learn from and avoid in the future."

I nodded with an enthusiastic vigor of a bobblehead riding a dirt bike.

"Good." Judas wrung his hands together and paced toward the door. He opened it, and I shot up out of my chair, sensing an escape.

"Thank you for stopping by, Mr. Gantry. Let us hope, for all our sakes, that your next visit brings better news."

CHAPTER FOURTEEN

I slogged through the maze of high-rise shanties in Scrapyard City, surprised at how many had been rebuilt. Firestorms were always a catalyst for new construction in my neighborhood. Abandoned homesteads due to the death tolls and countless collapsed buildings meant a free-for-all on building materials. Survivors improved what they had or started over if they had nothing. Everyone fell to a storm sooner or later. It was inevitable. I'd survived longer than most, but even I had taken my turn beating back the fire only to find myself consumed by the flames.

I thought my firestorm dodging days at the shop might be over, but Judas confirmed the fact that not all new recruits rated their own dorm or apartment in the Factory ... err Agency. He said getting me a place would only raise suspicion, so I should work on earning it for myself. Seemed like a half-truth was as close as Judas ever got to the real truth. Agents get a place to live, but only if you earn it first. You will be assigned a partner to work with and show you the ropes, but she will be a psychopath control freak who has a penchant for working alone. Joining the Agency under Judas was like winning a twenty-four-hour shopping spree and then getting dropped off in the middle of the Sahara Desert with a canteen and a pair of sneakers—all you had to do was make it to the store.

I scrambled over a large pile of crumbled beams, sheet metal, and old piping in the road and found myself face to face with a Woebegone brandishing a makeshift knife made out of some of the same scrap treasure I stood on. The man towered over me and appeared about as crazy and desperate as a cat trapped in the spin cycle of a washing machine. His rag tag outfit hung from his arms, legs, and torso, exposing strips of blistered, bloody burns. The acrid stench of burnt flesh and over-ripe sweat wafted off his body. The smell alone drove me back several steps.

"Mine." Mr. Smelly's voice came out high and squeaky, not at all matching his Hulk-like demeanor. The duality caught me so off guard I choked out a laugh. He wiped the grin off my face when he swiped his knife at my midsection. I should have insisted on accommodations at the Agency, at least for the night. There was a reason Woebegone would kill for a job at that place.

Mr. Smelly's swing didn't come close, but he made me flinch. I put my hands up and tried to peer past the rags he'd wrapped around his face to ward off the cold. I didn't recognize him. A new guy who didn't understand all the rags in the world wouldn't make him any warmer. Even with my shop in the area, it was a fair bet he didn't recognize me either.

"I don't want any of your stuff." I sidestepped, giving him a wide a berth. "I'm trying to make my way home. That's all."

"Mine." Mr. Smelly was more insistent this time. Move on or become a permanent part of his collection.

He took another couple of swipes at me, much closer this time, forcing me to jump out of the way.

"Knock it off." I tried to sound loud and intimidating, but my voice cracked, and I backed away a little too quick. "I told you I don't want any of your crap. You see I'm leaving, right?" I held my hands out and kept walking, but I didn't turn my back on him. Mr. Smelly responded in kind by sticking near his treasure trove. I didn't want any trouble, but this was The Nine. This place was the very definition of trouble.

I walked backward until I went around a corner and Mr. Smelly passed out of sight, then I spun on my heels and ran. I made a mental note to carry my Knuckle Stunner when I huffed it back and forth to work from now on. At least walking might get me in better shape. Half a block and I already wheezed like a doggie chew-toy.

I lumbered through a few more turns, passing several shifty-eyed squatters, and I loped around a curve until I recognized a familiar area of my neighborhood. The high-rise shanty that housed my shop had been beheaded by the storm, but most of the body was still there, due in part to many years of reinforcement by yours truly. The place looked like you could contract tetanus by sneezing at it, but that shop was home sweet home.

I wasn't all that shocked to see the shop was still there, but I was surprised to find the place open. Stray leaned out the front window, chatting with one of my better customers, Jonny. A particularly successful snoop when it came to sniffing out information.

I watched Stray pass something to him and realized she just made some sort of deal. I couldn't decide whether to be enraged, shocked, betrayed—or all of the above. To make things worse, I was pretty sure he scored my last two cans of Dr. Pepper. Jonny turned and walked away, pocketing his stash while I headed for Stray and my shop. I only made it a few steps before I tripped over a balding Woebegone crouched beneath a pile of ragged blankets. We went over in a tumble, and my ribs reminded me about the little party they had had with the floor a few hours earlier. I winced and rolled to get to my feet. The other man did the same. He was squat and fat, dark-skinned with a ridiculous three-strand comb-over.

He sprung to his feet faster than I did, but he didn't bother to help me up.

"Sorry, man. Sorry." He waved his hand at me as he backed away.

"It's all right. No harm done." I lied, thinking about my aching ribs. "Don't worry about it."

The Woebegone pulled his blankets over his head and clasped them below his nose as if he didn't want me to see what he looked like. "I was just resting. I'll get outta here. Sorry."

Blanket-man turned tail and ran like mugger making a getaway. The crazies were definitely out today.

I headed for the shop again, checking for any more human speed bumps along the way.

Stray saw me coming and waved, looking a little friendlier than the last time I'd seen her. Of course, I had to knock her unconscious in the middle of a firestorm and drag her into my shop where a lunatic had tried to beat down our door. That could make anyone a little cranky.

She walked out and met me in front. She seemed so happy I had a difficult time being angry.

"What are you doing?" I asked. "I told you to hide out inside, not open the place up. And what did you give away to Jonny?"

Stray held her hands out and stared up at me, a grin so wide it hardly seemed containable. "Just hear me out for a second. After you left, the storm died down. I wanted to find out if anything had been damaged. I thought it might be nice to fix the place up before you got back. While I checked things out, someone came by and said he had information you were waiting for."

I groaned again, rolling my head around in a tortured circle.

"No, no ... it's alright." She put her hands on my arms, still looking up at me with those innocent blue eyes. I wanted to ... I wasn't sure what I wanted to do. Yell, scold, throw my arms in the air, or flop down like a fed-up toddler. Instead I pressed my lips together and bit down on my tongue.

"He said you offered him half a dozen Twinkies for the information."

Another pained groan.

Stray rolled her eyes. "Don't worry. My memories might be gone, but I'm not stupid. I talked to him, and after a while he admitted you really offered him two. He apologized and said he would take one since he'd lied. He also told me more about the— situation you inquired about. I think I'm good at this. I don't think I've ever been this good at anything."

"Look." I smiled and tried not to sound like a condescending jerk. "I'm glad you had some luck with one of the local Woebegone, but ..."

"No." Stray took me by my hand, dragged me inside the shop and threw open the door to the secret store in the back. My mouth gaped. Somehow Stray had managed to almost double my inventory in only one day.

"How ...?" I shook my head and tried to think of something to say but couldn't. It had taken me a month to build up my meager supplies.

"I met a nice Hellion yesterday before you found me. A crazy Woebegone tried to grab me, and for some reason, the Hellion helped me escape. I ran and didn't see either one of them again. I guess the demon came back to find me after the storm. He showed up here at the shop after you left."

"This *nice* Hellion wasn't driving a VW Bug, was he?"

One of Strays brows went up. "Ummm, no. He was tall with white hair and red eyes. Super scary, but he acted very kind. Sort of shy, though, like he didn't want to be seen or something."

I smiled. "Yeah, I'll bet he didn't. So, he gave you all of this? For what?"

"He said he knew something about my situation and that I might be doing things on my own for a while. He said I should try and keep things open while you were gone, and if he ever needed any information, he would consider this a retainer for future services."

I rubbed my head, wondering how far I would fall through this particular looking glass.

"And the deal you made with Jonny a few minutes ago?"

Stray's gaze went down to the ground. "He needed a little help. He asked if he could bargain for double the goods if he promised to do twice as much on the next job. I didn't know him, but he knew quite a bit about you."

Stray smiled and glanced back up at me. I began to wonder what Jonny told Stray about me.

"He wanted the sodas to trade for a safer place for some friends to live while he rebuilt their shanty. I traded him for the information he had and said we would square up later for the rest."

Stray seemed on the verge of tears. "I swear I haven't done that before, and I wouldn't have agreed this time if it hadn't been for a good cause."

I smiled at her. "I think you're right. You are good at this. I would have done the same thing."

Stray stood up straight. "Really?" She hopped on her toes and bounded up to give me a peck on my cheek. "Thanks."

She backed away and leaned on the window with both elbows. "That was for saving me. I don't know why you did it, but if you hadn't dragged me in here, I would be dead—or at least suffering in those horrible burning sulfur pools at the Gnashing Fields."

She looked so young, so innocent and unassuming. I smiled and reached out to touch her face. My finger brushed her lip and both of our smiles fell away.

I dropped my hand and forced my smile to return. "You just needed a little help. Like Jonny, that's all."

I stared at her, standing there, so trusting, leaning back in her thin white t-shirt. She had regained her smile as well, but hers was truly jovial, maybe something more. I sighed and shut my eyes, trying to clear my head.

"Listen, Stray. Things are not all peaches and honey out there. Sooner or later someone will try to turn on you. If you aren't careful, some Woebegone will take you for everything you have, maybe do horrible things to you. And this little shop I have worked so hard for? It will be nothing but a burned-out memory."

I opened my eyes. Stray's smile had disappeared again, and her shoulders fell. It felt like looking into the eyes of a child and telling her the boogie man was real. My heart crumbled, and I reached out to touch her arm. "I'm sorry. That may have been a little much, but you have no memories or experience to go on. You are as sweet and kind as they come and down here ... Well, sometimes the Woebegone take advantage of that."

I rubbed her arm and leaned down a little to peer into her eyes. "I want you to be careful, that's all. I don't want you to get hurt. All this," I waved my free hand around, "all this can be rebuilt or replaced. I didn't risk the pools to save this shop. I risked a trip to the Sulfur Saunas to save you, and you were worth every burn, bump, and bruise I got doing it."

Stray regained a little of her smile.

"Except this one." I pointed to a random spot on my arm.

Stray seemed concerned and leaned in, then she slapped the spot with the palm of her hand. "There, all better."

My mouth gaped. "Did I say sweet? I meant mean, and cruel, and hurtful ..."

Stray laughed and peered out the window again. "Thanks, Gabe. For everything."

I smiled and stood beside her taking up a similar pose. "Just buy me a Harley or something, and we'll call it even."

Stray laughed again. "You? On a Harley? What about a Honda? Or a tough looking bicycle."

I clutched my heart and gaped at her. "This is how you show your thanks? By crushing my dreams?"

"I'm sorry." Stray peaked her eyebrows in a convincing look of concern. "You can still dream of owning a Harley. I just meant you shouldn't ride one."

I started to laugh, but she stared at me with an expression of such sincerity that I wondered if she was serious, then she snorted and let me off the hook.

I shook my head and laughed with her. "Cruel and hurtful."

"Oh, come on, I was kidding," she said. "You would be great on a Harley. You have a real bad boy thing going."

Stray pinched her lips into a line until they became white trying not to burst out laughing.

"You aren't helping," I said.

We both let out another laugh and resumed our survey out the window.

"So, have you regained any of your memories?"

Some of the pleasantness she wore on her face fell away from her eyes, but she kept her grin. "Not yet. I can't even remember my real name. I just tell everyone to call me Stray, like you."

"Don't worry. It'll come back. It always does if you give it time."

I peered through the window at Scrapyard City and watched the Woebegone wraiths wander the catwalks, pathways, and streets. The corrugated steel buildings formed such a patchwork labyrinth it was difficult to tell where pathways started and came to an end. Many led to drop offs or blank stairwells. If you didn't know the specific combination of paths to take to your destination, you could get lost for hours and never make it to where you were going.

It didn't help that the steel landscape was ever changing, rebuilt after every firestorm, further confusing the web-work of shelters and shops. Madness chipped away at the mind of every Woebegone, and there were plenty of ways to go mad in The Nine. My secret had always been finding a way to remain discreet, private, and out of the way. A rule I had thrown right out the window over the last day or so. I wondered what had changed, then something caught my eye in an alcove to the right and one level up. The moment I laid eyes on the movement, the Woebegone tried to move back into the shadows, but I already had seen who he was.

Blanket-Man. He hid in the dark, watching the shop—watching ... Stray?

"It's getting late. Why don't you close up? I'm going to run a quick errand. I'll be back in a few minutes."

Stray shrugged and nodded her head. "Need any help? Closing up'll only take a second. I can come with you."

"No, I'll be fine." I opened the false panel under the counter and retrieved my Knuckle Stunner, waving it in the air. "I have plenty of backup."

"All right. Be careful."

I found it a little funny that she was telling me to be careful.

I left the shop and headed in the opposite direction of Blanket-Man, being careful not to glance in his direction. I thought I had noticed him circling around before Stray and I had gone back into the shop, then on the street when we came out of the back, then in that little hidey hole on the second level across the way. That was too many coincidences.

I turned a corner to race up a catwalk to the second level, hoping the path would still lead around to the other side of the building. I tried to move quietly, but I didn't want him to escape either. I took the long way around. If Blanket-Man wandered off before I got there, my little cloak and dagger routine would be for nothing. I kept running, sacrificing stealth for speed.

My rash decision was rewarded with a blast of pain to my midsection. I never was a quick learner. I flew into the air and for the second time that day, I wound up flat on my back, gurgling in pain. A metallic tink, tink, tink passed by my head as Blanket-Man beat a hasty retreat, his blankets flopping behind him like a dirty superhero cape.

Perhaps I got a bit too close after all.

I rolled over and got on all fours. "I am really learning to hate that guy."

A hand fell on my shoulder, and I spun, knocking it away, aware of my vulnerable position.

"Easy." The voice came from my left. Jonny stood back with his hands in the air, giving me enough space to stand up and regain my bearings. "I wanted to make sure you're all right. What are you doing up here?"

I massaged my ribs and stretched my back, popping about a dozen vertebrae back into submission. "Just thought this looked like a comfortable place to take a nap. Did you by any chance get an eye on the freight train that hit me?"

Jonny took a few steps in my direction and put a hand on my shoulder. He was a small and unassuming guy, but smart enough to use that to his advantage. Blending in, going places, and seeing things he shouldn't was Jonny's specialty. He was the best guy I knew when it came to investigating those little secrets that were so good for business.

"I didn't see anyone. Only you crouched there on all fours. You sure you're all right? You don't look so hot."

"I'm fine." I forced myself to stop clutching my ribs, but I couldn't help but wince a little when I straightened my arm to drop it back down to my side. "Stray told me you worked out a little deal ..."

"Look, I never meant to take advantage, and they aren't for me. They're for someone else."

I held up a hand to stop his frantic explanation. "Calm down. It's fine. I thought of a way to make us square, that's all, but you have to keep it quiet."

CHAPTER FIFTEEN

My trip back to the Agency the next morning was a little better than the trip home. No one threatened to kill me with jagged hunks of metal during my long walk, though I was propositioned with offers ranging from a good time to some pretty imaginative ways of pulling one's head out of one's own ass.

This situation had to improve. Even if I earned new digs at the Agency, I would still want to go back and check on Stray at the shop. I made a mental note to find out how Procel scored that old VW. Maybe I could find an old motorcycle or something. Sporting a Harley around Hell wouldn't be bad for my reputation. Might even be good for business. Right now, I was stuck wearing out my old tennis shoes, hoping I could commute back and forth without losing any major appendages.

I headed up the black stone stairs to building three and noticed two characters exiting the huge mirrored doors. They looked like a trailer park version of Laurel and Hardy. The skinny kid wore a baggy set of olive-green fatigues from the Vietnam era, but managed to disrespect the uniform in every way. The hat faced sideways, the sleeves were pushed up above his elbows and one of his pant legs was bloused up to his knee while the other hung loose over his combat boot. He had one patch sewn onto his sleeve. An American flag on his right shoulder. He had attached it upside down.

His partner didn't have the same flair for the theatrical. He wore a set of greasy, pinstriped coveralls, but I suspected this was because coveralls were the only thing that would fit his generous proportions. The man had to be over four hundred pounds, though he carried it well. I couldn't picture him running a marathon, but the man moved with an easy, if not rumbling, grace despite his immense girth.

The duo locked in the moment they laid eyes on me and altered their course to intercept.

Why did this always happen to me? I would try to make nice, and they would tell me how they didn't like to share their toys. Next thing I know, everyone's punching me in the face, and I'm getting blamed for the whole thing. It was like grade school all over again, and college, and that time I tried to learn ballroom dancing.

As I got close, Laurel nudged Hardy's arm, and he gave me a nod. "You the new recruit?"

I smiled and gave him my make nice nod. "I guess that's me."

I held out my hand to shake his, but Laurel didn't even glance down. Not the shaking type at all.

"This is Max, and I'm Jake. We've been around here for a long time, so we know how things work. To start, snot nosed recruits don't talk to senior agents without calling them 'Sir.'"

"Must be why you're such a fan of the military."

Laurel ... err, Jake took a step toward me. "Was that supposed to be some sort of crack?"

I examined the greasy locks of brown hair that spilled out from under his hat. "No...Sir." I drew out the word a little longer than necessary, and their smug grins disappeared.

"I was wondering, wouldn't Daddy be upset if he knew you

played dress up in his clothes? You should at least get a haircut or wash it—something. Maybe put it up in a man-bun. That would make him real proud."

Max, the walking earthquake, stepped forward to match his buddy and bumped me with his belly. I tried to stand my ground, but it was like being rebounded off a mail-truck. I fell back a step but managed to halt my forced retreat there.

"I hoped we would have to teach him a few things." Max had a huge tag sewn onto the chest of his coveralls with his name in oversized letters. His top buttons were undone, making him resemble an auto mechanic that would give Deliverance fans nightmares.

"Teach me what?" I asked. "How to power eat? No thanks. I'm trying to watch my girlish figure."

Max's expression twisted into a pudgy-pinched pit of anger. I had pushed the launch button on this freak show duo. This was the part where my face got acquainted with lots of punchy things, but I never backed down from a bully, no matter how many poundings I had to endure. It was all part of my endearing charm.

I slid to the right and stepped up to Max, putting him between me and skinny Jake. I figured he would swing first, then the tooth-pick would try to flank me, but I was not about to let that happen. I would orbit planet Max as long as I could to keep Jake trapped on the dark side of the moon and the odds more even.

Jake seemed unwilling to retreat down or head up the stairs, so he looked over his partner's shoulder instead and waited for the show to start.

"Hey."

None of us were stupid enough to turn toward the voice. The big guy was smarter than I thought. Alex's blue hair and tattoos entered my peripheral vision, and Max's expression changed. Not a lot, something around the eyes. I'd made deals in my shop long enough to realize when something tipped the scales in my favor.

"Hi, Alex." I kept my eyes locked on Max, but I lifted a foot up to the next stair to give me an edge if Mr. Skinny was dumb enough to make a leap for my partner. "I was saying hey to some friends of yours."

"I don't make friends with piles of shit."

So much for sarcastic monologue.

"Beat it." Alex didn't stop until her face was inches from Max's pudgy cheek. "You want to hassle my partner, you can hassle me too. Just don't forget you won't heal down here like you do up there." Alex jabbed a finger into the side of Max's neck. He refused to turn and face her.

I stood there and tried to seem menacing, but compared to the spit-fueled fury of Alex's burning stare, I looked like a wide-eyed kitten on the front of a Hallmark card. I continued to menace anyway.

There was a moment of silence, then Jake smacked Max on the shoulder. "Come on. They're not worth it. We'll catch 'em Topside sometime and finish this up there."

A bit of Max's smile returned, though he never unlocked his eyes from mine. "I guess we'll see you later."

Jake pulled at Max's shoulder, eager to make his escape. Max obliged, stepping back without turning away. "Next time, this exchange will be different."

"Sure was swell to meet you fellas." I raised my hand and waved goodbye with a finger. "Have your people call my people, and we'll do lunch, okay?"

Max grinned and flipped me the bird before scurrying away with his little GI rat wannabe.

Alex grabbed my arm and forced it down. "What is wrong with you? Do you have any idea who those guys are?"

My eyebrows twisted, and I stared at her. "How would I know? They came down to hassle me. Maybe they got wind of my rep after our last operation and couldn't wait to meet me."

Alex gave me what was becoming her trademark deadpan stare and let go of my arm before heading back up the stairs.

"What?" I yelled a little too loud. "We rocked that mission. Don't be modest."

She kept walking, so I jogged up to follow her inside. "Look, I don't want to sound ungrateful or anything, but why were those guys so scared of you? I mean you have an intimidation factor that would make Mr. T jealous, but that guy could belly-bust a tank. He was ready to throw down until he heard your voice. Then both of them all but peed themselves trying to figure out how to get away without losing every trace of their manhood."

Alex stopped and peered at me with those piercing hazel eyes. "Let's just say you'd rather not make me angry down here or anywhere for that matter."

"But why? Are you some sort of super warrior or something? Do those tattoos represent the political leaders you assassinated? Come on. What is it?"

Alex grinned and patted me on the cheek. "Someday." Then she walked away.

I badgered her all the way through the loud bustling halls and into the locker rooms, but I didn't get any other answers. She just wandered along as if she were alone and no one was speaking. I got so desperate for a reaction I considered proposing, but I decided that might make things weird later, what with splitting up the wedding gifts and all.

We got to our locker, and I suited up in my homeless garb again with one improvement: I managed to find a rain boot that fit my right foot, though it was still a different color than the left.

I walked around the corner of the lockers and found Alex tucking her little Derringer into her boot. She glanced up at me and shook her head. "You look ridiculous."

It was my turn to return her deadpan stare. "If you have a problem, I suggest you speak to the designer of this particular ensemble."

Alex rubbed her chin and gave me a once over. "This served its purpose last time, but people could see us on this mission. Look at me. I can't be seen with—this." She motioned toward me, head to toe. "We have to find you something else to wear."

Alex turned, and we headed for the elevator room. "Come on, let's go shopping."

CHAPTER SIXTEEN

The Splice Alex chose for this trip turned out to be a half-full fast food dumpster. My foot slipped, and I went down in an aromatic pile of rotting grease and faux-vegetable matter. I tried to stand, but I felt like a cat trying to gain traction on buttered linoleum. The bottom of the dumpster was coated with a substance slick enough to solve every friction problem NASA and the porn industry ever had. I grabbed for the edge of the dumpster and noticed Alex perched on the corner beneath the night sky, one foot balanced on each rail.

"What are you, a ninja or something?"

She grinned and held out a hand. "You could stand to work on your balance."

I reached up and pulled myself to the edge, abandoning any hope of staying out of the greasy mess. "Well, I definitely need a change of clothes now. I smell like a french-fry street gang took a dump on me then flushed me into the sewer."

"Thanks for that visual." Alex hopped off the edge and landed on the asphalt without a sound.

I threw my weight over the side of the dumpster, smacking my foot into the plastic lid on the other side. The thing banged and vibrated like a bomb going off, then my pant leg caught something sharp on the dumpster's rim, and I went over head first with a grunt. My body dangled upside down for a moment, then made an ungraceful splat landing on the ground when a section of my pant leg tore loose and let me go.

"Wow," Alex said. "Did you take dance when you were a kid? That was really...something."

"Parkour, actually." I reached up, jerked the length of fabric my pant leg left on the dumpster, and put the strip in my pocket as if it were an important part of my ensemble. "You know that thing where all the kids run around flipping from building to building?"

Alex looked stunned. "How do you know about parkour, but you've never heard of a GPS?"

I made a show of brushing myself off. It did no good whatsoever. "I met a guy in Scrapyard City. He did all these crazy flips and jumps all over the place. Wasn't very good though. Missed a jump and ..."

"I get the picture." Alex held out a hand to stop me then made her way toward the street.

"You asked. I gave you an answer. Where are we anyway?"

I followed her as she walked along the grungy cobblestone alley, headed for the bright lights and asphalt of whatever town we had landed in. She disappeared around the corner and when I got there, I discovered the streets were deserted. It must have been late because there wasn't a soul to be seen. The dusty old town had quite a bit of life in it. At least during the day. The buildings were occupied with merchants, and not tourist traps, pawn shops, and run-down liquor stores. There were clothing shops, a large tack and feed store, and a couple of nice restaurants. I even noticed an old-time drugstore with a huge picture window. If you gave the fifties a modern makeover, this would be Main Street. The sign in the drugstore said they sold something called a fifteen-dollar burger. Guess prices from the fifties got a makeover too.

The town hadn't celebrated their first stop light yet, but we seemed to be on the main drag. Alex led us past a number of small shops, peering at each window display as we walked by. Something at an outdoor sports and hunting shop caught her eye, and she stopped to look inside. I pulled up next to her to see a bright silver mannequin posed before a fake fire and surrounded by midget trees, plastic bushes, and Styrofoam logs. The chrome model sported a gawk-worthy outfit the likes of which I had never seen. From the knees down, the pants were made out of some sort of grey rubber. Above that, the left thigh was cut from a slick brown fabric while the right came in a rusty orange. A patchwork of pockets covered both legs and closed with exposed yellow zippers. The moron ensemble was rounded out with a matching jacket and a silky long sleeve pullover.

I snorted. "That might be the most ridiculous outfit I have ever seen. Rodeo clowns dress with more dignity."

I stopped laughing. When would I learn?

A wry grin grew on Alex face, and I shook my head. "No."

Alex nodded and grabbed my arm. "Oh, yes."

She pulled me around to the back of the store, and within a few seconds, we were through the delivery door and inside. After twenty minutes of my whining and her laughing, the mannequin was naked, and I had a new set of clothes. The pants fit so tight I had to tuck them into the ankles of the matching lightweight boots. Alex said they were called skinny pants, but they looked like something out of a woman's fashion magazine and felt like wearing wedgie specialized sausage packaging. The whole outfit was ridiculous.

"You look fabulous, darling." Alex grabbed my arm and spun me around in a circle. "Trust me, this is way better than that old rain jacket. And this is all waterproof."

I touched the slick fabric.

"Something called Gortex," Alex said before I could ask. "Same thing my jacket's made out of. Way better than plastic."

I sighed. "Whatever, as long as Gortex keeps me from melting."

"It will. Now let's go, we're running out of time."

"Time for what?"

I followed Alex out the door and through the alley to the street again.

"You didn't think we were just out on a shopping trip, did you?"

I shrugged. "I'm trying to go with the flow. You said we were going shopping, so I thought we were going shopping."

Alex huffed and turned off the main drag, entering the outskirts of the little town. The places reminded me of the old neighborhoods I hung around growing up. Small and square with friendly looking porches and unfriendly looking fenced-in yards. They weren't run down, but no one in this town got rich either.

We passed a row of bright colored houses converted into businesses. The only one not spreading the spring painted cheer was the office of an accountant who chose to keep his home a brown as staunch as his profession. I could almost picture a wrinkled, yellowed eye peering at me from behind the darkened curtains. The absence of even a cricket's chirp began to work at my nerves. Before long, I imagined eyes all around us. Alex opened the rear gate to a little white house with a gigantic swing set in the yard.

"Here we are." Alex stepped onto the grass, shattering the night with her whisper. "Keep your eyes peeled. We don't want to be seen messing around in a local's yard."

Adrenaline spiked every hair on the back of my neck. I wasn't sure what to look out for, but if this were a horror movie, this would be prime time to bring on the zombie dinosaurs.

My breathing got faster, and I tried to close the gate without making any noise. A squeak reminiscent of a 72' Monte Carlo's worn out fan belt echoed through the neighborhood anyway. Alex didn't seem to take notice, but the deafening screech seemed to be a dead ringer for a zombie mating call. If my nerves got worked up any more, my heart would pass out from exhaustion.

I took a deep breath and tried to calm down as I followed Alex up to the back porch of the house. Alex was a pro. She wasn't going to get us caught. I just needed to shut up, follow her lead, and make sure she wasn't doing anything I needed to run interference for.

Alex opened a wooden box set to the side of the door on the porch. The inside contained three plastic half-gallon jugs of milk. I tried to work out what she had in mind. Alex painted a pretty clear picture when she reached for an inside pocket and pulled out a small case containing a syringe. It was drawn to the top with a cloudy white liquid. The perfect implement to spike the milk, and I could make a good guess as to what the ominous liquid had been derived from.

The poo prize we had collected the night before must have been distilled into the mystery substance Alex carried in her little care package. I had no idea what the sample had been turned into, other than a disgusting poop cocktail, but that's not what bugged me. The question that really made the sweat beads crawl down my neck was, do I need to stop her?

CHAPTER SEVENTEEN

Alex reached for the syringe, but I grabbed her wrist. She looked at my hand and then into my eyes, her mouth twisted into a sneer. "I do not like when people grab me."

"I'm sorry." I couldn't quite make myself let go even though I had a feeling holding on much longer would be tantamount to suicide. "What are you going to do with that?"

"I am going to jab it into your neck and use the needle as a stir stick if you don't let go of my wrist."

Definitely suicide. I let go, but I didn't back off. Alex relaxed her shoulders, her hazel murder eyes not leaving mine. "We are here to do a job. If you don't have the stomach for this, you better call it quits now. I can promise this is about as G-rated as things get around here." Alex uncapped the needle with her teeth and held the syringe up high, like a serial killer.

"Do you know what's in that thing?" My body vibrated with apprehension. It took considerable focus to calm down enough to hide it.

Alex parted her lips and caught the cap in the case with her free hand. "Yes, I know what's in here; it's the sample we picked up the other day. Now back off so we can finish what we came for."

Something in my head screamed for me to stop her. I wondered if Alex had any real idea what the substance would do. Uncertainty fogged my mind and turned my arms to jelly. I couldn't decide what to do. Short of pulling down my pants and mooning her, a decent distraction didn't even come to mind. I considered the possibility for a moment, then decided my butt would be too tempting a target for her syringe.

Alex stared at me, her eyebrows knitted together as if she had just seen a lunatic. My internal dialogue left me standing there, staring at her like a wide-eyed idiot. She probably wondered if I had lost my mind.

She crouched down, moving slow and keeping her eyes on my face as if she were afraid she might spook me or something. I dropped down with her and flipped the lid to the milk crate closed with a thump, catching my thumb under the rim.

"Are you serious right now?" She went to open it again, but I jerked my thumb free and slapped my hand on the top, ignoring the throb that now pulsed with my heartbeat.

"How can you just follow orders without knowing what you're doing?" I said. "You don't even know what this stuff will do to these people. They could be good people. A family. Geez, there could be kids in there, and we're going to pump them full of bat crap and see what happens?"

"Look, you're not going to screw this up for me. It's a miracle that I got a second chance at this, and I'm not going to blow it because my new partner has a conscience."

I narrowed my eyes and cocked my head to the side. "Wait, go back. What do you mean you got a second chance? Do you mean you got in trouble, and they gave you a second chance? Or that this is only your second ..."

Alex's face went from badass to looking like a toddler with her hand caught in the candy drawer.

"It is." I smacked my head with my palm. "This is only your

second job. And you screwed up the first one. You're almost as green as I am in the field." I let out a cynical laugh.

"This is my second op," Alex said, "but I am nowhere near as clueless as you are. I've been a Topside courier for the Agency for a long time. I know how things work up here."

I laughed again. "Great. I've been getting my balls busted by the mail girl. This gets better and better."

Alex recovered her murderous stare and leaned toward me. "Remember when I told you water was about the only thing that could hurt us up here? Well, our powers can do the job pretty well too." Alex's hand flared to life and bright orange flames consumed her wrist and hand. The heat was so intense it forced me to lean back. "If you like, I can fry you to a crisp and carry you back to The Nine looking like an overdone marshmallow."

I put my hands up in surrender. "No need to get nasty. A little honesty would have been nice though."

Alex extinguished her inferno hand and stared at me for a moment. "We're here to test a simple contagion, that's all. This is done all the time. The people who live here are supposed to possess some sort of genetic immunity to the stuff in this syringe, but there is only one way to find out for sure. The powers that be don't like to waste time with medical trials on rats and monkeys. They go straight to the source. I can't tell you exactly what's in this syringe. But I can tell you, they would not entrust a couple of rookies with the modern introduction of the Black Plague—especially on their maiden voyage. Nor would they do it in some hayseed town in the middle of nowhere."

I nodded. "Thank you. Was that so hard?"

"More painful than you could imagine," she said. "Now are you going to take your hand off the top of this box, or am I going break it off and leave it inside as a parting gift?"

"That's ridiculous." I pulled my hand away and tried to massage the throb out of my aching thumb. "They would never drink milk all covered in severed hand. It's unsanitary. Think through your threats a little bit, will you?"

I tried to appear nonchalant while Alex examined the milk containers for the most inconspicuous place to use her syringe. I didn't like what we were doing, but I couldn't argue with her logic either. Why would they send a couple of know nothing rookies on a crucial mission? The price for failure would be too high. Testing a new flu virus on an innocent family wasn't all that ethical, but they were supposed to be immune. If I let her do this, I gained her trust and the Agency's trust. I'll be set to stop bigger jobs down the line. It was a dangerous risk, but no one said this would be all peaches and cream.

Alex found a good spot and punched the small needle through the plastic. I watched the cloudy liquid pervade the fresh white milk as Alex pushed down the plunger. Doubt raised a chill of goose bumps on my skin. I stood there watching Alex do the very thing Judas had hired me to prevent. As mistakes went, I hoped this wasn't a big one. She sealed the tiny hole with a heated finger and stood up. My chance to stop her with any sort of subtlety had passed. If I wanted to prevent anything now, nothing short of picking up the jug and smashing it on the ground would do.

"I'm sorry I lied to you," Alex said.

I peeled my gaze away from the milk box and looked at Alex. A pang of guilt twisted my stomach. "We all have secrets. Let's just try to keep them—and dismembered hands—to a minimum from now on."

CHAPTER EIGHTEEN

G etting back to the shop that night proved to be an even
bigger challenge than the day before. I got out of the
Agency late, and it was dark. In The Nine, nighttime was never a
good thing. Hell was bad enough during the day. At night, all the
things that went bump came out to play. The Nine transformed into
an evil comic book mashup of Hollywood Boulevard and Saigon
Alley. Desperate Woebegone walked the streets, offering lewd acts
to low level demons in return for trinkets or protection.

Laughter erupted from inside a building to my left, and a
Woebegone man flew out of the window three feet in front of me.
He cleared the drug coma flesh pools slumped against the corrugated steel wall under the window and landed with a thump on the
street. He rolled, flopping his limbs as if he'd jumped off a
moving truck, and came to a dusty halt in a position reserved for
pretzels and freaky Asian contortionists. This guy didn't look like
either.

Two young Woebegone women appeared at the window, their
expressions as naked as they were. They stared at the man in the
street with perplexed horror, but neither made a move to come out
or run away. They were confused and innocent. The real bad guy,

err … bad *girl,* appeared behind them. A female Hellion wearing nothing but a sharp toothed grin.

"Don't worry, ladies." She wrapped her hands into the Woebegone's hair and jerked them back until they pressed against her dusky grey skin. "We're going to have more fun without him." The Hellion's yellow eyes shot toward me. "Unless you'd like to join us."

I stared at the terrified looking girls. My hand found its way into my pocket and my Knuckle Stunner. Attacking any Hellion was suicide, but if she's alone ...

The hellion giggled and disappeared into the dark confines of the sour smelling hovel. I took a step forward, but a professional wrestler/burn-ward crossbreed stepped out of the shadows and stood in my way. He looked like he had gotten into a fight with a meat grinder—and lost. He didn't bother to glance in my direction. The message was clear. Move along or I would find my own meat grinder to wrestle with.

I sighed and kept walking. There were hundreds—thousands— of other matchups like the one in that dark hovel, and they were all organized and run by Woebegone like that meat grinder.

They were called Disposable dealers, scum who trolled the outskirts of the Gnashing Fields for fresh born to kidnap and lease out as their newly acquired slaves. They sold fresh born Woebegone like disposable property. Buyers would use them to do dangerous or ill-advised jobs, use them in graphic or violent sex shows, or as a toy for themselves. When the buyers were done, they cut the Woebegone's throat, if they weren't dead already, and sent them back to the Gnashing Fields, never regaining their memory or becoming the wiser when the Disposable dealer showed up to collect them again.

Hell was still Hell. As much as some of us tried to make something livable out of The Nine, human life was all but worthless here, and the streets were only the beginning. The real scum hung out in private clubs and bars where unspeakable things happened, and Hell earned its reputation for being every jagged-edged nightmare promised in the big black book. Too bad the print version waters down its descriptions the way bartenders water down beer on ten cent draft night. If the good book preached even one uncut version of the world down here, people might not be so eager to line up at the fiery gates and take their chances.

The shop was all buttoned up for the night when I got there. I rapped my fist hard against the door, but the solid metal did little more than emit a dull thud.

"It's me. Open up." Something rustled around inside, then the door opened a crack. I shoved it the rest of the way open.

"Rule number one. Never open the door at night without checking to see who's there. Anyone could have ..." I stopped talking, letting my mouth hang wide when I noticed the Whip-Crack in Stray's hand.

"All right. Easy. That thing is very dangerous. If you flick the handle the wrong way, you're going to take my leg off or worse." I crossed my hands in front of my crotch and wished for an armor-plated sports cup.

Stray rolled her eyes and snapped the Whip-Crack. My legs flexed on their own, and I jumped high enough to crack my head on corrugated roof of the shop. I managed to land on my feet and reached up to rub my head. I did a quick inventory of all my appendages. To my surprise, they were all there. More surprisingly, the Whip-Crack had coiled and receded back into its holstered position at Stray's side.

"Relax," Stray said. "I had one of the Hellions show me how to use this in case I needed to protect myself when you're not here."

"You just asked a Hellion to teach you how to use this incredibly illegal weapon that no Woebegone has any business owning, for any reason?" I peeled my hand off my still aching head and examined my palm to be sure I wasn't bleeding.

"Yeah." Stray shrugged. "He was nice."

I let out a stream of hysterical laughter. "Stray, you are one of a kind."

"Thanks. I like to hope so."

"Oh, that reminds me." Stray clapped her hands together and did a little hop. "I have a surprise for you. Close your eyes."

I narrowed them instead. "What did you do?"

Stray scissored her fingers and pretended to poke me in the eyes. "I said close them or no surprise."

"I hate surprises."

"Just close your damn eyes and stop being an ass," Stray said. "I did something nice. You could try to be a little gracious."

"All right, all right." I closed my eyes, leaving them open a crack, but Stray moved around behind me and slapped her hands over my face ... hard. "No peeking."

She guided me through the rear doors to the bus storeroom and giggled. "Are you ready?"

"Yes," I groaned.

"Are you sure?"

I reached up and pulled her hands away. "All right, just tell me ..."

As I peered down, words left me. There among a field of sea-foam green sheet-metal and school bus windows sat a Vespa 98 scooter. Remnants of its bright blue paint job showed through here and there, but the little scooter had sustained lots of bumps and bruises. Age had browned it around the edges and in-between. The chrome had been blacked out and the street tires replaced with some sort of insane off-road rubber that would be right at home on an armored personnel carrier. It was no Harley. But the little rusty ride was about as incredible a gift as anyone could receive in a place like this, and somehow Stray had scored it for me.

"How ... who ..." I slapped my hand over my mouth and tried to reset my brain.

"Do you like it?"

"Are you kidding? This is incredible. How did you do this?"

My excitement made me want to squirm like a kindergartner who went too long without peeing, but I throttled it back to a grin wide enough to double as the front grill on a Cadillac.

"This little guy wasn't cheap. But you needed something to drive around, and walking is going to get you killed, so ..."

"Yeah but how?"

"Luck really. Someone came by with it. He found the Vespa after the firestorm, but he was terrified someone would cut his throat for it. I made a pretty good deal, considering."

I reached out and caressed the rust-pitted handlebars. "You are one of a kind." My eyes went a little watery, so I cleared my throat and pretended to scratch some sort of nondescript moving itch on my face.

Stray beamed. "It was the least I could do after all you've done for me."

I shrugged. "I was in the right place at the right time."

"Whatever." Stray smacked my arm. "Anyone else would have left me for the Fields. Plus, you took me and in and gave me a place to stay. I wanted to say thanks."

I smiled, "You're very welcome. I think I'm going to go out and get a little air before I turn in."

"You found cigarettes, didn't you? Give."

She held out her hand, and I placed the pack, minus one, in her palm. Stray didn't want to smoke them, she wanted to trade them. They were one of the few things more valuable than Twinkies.

"I can't believe you were going to hold out on me." She sounded serious, but the smile never left her face.

"Me?" I winked. "I would never do something like that. Now if you will excuse me, I am going to head out and smoke some of the merchandise."

"That's going against one of the golden rules," Stray admonished.

"I know, but I like the way these make me cough like I'm going to lose a lung."

Stray reached for something and tossed me the Knuckle Stunner I had set down when I went into the shop. "If you're going to stand out there, you might want this back. Just in case."

"Thanks." I shoved the weapon into my pocket and walked out the door. I put the cigarette in my mouth and realized I had no way to light it. Stuck in Hell and I couldn't even find a flicking flame to light a cancer stick. If that wasn't the true definition of perdition, I didn't know what was.

I turned to go in and find a couple of sticks to rub together when I saw someone slink out of the dark and head my direction. My hand found its way into my pocket, and I slipped my fingers around the Knuckle Stunner, ready to give my new visitor everything it had.

"Gabe."

I relaxed a little and squinted into the dark. "Jonny, is that you?"

"Yeah, I tried to catch you on the way in. I didn't want to knock. I have some information for you, about ..."

"Really? That was quick."

"Wasn't hard to find." Jonny lowered his voice and took a step closer to me. It made me a little nervous, but I didn't back away. "Look, I'm just giving you the information, okay. Don't be mad at me."

"Yeah, yeah. Spill it. What did you find out?"

Jonny hesitated. "I think your girl in there is a Disposable."

I faced him. "What?"

"Yeah, word is, there's a big ring operating out of the Skin Quarries. They lost a couple of their slaves." Jonny leaned back again, seeming to realize he still stood too close, and wrung his hands as his eyes shifted from side to side. "They're looking to get them back, but right now, I don't think they know where they all are. Someone known as the Scarecrow is hunting for them. Those guys use all kinds of names. If they're out of circulation much longer, they're going to regain their memories, then they won't be worth much to anyone." Jonny cringed. "Sorry, you know what I mean."

I sighed. "Yeah. After years of violent abuse, torture, and death, getting your memory back may not be such a good thing. I can't believe this."

"I'm sorry," Jonny said. "If I can do anything ..."

I flipped him my unlit cigarette and gave him a weak grin. "Thanks for your help, Jonny. If you come across anything else, give me a shout."

CHAPTER NINETEEN

The ride into the Agency the next morning was amazing. The Vespa, officially dubbed The Rusty Rocket, smoked like an oil rig fire and sounded like a chainsaw cutting its way out of a 55-gallon drum. The thing also screamed down the road like it had eaten a bad burrito and the nearest bathroom was a hundred miles away. When the streets ahead became congested, all I had to do was down-shift, and The Rocket backfired like a twelve-gauge shotgun, scattering the loitering riffraff out of my way. A ninja, The Rocket was not. As fun as it was, I would have to find a way to quiet it down. I didn't want to run into little Vespa pit traps set by Woebegone irritated by The Rusty Rocket's outgoing personality.

I parked behind tower three and made my way up the rarely used stairs to Judas's office. He listened as I ran through the events that transpired the night before, and my reasoning for not interfering. When I finished, he sat back in his chair, steepled his fingers at his lips and closed his eyes.

Procel and Mastema flanked him, occupying their usual corners in the room. I wanted to ask Procel if he was the mysterious Hellion who had helped Stray, but it wasn't the time. Mastema crouched on her pedestal as usual, blindfolded and following my every move like a grinning raptor out of a horror movie. She creeped me out so bad I couldn't even look at her. I wanted to hold up my hand and pretend we had an imaginary wall between us to block her murderous grin.

Judas remained silent. He sat behind his desk with his eyes closed, breathing deep and looking angry enough to feed my balls to a herd of rabid llamas. My attention slipped. I thought about a documentary I saw about llamas. Something about the males gnawing off one another's dangly bits to maintain breeding superiority. Barbaric little beasts. I hoped Judas didn't own any llamas.

"So, you are telling me," Judas said, interrupting my llama rumination, "that you sat there while she injected an unknown contagion into a gallon of milk, introducing it to the world population." Judas leaned forward and slapped his hands down on his desk. "Is that what you are telling me?" The sharp noise made me jump. I took a step back, raising my arms in defense.

Mastema let out a giggle and followed his movements with a sensual bob of her head. "Because I thought we discussed the fact that you were chosen to prevent that sort of event from occurring." His voice boomed and his eyes bulged, red and irritated. Judas stood up. I took another step back.

"Anything could have been in the syringe. A bad case of dysentery or the next Ebola virus. You had every opportunity to spill the milk, break the syringe, pretend to inject the bottle yourself, a thousand things to stop this from happening, and yet you did nothing. You just watched her do it."

Judas walked around the desk, stalking toward me, locking me into his gaze. My chest tightened and breaths came in shallow little hisses. The door wasn't far away. The window was even closer. Diving out almost seemed like the better option.

"And why?" Judas continued. "Do not tell me you failed to act because you believed you were right. I've been around a long time. Heard every excuse. I do not need to hear any more of yours. Fear stopped you, nothing else. You feared being caught or ruining your partner's career. The career based around cultivating misery and death."

Judas closed the gap between us, and I reflexively dropped my hands in front of my crotch because, well ... llamas.

Judas turned his wiry bearded chin up, accentuating the insane look in his eyes, and seemed to peer right through me and into my head.

"I know the doubt and fear that lives in your mind." He spoke through clenched teeth as if it were the only way he could keep from yelling. "I know how they lurk, waiting for you to weaken, hoping for a chance to make you turn away when you have a duty to act. I have exploited that weakness to destroy families and crumble nations. If you can't overcome something as simple as childish doubt, then you have no place here in this Agency and even less in my personal employ."

Judas stood for a moment, staring at me. When I didn't respond, he barked out, "Well? You have nothing to say?"

"I agree with everything you said," I choked out the words in a speed-yodeled panic. "And I would just like to thank you for not feeding any of my bits to your llamas, if you own any."

Judas eyed me then turned away, calming his voice a bit. "Needless to say, the sample you provided for us to test was inert. Had you not mixed them up, and kept the correct vial, Sabnack would have considered the entire mission a failure and moved on. Instead, he has a contagion we still know nothing about, and it is now out among the populous."

"I am sorry." I cast my eyes to the ground and put a hand to either side of my head, rubbing in slow circles. "You're right. I screwed up bad. I was afraid I couldn't stop her without getting caught. I thought ... I don't know what I thought. I can only say that it won't happen again." Weight fell heavy on my shoulders, and I couldn't shrug it off. Nothing Judas said now would make me feel any worse than the realization that I was a coward and now countless people would pay.

"This could decimate populations," Judas said. "Disease, war, and famine are the worst of the mortal threats. If one gets out of control, hundreds, thousands, millions could die."

I shuddered and wanted to sit, but I didn't deserve to.

"Saying it won't happen again is not enough." Judas crossed an arm over his chest and used the other to illustrate his words as he spoke. "You must understand. This is how these things always begin. An infected bird, a mosquito bite, a tainted glass of milk. It's always something small, and almost always set up by this Agency, The Disaster Factory. One infected individual. One person placed in the right place at the right time, and an infection becomes an epidemic. Remember that next time you think that a gallon of milk is of no consequence."

I dropped my hands to my side and managed to nod but still couldn't meet his eyes. It seemed to be enough. Judas rounded his desk, lowered himself into his chair, and started to write something on a stack of forms. I stood for a moment, wondering what I should do, then I glanced up at Procel. He tilted his huge horned head, gesturing me toward the door.

I took a breath to say something and caught the words in my throat. I didn't know what I would say. Odds were, it would be wrong anyway. Procel was right. Making a quiet exit while Judas had his attention focused away from me was best.

Procel nodded toward the door again, and I backed away as quiet as I could. When the door swung closed behind me, Judas chuckled. I turned back in time to hear one word—llama.

CHAPTER TWENTY

I stepped into the cavernous hall outside the reception area to Judas's office and reached back to keep the door from making any noise when it closed. He wouldn't hear anything this far away, but I couldn't seem to stop slinking. I could have blamed everything on Alex, saying she kept a close hold on things or wouldn't allow me to have any part in the op, but morals kept getting in my way. The very idea was laughable. I lived in The Nine. No one thrived on morals; we survived on opportunity. But if I lied to Judas, who would I tell the truth to?

I made my way through the empty hall, staring at the intricate black marbling at my feet. The dull echo of my shoes bounced off the walls and, after a second or two, a smile tugged at the side of my mouth. I realized something. Bad as the situation was, I owned up to it and survived. In a place where a little mistake could buy you a trip to the Gnashing Fields, I did all right.

The elevator opened, the one that takes people between floors, not the tilt-a-whirl dimension masher, and I got on feeling a little better. This was a new start. All I had to do was make sure nothing went sideways from here on out. When the doors opened on the first floor, the universe laughed at me.

"What are you doing here?" Alex stood not three feet away, waiting for the same elevator I was on. Sideways, here I come.

I stared with my mouth half open so long the doors began to shut, threatening a blissful reprieve. No such luck. Alex stuck her arm in the door. They rattled and groaned before bouncing open again.

"I was upstairs doing some in-processing stuff." I blurted the answer way too fast and prayed there was at least one upper floor where my story might be plausible.

The elevator let out an annoyed buzz and tried to close again while Alex stared at me, narrowing her eyes. "Are you getting off, or are you just going to stand there in the way?"

I had forced my mouth to move but not my feet. So I stepped forward, causing Alex to take a step back, and let the doors close behind me. Alex's lips tightened into a thin line. "I wasn't waiting for that or anything."

If I were any smoother, I'd be concrete.

"Oh. Geez. I'm sorry." I punched the up button like an epileptic junkie.

"Forget it." Alex grabbed my arm and pulled me around toward the front doors. "I hoped I would run into you anyway."

It took a few steps for me to match her rapid pace, but I managed to catch up before she got to the doors.

"Look, I haven't been very nice to you."

"Really." I put on a shocked face. "I hadn't noticed. I just told the guys upstairs about the Agency fruit basket you put together for me."

Alex glared at me out of the corner of her eye. "Don't interrupt me when I'm apologizing. This is hard enough as it is. And if you tell someone I bought you a fruit basket, I will kill you."

I made a motion to zip my lips and then pretended to peel a banana.

Alex cast her eyes forward, ignoring me and leading us on the familiar path toward tower three where we worked. "Like I said, I could have been nicer, and I wasn't all that honest about my experience. I guess I wanted the chance to prove myself on my own."

I waited a moment, grinning. "And?"

"And, what."

"And you're ssss ... come on you can do it."

Alex pursed her lips which made me laugh.

"Fine. I'm sorry. Are you satisfied now? You know you aren't making the rest of this any easier. I wanted to take you somewhere cool to make up for everything but ..."

"You mean we get to go Topside and do something fun? Oh please, please, please, please, please, please, please." I clasped my hands together and turned to jump in front of her, jogging my feet like a toddler. "You can torture me all you want. Let's just go do something real up there."

This time Alex grinned. I think it was the first time I saw a genuine smile on her face. It was bright and kind and made her eyes wrinkle a little at the corners. She revealed a hint of what or who she was under all that ink and hair dye; a good person, stuck in a bad place. Maybe we had more in common than I thought.

She made me grovel another thirty seconds, then said, "Fine. But no more talk about stupid fruit baskets."

I spun back around and fell in step next to her. "I don't even like fruit." I twisted my face in an expression of mock disgust. "Fruit is revolting, all that sweet, delicious juice rolling over your tongue and down your hand ... yech." I pretended to shiver and actually got a giggle out of her as she opened the door at tower three.

"Shut up and go put on your going-into-town clothes."

I got into my patchwork rusty orange and brown skinny superhero outfit. Alex guided us to a less than horrid landing in a lesser used outhouse storage area. Thankfully, the outhouses were either clean or so old and crusted that they no longer smelled. I didn't care enough to open the lid and check when I stepped out of my green plastic Tardis.

When we got to Alex's surprise, overwhelmed didn't quite cover it. She had found an expo that outlined the most influential advancements over the last forty years. I couldn't have come up with a more amazing outing if I tried. We walked up to a ticket counter, and Alex pulled out her Android television-phone and showed the lit screen to the person standing at the door. I was amazed by that technology alone, but the man blocking our way seemed less then enthralled. Before we could react, he drew a big square laser gun from under the counter and shot the defenseless Android in Alex's hand. I leaped back and waited for Alex to pull her automatic and return fire, but she didn't. Instead they both stared back at me as if I were the lunatic.

Alex rolled her eyes and gave me a wave. "Come on little kitty. Everything's safe." I shot the man a weak smile as I walked past him and followed Alex into the building. I felt like a kid from the old west dropped into the middle of a modern-day shopping mall. Alex was right. I never had a clue.

We spent the next few hours learning about Stealth Bombers, Drone Aircrafts, and Seedless Watermelon, which I had missed by a year.

Sucks to be me.

There were cameras that took pictures and displayed them on obscenely large televisions with a clarity that appeared almost three dimensional. I still had a hard time believing anyone would have something like that in their house. My last television had been a thirty-six-inch Zenith, and that behemoth had weighed more than my couch. The T.V.s now would take up more of my bedroom wall than I had wall.

Lightbulbs had changed into some sort of soft serve ice cream looking things—old Tommy Edison would be proud—and there was something called Amazon and the internet that I did not understand. Alex tried to explain the internet as a huge library where you could find anything you wanted, minus any actual books. Unless you went to a store like Amazon that sold pretty much anything, including books, but you couldn't drive to the Amazon store. They drove to your house to give you the stuff you bought without going to their store. I asked what happened when you finished the internet. Alex almost fell over laughing at that one. I still didn't get it. There was also something called a Facebook and a Twitter, but Alex refused to try and explain those.

I had missed compact music disks, DVDs, iPods and MP3s, but I would catch up on that a little. I saw something that looked like Alex's robot phone that played all kinds of music. Oh, and the music. What happened in the nineties? Did everyone take Quaaludes and start suicide clubs? Geez. Disco wasn't even that bad.

At the end of our visit, we stood in front of a proud auto display. Mankind's creativity and resources had come together to build and create incredible things, and at the end, one of the world's most powerful industries used that technology and knowledge to create what now stood before me.

My shoulders sank. "A Nissan Leaf? Does it fly?" The tiny speed bump of a car ran on electricity instead of gas and looked like the unholy union between a Ford Pinto and an AMC Pacer.

Alex shook her head, looking as let down as I was. "Nope."

"It took them forty years to figure out how to make a car run on batteries? I had toys that did that."

Alex nodded.

I stared at the ugly, bulbous hunk of ... I wasn't even sure the thing was made out of metal. "Back to the Future, my ass. Doc Brown must have rolled over in his DeLorean when this puppy vomited off the assembly line."

Alex seemed to want to say something, but she just smiled and walked away. "We should go."

I took one more look at the car, crinkled my nose as if it had farted, and followed Alex toward the exit.

"Thanks for this," I said. "This was great, and it helped. Even if I didn't understand everything."

"You're welcome. No reason why we shouldn't use our perks every once in a while, right?"

I held the door for Alex, and we headed back toward the short cut through a mechanical space to our Splice point. "They are gearing up to host the Olympics here in a few weeks too. Maybe we can come back and check things out. Might be another good opportunity to learn and blend into modern society."

I nodded. "That would be cool. I've never been to the Olympics. Do they still have Women's beach volleyball?"

Alex sighed.

"What?" I straightened and tried to look appalled. "Those women are incredibly athletic. It takes years of dedication to play at that level."

"As long as we go see the men too," Alex said.

"Deal."

We rounded the rear corner of the building and strolled through a forest of silver piping and ventilation ducts that made up the expo's HVAC system. Greasy water flowed in a slow trickle to a rusted drain, and steam rose out of every corner, producing trees of short-lived fog. I sniffed at the air, catching something on the wind, and glanced down at Alex. She peered back up at me. "What?"

"Well, well, who do we have here?"

I turned and was forced back several steps by the wall of odor that overtook us from behind. Max and Jake held some sort of strange, spiky looking fruit in their hands. Again with the fruit. I was sorry I ever mentioned it.

"Fancy seeing you two up here." Jake took a sloppy bite, and I retched in disgust.

I seemed to be the only one smelling this stuff. My olfactory senses had been ramped up to a million but only to smell this putrid mutant fruit. It was like having the worst super power ever.

The thought stopped me in my tracks. The denarius. Judas said the coin would give me a special power. One I would need at the right time.

I peered down at the pale slice in Jake's hand. "You've got to be kidding me."

Jake followed my eyes down. "You don't look so good. Maybe you need a little something to eat. Why don't you try some of my durian fruit?"

I tried to breathe through my mouth, but I could cover my whole face and the greasy odor would probably crawl in through my ears. "You smell like you've been French kissing the wrong end of a dead hippo."

"No." Max shook his head. "We haven't seen your mother today, but if we do we'll be sure and tell her hi." He made an obscene thrust of his hips, and his huge belly flopped out and back down.

"Right. You haven't seen that thing in centuries." Alex wagged a pinky at Max and raised an eyebrow. "You wouldn't know what to do with the little thing if you could find it."

He turned to her and bared his teeth in an evil leer. "I don't have to see the piston to know the engine's still running. I'd be glad to give you a peek under the hood though." He took a step in Alex's direction. I moved to step between them, but before I could, Jake had his rotted durian fruit shoved in my face.

"Why don't we leave the two lovebirds alone? You and I can sit down and have a bite to eat while we enjoy the show."

The smell overwhelmed all my senses and clogged my reasoning. Jake wore an olive-green overcoat that hung on his skeletal frame. I grabbed the collar, balled up my fist, and hit him in the jaw with everything I had.

Something went crunch. Jake fell back a few steps, dropping his fruit to the concrete, but he didn't fall. I still smelled the horrid stuff, but it no longer clouded my whole world. Jake's jaw hung at a grotesque angle. As I worked to wipe more of the durian out of my eyes, I realized what I had incited.

Jake's face began to mend and crack back into place almost instantly, revealing a knowing grin. We were in an out of the way area, so there weren't many bystanders, and none were paying attention to us.

"Nice shot, rookie, but wrong place, wrong time. Now it's my turn."

I steeled myself, waiting for Jake to launch himself at me, but he just stood there, grinning, with his yellow teeth and foot breath pumping in and out of his lungs like an overworked race horse.

I heard the threat before I saw it. Max made a casual circle around Alex, or she circled him, I couldn't tell. It didn't matter. I had my own problems.

Above my head, a growing cloud of hornets took an unnatural interest in the area where I stood. I didn't know how he did it, but skinny Jake seemed to be the bug whisperer. And he had just declared war on Gabe.

CHAPTER TWENTY-ONE

I backed away from Jake and into the chrome railing of a stairwell leading into some sort of basement access. The depth into which I had sunk in over my head staggered me. Like a kitten trotting through a dog fight, only the dogs hadn't eaten in a month, and the kitten wore its favorite bacon sweater.

Jake shoved his hands into his pockets and sauntered toward me, grinning as if he had a secret to share.

"That's all the fight you've got, newbie?" He worked his chin in wide circles, illustrating the fact that his bones were healed and all but daring me to take another shot. "You should teach your brat a little better, Alex. He needs to learn who he can mess with and who's going to make him pay."

Jake looked up, and I followed his gaze toward the sky. The odd gathering of insects grew into a dark humming cloud. As soon as I laid eyes on them, the mass descended and swirled around me. I latched onto the rail at my back, too horrified to move. Stinging insects of every kind cycloned past, whizzing inches from my face. Fat bumblebees, long skinny wasps, and innocent looking honey bees joined their hornet brethren, prowling the air near my body.

I told myself I would not scream.

Next time, I'd remember to cut him in half and run before he had time to regenerate. And there would be a next time. After this party, I would take a personal interest in squashing this little bug-boy.

I forced a smile. It must have been convincing, because Jake twisted his head in confusion. "Something funny?"

I yawned and tried to seem bored, praying one of the little critters would fly into my mouth and choke me to death before his friends started stinging. I didn't think Jake would buy the whole act, with me peeing in my pants and all, but I wouldn't give the little cockroach the satisfaction of knowing I was terrified enough to crack a walnut in my butt cheeks.

"Could you skip the cheesy super-villain banter and get on with it? I'm sure you two worked out some sort of dastardly duo routine —the grease-burger and his side kick the swizzle-stick—but I'd like to get this over with."

"I am not a sidekick."

I laughed. "You are a ninety-pound dork playing Army dress up in his grandpa's P.J.s. You barely qualify as a sidekick. What's your trademark move? Hopping around your buddy like a little chihuahua asking if you can be his friend?"

The cloud of insects parted, leaving a clear space between Jake and me. His face twisted into something dangerous.

I hadn't helped my situation, but I wanted to give him something to think about while I was gone.

"I am going to enjoy watching you suffer."

"Blah, blah, blah, more bad guy banter." My eyes flicked to where Alex stood, and I fought to keep a laugh from escaping my throat. "You might want to check on your big boss over there." I leaned in close and whispered. "By big, I mean fat." Jake gave me a shove backward, but I didn't go anywhere. The rail was still behind me, and despite my tough guy act, I hadn't convinced myself to let go. "You are falling down on your sidekick duties, is all." I blurted out the words before he had a chance to back away and launch his super-bug attack. "He appears to be in a bit of trouble."

Jake snapped his head around as if he had forgotten all about his partner. Alex held Max's face down on the ground, wrapped up like a doughy pretzel. Well, most of him touched the ground. His legs were splayed back on a wall as if he had been thrown through the air, splatted against the bricks, and then sort of melted down the concrete until his face stopped his momentum. He had no way to leverage his bulk against Alex. She had his arms in some sort of wicked ninja hold, preventing him from moving one way or another.

"Back off of him, Jake, or the news will have two stories to report in the morning."

Jake faced Alex. The stinging squadron of attack drones closed in and slowed their taunting swirl. I squeezed my shoulders, crossed my ankles, and tightened my grip on the rail in a fruitless attempt to cave into my own body and disappear. I couldn't even bear to keep my eyes open. I was being vacuum packed in a bug Ziploc, ready to be poked full of holes.

"Let him go," Jake said. "Or your boyfriend here is headed for the Pools."

I risked a peek. Alex's eyelids drooped at the absurd threat. "So, you're saying you'll do exactly what you planned to do a moment ago anyway? You two need to work on your bad guy game."

I cracked a smile then snapped my lips shut to discourage an overeager bumblebee. I didn't want my choking and screaming to ruin the ambiance Alex had worked so hard to establish.

"Scatter your little entomology experiment, or Max is going to learn something about spontaneous human combustion." Alex smiled and manifested a bright red fireball behind Max's head.

"Let him go, Jake." Max sounded like he was wheezing through a stack of old pillows, but his cracked voice came across loud and clear. "They're not worth it. We have a job to do, remember?"

"Yeah, Jake." I risked some tight-lipped speech but didn't dare to open my mouth and eyes more than a few millimeters. "You have a job to do. You can't do your job, and we can't do ours if you keep douching things up every time we see you. Let bygones be bygones. Release your creep hoard, and Alex will let your boss go. You two can kiss and make up and everyone will be happy."

Jake turned and glared at me through the writhing wall of insects. It occurred to me that if I had to kiss either of those two rejects, I would rather be stung to death.

"You wanna speed things up?" Max mumbled. "It's a little hard to breathe like this."

Jake's shoulders fell. "Fine." He waved a hand, and the growling swirl of flying harpoons took off like they remembered they were late for a lunch date. Both of my knees betrayed me. They buckled, but I managed to keep my grip on the rail. The effort wasn't enough to keep the smirk off of Jake's face though.

"Let him go." Jake faced Alex again.

She hesitated.

"You know what I can do and how fast I can do it." Jake's face became grim. "If you want to cause a scene, I am in the mood." He gestured back the way we came, toward the crowds of adults and children who had no clue about the supernatural throw down going on around the corner.

Alex smiled, patted Max on the back, and then let him go. She took a few quick steps to be sure he didn't decide to make a quick grab for her feet, then the rest went down like a weird foreign prisoner exchange. Jake moved to help Max, and Alex made her way over to me. Neither took their eyes of the other as they crossed paths, turning so they could keep the other in sight.

"There will be a time to finish this." Jake stared right at me. "I always pay off my debts." He made a show of rubbing his chin, and Max clapped him on the shoulder.

"Let's go. We have work to do."

The two of them walked away, licking their collective wounds, and I peeled my fingers off the rail behind me. I was pretty sure the feeling in my hands would come back at some point, but the joints had locked in for the long haul. We watched the evil duo until they disappeared around the corner. Then my shoulders fell, and I tried to rub my fingers back into submission.

Alex glanced down at the rail and let out a laugh.

"What?" I turned around and saw two perfect hand-shaped rust spots etched into the railing. The chrome had flaked away in speckled chips and revealed heavily rusted iron underneath. The rail wasn't rusted through, but there was a noticeable indentation where my fingers and palms had been.

"Well, looks like we found your Topside power." Alex ran a finger over the railing, brushing away more of the shiny flakes.

"What do you mean? Making things a little rusty is not a power. That's more like an annoying side effect, like getting cavities from eating sugar."

Alex laughed. "Your power might develop if you work with it. Maybe this is just the start." I appreciated the words Alex tried to use, after all, encouragement wasn't her forte, but she couldn't hide the smirk on her face.

I stared at her, and her smirk became a little laugh. "Look, we don't choose what manifests up here. Nobody knows why we get anything at all. You'll figure out something."

First, I acquire the delightful ability to enjoy bionic fruit funk, now this. I prayed the super smeller came from the coin. At least that would be temporary. I'd rather have the power to fit my head up an elephant's ass than deal with a smell of that fruit for the rest of eternity.

"What did you do when you lived up here?" Alex asked. "I mean, when you were alive."

A momentary panic washed through me. After all this time, the secrets of my past still catch up to me. "I worked in a junkyard, with my cousins." My voice came out rushed and stammered.

Alex raised an eyebrow. "Okay ... Maybe that's where this ... rust thing came from. Junkyard ... rust ... makes sense. We'll work with it."

"Thanks." I ignored the guilty pangs in my stomach for telling Alex the lie—or at least the half-truth. "I appreciate that. At least things can't get much worse. If I work at it, I might be able to rust out the rear quarter panel of an old Ford truck."

Alex laughed and started walking. "Good luck finding one that's not rusted already."

I nodded. "Maybe I should set my sights on something a little more challenging."

She laughed again.

We passed through a tight alley, and Alex tossed a homeless guy the last of our cash. He caught it and scrambled to his feet, nodding his thanks and waving the cash as he headed for a convenience store. Alex never glanced back at him.

"So why don't you develop your power?" I asked, politely ignoring her shocking generosity. "I mean it seems like you have one of those strap-on-the-cape-and-tights abilities to fight crime and strike terror into the hearts of pimple-faced teenagers everywhere."

Alex jerked her head in my direction, and her eyes grew red, watered and furious. For a second, I gave serious consideration to turning around to join the homeless guy, but then she sighed. "If you're going to be my partner I guess you have the right to know." She turned her face forward again, not looking at me as she spoke. "Before I died, I had a brother. He was autistic, and we were pretty much on our own. We didn't have the best parents, so I made it my job to look out for him." Alex crossed her arms, and the hard-edged woman melted into a vulnerable little girl. "See, my brother, he liked to watch fires, any kind of fires. Matches, fireplaces, barbecue grills, campfires, didn't matter. It calmed him down and put him into a sort of Zen place. I didn't see the harm as long as I kept things under control."

Alex kept walking, but her head was down, and her voice got small. I had the feeling she wasn't so much talking to me, as to herself. "But then things got out of control anyway. Sean found a book of matches and started our living room couch on fire. I took the blame—and the beating. That just upset Sean more. Me getting in trouble, I mean. He ran out and threw his lit matches into a dumpster. The dumpster happened to be sitting next to our ratty, old apartment building, so before we knew it, the whole place went up. My brother ran back in to find me, but I was already out. I went back in several times looking for him. The place didn't even have fire alarms. I screamed for everyone to run, going door to door for as long as I could, hoping he'd gone to the wrong place. A lot of people got out, but I never found my brother."

Tears rolled down her face and trailed the ground, but her voice never cracked. "I'm sorry," she whispered, then she fell silent.

I lifted a hand and almost laid it on her shoulder, but stopped at the last second, unsure if she would appreciate or resent the comfort.

I thought about the skeleton in my own closet, and another pang of guilt twisted my insides. She had trusted me with her darkest secret, her deepest sorrow, but when I had the chance to do the same, I glossed right past out of shame.

"I'm sure you know this, but none of that was your fault."

Alex peered up at me, a mix of anger and sorrow in her eyes. "Wasn't it? I was never a stranger to unhealthy vices, I mean look at me. I'm not exactly Betty Crocker, but I should have warned Sean off his obsession with fire. I knew where something like that might lead, but I never stopped him. It was easier to let him have his security blanket."

I shook my head. "Life doesn't work like that. You can't control someone's actions, not even your brother's. Not all the time, anyway. You could have sent him to every therapist in the country and never changed what happened. You can't look back and wonder what you could do different. You can only look forward and figure out what you can do different now."

Alex stared at me. "Tell me you read that in a fortune cookie or something."

"The back of a cereal box, actually."

"That must have been some horrible cereal."

I nodded. "Bound me up for a week. I was never the same again."

That made her laugh.

"Thanks," Alex said. "I still think you're full of crap, but it helps a little."

"Well, it's the least I can do after you got me this incredible outfit." I did a little spin and showed off my patchwork ensemble.

"It fits you, what with the whole rust thing and all."

I glanced down at the rusty orange, brown and grey squares. "Maybe you should be the one making fortune cookies."

"I think I'm more of a fortune pizza sort of girl."

"Pizza's better; you can print the fortune on the bottom of the box."

Alex nodded. "Thanks for listening. I'm sorry to unload on you. Feel free to toss any of your baggage my way if you feel the urge."

I paused.

"All my baggage is checked for now." I forced a confident smile that felt more like a total fraud.

"But I'll let you know."

CHAPTER TWENTY-TWO

Nine days had passed since our trip to the Salt Lake City Tech Show and our Battle Royal in the back lot. My life in the shop always made me happy, but it surprised me how much I wanted to return to the Agency. At least being away from the spy biz gave me some time to spend with Stray at the shop. She had a knack for making deals and seemed to be in line with my way of thinking when it came to helping those who might need a little extra push. I couldn't believe anyone could use her as a Disposable. She possessed an innocent and giving personality that drew people like a magnet. I couldn't help but wonder how much her personality might change when her memory returned.

I considered going out to search for Scarecrow, Stray's supposed Disposable handler, on my own, but without a lead, finding him would be like wandering around New York City hoping to recognize some guy who held a door for you two weeks ago. I had to dig up information at the Judas Agency or hope the Disposable dealers had assumed she had regained her memories and had cut their losses.

I doubted the latter would ever be true.

I glanced at Stray. She stood at the counter talking to a local

Woebegone, smiling as if she didn't have a care in the world, and I guessed she didn't. She still had no idea who she was or what she had been used for, and I had no idea how I could ever tell her.

Stray giggled, and I watched the other Woebegone relax, uncross his arms and smile. He dropped his guard.

Stray had something the Woebegone wanted more than anything my shop could offer. She had love, and she shared that love with everyone she talked to. I wanted her to hold on to that for as long as possible.

I realized I had a moment alone. Stray was occupied, and no other Woebegone wandered around the shop looking for a deal. I went to the outside wall and laid a palm on the corrugated steel. The icy metal felt rough under my hand, and I almost felt the years of torture it had endured. I closed my eyes, shutting out any distractions. The odor of rotted earth filled my nose, and the clanging bustle of Scrapyard City tried to beat its way into my ears, but I took a deep breath and pushed the diversions away. I focused all my energy into a single spot on my palm. A trickle of warmth, either power or my imagination, rolled down my arm and into my hand. I focused harder, squeezing my eyes closed and pressing my weight into the metal.

"Hey, Rookie." I jumped at the familiar voice and spun to face her. "I told you that doesn't work down here."

Alex made her way across the road and grinned at me.

"I wasn't ..." I stammered. "I just ..."

"You were just thinking real hard about holding up that wall? Concentrating on what you wanted to buy me for Christmas? Have to take a ..."

"Alright, alright," I said. "What are you doing here?"

"We're back in." Alex grinned and glanced at the hand I still held against the wall. I jerked my arm down, and she let out a little snort. "I really need to talk to them about getting you a place. I'm not coming all the way out here every time we have a job."

I tilted my head and looked around. "What's wrong with this? You too good to come out and slum it with us little people?"

Alex laughed. "Nope, but all this walking is murder on my boots." She bent her leg and peered over her shoulder at the dirty blue leather. "Look at what this place is doing to the heels."

"I'll buy you your very own can of blue shoe polish when we get back. I might even pay for a shoeshine." I winked.

"Like you could afford it." Alex turned toward my shop and walked toward Stray, who was already meandering out the door. "So, this your place? Looks like you got a little side thing going here."

She peered at Stray, and Stray aimed a dangerous expression in Alex's direction. It was the first time I had ever seen anything approaching dark or sinister color Stray's features.

"And who is this?" Alex walked toward Stray, and I got the sudden sense that static electricity was about to spark over a tank of gasoline.

"I'm Alex." She held out a hand toward Stray, ignoring the Woebegone who now seemed content to retreat at a sprint. "And you are?"

Stray shook her hand. "I have no idea, but we're working on it."

Alex nodded. "Interesting."

"Stray's been helping me out while I settle in at the Agency. She stays here and takes care of the place while I'm gone."

"And what does she do when you're here?"

"We sleep together," Stray answered, a little faster than she had to.

She let the statement hang without further explanation.

"She means in the shop."

"Right," Stray said. "We sleep together in the shop."

Alex raised her eyebrows and peered back at me again.

I felt a sudden compulsion to lock myself into the back room and probe my major arteries with a sharp pair of scissors.

"Well, we should go." I motioned Alex away from the shop. I got the idea touching her might cause me to lose a limb.

Alex nodded. "We should." She shot a plastic smile toward Stray and waved a princess parade goodbye. "Nice to meet you. I'm sure we'll see each other again."

Stray, to my shock, one-upped Alex in the fake smile department and waved back. "Can't wait. We'll get together for some girl talk."

Alex's smile faltered a bit. "Right, well let's go, Gabe. We have a long walk." She laced her arm around mine as if I were her date for a night on the town.

A jolt of simultaneous pleasure, topped with a double shot of dread, surged through my body and forced a nervous squeaky giggle to erupt from my throat. I tried to block our arms from view, but I moved too late. Alex made sure of that.

I smiled, acting as clueless as I felt, and pointed toward a small recess in the sheet metal wall. "We don't need to walk. We have a ride."

Stray stared white hot laser holes into my head as soon as the words came out of my mouth. What was it with these two?

Alex leaned to the side and followed my gaze until she saw the Vespa 98. "You have got to be kidding."

"I can't tell you where I got her. That would be unethical, with that whole no owning property rule and all, but she runs like a rocket on greased rails. I promise it'll be a lot better on your heels than this dirt."

Alex's lips tweaked into an expression of confusion and disgust, then she seemed to catch a glimpse of Stray's reddened face.

"Looks like fun." Alex smiled and waved me toward the scooter. "What are we waiting for?"

I glanced at Stray and waved, trying a smile of my own, but settled on bewilderment. She waved, crossed her arms, and disappeared into the shop.

I took a step to go after her, but Alex snapped her fingers. "Come on. If we're going to ride this pig, let's go."

I hesitated for a moment, then turned toward the scooter. The conversation would wait until later. I kicked The Rusty Rocket to life, and the rusty tailpipe belched out enough smoke and fire to make a coal train jealous.

I jumped on, and Alex sat on the rack behind me, scooting in close to hold me around my waist. "If you kill us, I am making a note to kill you as soon as I remember how we died."

I threw The Rocket into gear. We rocketed into the shanty nightmare like a low budget missile on knobby tires, leaving Stray and my shop behind.

CHAPTER TWENTY-THREE

I spit a feather from my mouth and peered out of the corner of my eye at Alex. We'd landed in a gigantic open barn filled with thousands of huge, red headed, waddling turkeys. Our sudden appearance initiated a cacophony of gobbles that echoed off the open metal rafters, redoubling in volume like some twisted sonic holiday weapon. The assault was relentless.

I tried to hum a soft lullaby, hoping to soothe the gobblers into a quieter mood, but all that came out was a cracked rendition of Jingle Bells. My throat was so tense, it choked the squeaky tune into Minnie Mouse range, but I couldn't stop. I feared my every breath could set off another gobble-ruption, or worse, attract one of the filthy scrotum heads toward me.

"What's wrong with you? Why are you ... squealing?" Alex spoke in a barely audible whisper, but the noise sounded more like a riot grenade in the barn where the Splice had dumped us out. I tried to relax. But my lips were sucked in past my teeth, and my arms were crossed tight enough across my chest to crack a rib.

"What—is—wrong—with—you?" Alex spoke a little louder, enunciating each word. A couple of nearby turkeys let out a feeler gobble. I shook my head side to side in jerky little movements, squeaking out the notes to *laughing all the way, ha ha ha.* I wished someone would zap me out of this Turkey Hell.

One of the over-ripe birds brushed its tail feathers against my leg. I jumped, turning the next few notes into a whimper. My movement, in turn, drew out a few more targeting gobbles. A smile grew on Alex's face that only meant one thing. She knew.

"Wait, you're afraid of turkeys?" Hysterical laughter exploded out of Alex's mouth, followed by the gobble thunderclap of a zillion wattle-dangling, feathered nightmares. They echoed her laughter at a thousand hiccupping decibels in true THX surround sound, making me want to claw out my eyes just to shove them into my ears.

I turned and sprinted the entire length of the massive barn with my hands cemented to either side of my head, parting the sea of pink-skinned scrotum heads, with a shrieking finale of my carol lullaby.

I stopped running and shrieking, once I was out of the Thanksgiving nightmare, and paused to hyperventilate.

Alex followed me out the door several moments later. She was out of breath as well, but I suspected it was from laughing rather than some frantic escape.

"Turkeys? I cannot wait until Thanksgiving." She snorted out another laugh. "Do you have any other fears you'd like to talk about while we're here? Santa Claus, The Tooth Fairy, Bologna sandwiches with extra mustard?"

"Do you know what they do to turkeys in places like that?" I said.

Alex pressed her lips together to control her laughter and raised an eyebrow.

"They inseminate them so they can have more turkeys, and I do not mean they turn down the lights and play Barry Manilow. They use hoses and tubes and syringes the size of bazookas. Turkeys are flopped upside down, stuff flies everywhere. I can promise poop isn't the only thing marring your fancy blue boots." I retched.

"If you're into Turkey porn or something, I don't want to know."

"A buddy of mine lived on a farm when I was a kid. He showed me once. I never got near a Thanksgiving turkey again."

"Look at my boots." Alex held a foot up for my inspection. I retched for a second time at the slimy concoction of turkey poop, mud, and nondescript goo that hung off the blue leather.

"That's going to take more than shoe polish." I held out a palm to obstruct the sloppy mess from view. "Put that down, you're not helping. The smell is enough to make your point."

"You're the one who didn't want to go through the dumpster again." Alex dragged the side of her boot along the ground as we walked, leaving a green smear in her wake.

I averted my eyes upward and tried not to breathe through my nose. "At the time, I ran under the assumption that there couldn't be a place worse than the greasy interior of a fast food dumpster. I now stand corrected. Thank you."

"You might want to clean off those disasters too." Alex pointed at my feet. "Check out your shoes. At least mine don't have treads. I think you're carrying half the barn floor with you."

I kept my eyes pointed toward the sky. "I'll take your word for it." I dragged my feet on the ground and stomped like a toddler throwing a fit, not wanting to see or even get a whiff of anything that came off.

"So, is there a name for turkey phobia, or ..."

"I do not have a turkey phobia—and it is called meleagrisphobia."

"Figures you would know," Alex said. "Will you just tell me if I got everything off my boots?"

She caught herself and tried to appear indignant. "Hey, what if I injured myself?"

"You would heal, but the image of your boot seared into my mind never would."

"Big baby."

I nodded. "You never told me why we're back here in town again."

An obvious attempt to change the subject, but Alex let me off the hook.

"We are heading back over there."

She pointed toward a house I recognized. It was the place where we infected the milk bottle with the cave contagion. As we got closer, Alex's face became strained, and her forehead wrinkled with worry.

"You all right?" I asked.

Alex held up a hand and made her way to the front door of the house. Last time we had approached the little white house from the back, walking through the fence and crossing the big yard. This time we circled around to the front, and I discovered, like many other homes in the area, part of this one had been converted into a business. A doctor's office. Maybe the only doc in town.

Alex opened the door and walked over to a little desk in the front waiting area. An older woman sat there in a conservative violet-colored dress with a silky white scarf tied around her neck. Her glasses were perched at the end of her nose, and she peered up at us with a smile as the jingle of little bells rang on the doorknob behind us.

"Is the doctor in?" Alex asked.

"He is, but I am afraid we are very busy today." Her eyes flicked around us, and we turned to find a waiting area hidden around the corner. Almost every chair was filled with miserable-looking people staring at the ground, looking at magazines, or struggling to keep their children quiet while the others basked in their own exhaustion.

"Wow, are you always this busy?" I asked.

"Not always," The woman said. "But we are the only office in town. When the flu hits around here, it hits us hard. You're not from around here." It was a statement, not a question. "Mind if I ask why you're looking for the doctor?"

Alex opened her mouth to answer, but she seemed to stall out, as if such an obvious question had never occurred to her.

The silence felt about as comfortable as an accidental fart in a crowded elevator, but I managed a smile and put a hand on Alex's shoulder. "We're just passing through on our way home to visit my parents. We stayed in a hotel last night, and I realized I forgot my prescription. I don't want to drive all the way back. So I hoped the doc might re-write it or verify it, so I can get a refill."

The nice Purple Lady never lost her smile. A real smile, not the smile you see down in The Nine where a smile meant you were up to something.

"Well, that shouldn't take long," she said. "Why don't you sit down, and I'll see what I can do for you."

Alex smiled back at her, and I noted hers seemed decidedly more Nineish, but it was still pleasant. "Thank you."

We sat down, and Alex resumed her worried expression. She rubbed her palms on her legs and stared at the wall as if something ate at her and wouldn't let go.

I put an arm on the back of her chair so I could lean forward and speak at a whisper. "I know we're not here for a millennium physical, so what are you up to? I've never seen you this worried. You're starting to freak me out."

Alex surveyed the room and leaned in my direction without turning to face me. "I found out what that sample contained. The syringe didn't have some little cold and flu bug. We injected that milk with a virus no one Topside has ever encountered. The Judas Agency wanted to know how effective it is on humans." Alex rubbed her face and glanced over my shoulder, searching for unwanted eavesdroppers. "They don't care if this guy is immune; they want to know if he gets sick. If he does ..." Alex's voice cracked. She stopped for a second and then started again. "If this contagion makes him sick, The Judas Agency has found an all but unstoppable disease."

My stomach dropped clear to my turkey poop shoes. I could

have stopped it—twice—and now we waited to see if the guy I had allowed Alex to infect would come out to look like patient zombie zero.

A door to an exam room opened, and a man walked out. He staggered and coughed, clutching a bouquet of tissues in his left hand and a stethoscope in his right. Stars swam into my vision. I wondered for the first time if I had the ability to faint. Alex had gone so stark white, her tattoos looked as if they were painted onto typing paper.

"Sorry, Doc," the man said. "I didn't mean to knock this out of your hand." He turned and faced someone else coming out of the room.

"No worries." Another man, this one wearing a white lab coat, appeared in the doorway and took the stethoscope. "No harm done."

I let out the breath I had stifled in my lungs with an audible whoosh. The way my luck was running, I'd make a boatload of money if we went to Vegas.

The patient made his way toward the desk. The doctor followed him out. He seemed to be in his mid-forties with a full head of salt and pepper hair and a short-trimmed beard to match. Best of all, the man looked to be the most fit person in the room, Alex and me included. The guy must compete in pentathlons for lunch every day. If he was sick, I wanted whatever he had. This small-town doc looked like the fountain of health shimmering among all the sick and wounded in the room. Color washed back into Alex so fast she looked like she had blushed. The heat of circulation returned to my skin too. My stomach even made the return trip from my feet.

"If you're still feeling bad in week or so, you come back and visit me. We'll do a few tests and see what we find, but I think this is something that'll run its course," the doctor said. "Stay out of those fields for a few days. Rest and drink plenty of liquids. You'll be fine."

The patient nodded and headed for the door. "Thanks, Doc."

Purple Lady raised a hand before the doctor had time to escape and waved him down. "David, can I bother you for one moment?"

She glanced over at us, and my panic resurfaced. Purple Lady was about to call our bluff.

Alex pulled out her smartphone and waved the little black Android, which I had yet to see, in the air. "I'm sorry. I just got off the phone with the pharmacy. They said we can have our regular doc call, and they will refill the prescription for us."

Purple Lady smiled and nodded. Doctor David looked confused. "Never mind, I guess we got everything worked out on our own."

She glanced back at us as we stood to leave. "If you need anything else, I'd be glad to help."

Guilt washed over me. Here we were trying to infect this poor office with who knows what, and this kind and unassuming woman wanted to do anything to help us. I needed to get a whole lot better at doing my job for Judas.

"Thank you, ma'am," I said, "but I think we have everything covered. I appreciate all your help."

CHAPTER TWENTY-FOUR

A lex and I headed back toward the Splice to report on the good doctor to the Judas Agency. I hadn't taken the time to notice on our way in, but the town still seemed deserted. We were here in the middle of the night last time. It had made sense for the place to be empty. Now, in broad daylight, the place looked downright desolate. The windows were clean, and the displays looked fresh and tidy. A few parked cars even lined the street, but there still wasn't a soul to be seen. I wondered how anything in the town managed to stay open. They didn't have much of a tourist trade. Most of their clientele had to be the local farmers and ranchers in the area, but business wasn't exactly booming.

One other thing didn't add up either. If the Judas Agency wanted to test out an infectious contagion, why do it in a town the size of a postage stamp? The best they might hope for was a few hundred infected people. Someone might pass through from out of town and carry the disease out, but that was a long shot. Anyone who got sick would hunker down and wait it out at home. Not exactly an epidemic befitting the Disaster Factory.

"You mumble." Alex stared at me as we walked.

"Sorry?"

"I said, 'You mumble,'" Alex repeated. "You quiet down and then start this indiscernible grumbling, mumble thing. Like a stalling engine stuck in a vat full of pudding. It is not endearing."

"Sorry. I didn't realize I was doing it."

Engine stuck in a vat full of pudding. Worst metaphor ever.

"You're mumbling again." Alex backhanded me in the chest. "What is wrong with you? Are you some kind of lunatic? I should have come up with a better metaphor."

Now she freaked me out.

"Can you hear ..." I made a vague gesture toward my head and squinted, wondering if I had grumbled my thoughts out loud or if she had read my mind. I decided against finishing the question.

"Forget it," I said. "Hey, can I ask you a something without you getting all defensive and fist-punchy?"

"With you, it may be impossible, but ask anyway."

"When we were in the office back there, you seemed awfully worried about the doctor, and about what it might mean if that virus had been a viable."

"Yeah, so? I'm not a monster."

"That's just it," I said. "You work for the Judas Agency—The Disaster Factory. How can you work for them and still have that kind of conscience? Isn't a handicap like that sort of detrimental to your career?"

We walked along without saying anything. I wanted to wait her out and let her answer when she was ready, but the silence wore me down. "Look, I'm sorry. I didn't mean ..."

"Not everyone can survive out in The Nine the way you do." Alex almost shouted the words, making me want to jump out of the way. "I spent a lot of time recycling through the Gnashing Fields while I lived on the streets of that burned-out, frozen junkyard full of killers, thieves, rapists, and abusers."

Alex clenched her fists, and I had a sudden urge to fall back out of her reach.

"I had to learn how to fight and claw my way out of the

gutters. The Judas Agency gave me a place to live and relative safety. I even own a thing or two. I have more now than I've ever had, and I earned every bit of it. If you're asking me if I feel guilty about doing my job? No. I do what I have to in order to survive. I just learned how to do it better than most."

Perfect. First, I make her think I'm a lunatic, and now she wants to kick my ass.

"It was just a question," I said. "No judging. I've done plenty I'm not proud of, both alive and dead."

I cringed, realizing what I had just implied. "That's not what I meant."

"I am proud to work for the Agency. Try climbing down off your high horse, and you might see that we're not all bad. You might even find you're not as perfect as you think you are."

"I'm sorry." I didn't try to refute her accusations. "Like I said, I was curious. That's all."

"Well, now you know." We walked in an uncomfortable silence after that. I was thankful we didn't have much further to go. Our conversation had carried us all the way down Main Street, up the short distance on the country road, and then to the driveway leading to our Splice location. Alex stopped at the top of the dirt drive and dug something out of her pants pocket. "I almost forgot. I have something for you."

I felt my face brighten. "Is it a gun? Or a knife? Some sort of fancy hellion weapon that makes me irresistible to women?"

Alex peered at me. "A fusion-powered pheromone bomb wouldn't be enough to do that."

I put my hand over my heart. "You wound me."

"Shut up. You make giving you things so hard." Alex grabbed my hand and slapped a small metal object into my palm much harder than she had to. It was about the size of a quarter. An obsidian J encircled by a brass compass.

"What's this?"

"It's a lapel pin. Be thankful I didn't decide to attach it to your chest before you opened your mouth."

I smiled. "Thanks, Alex, this is great. But I didn't get you any ..."

"I'm not giving this to you to be nice, freak."

"Oh, well ... none taken."

"This is a portal key. This lapel pin allows you to use the Envisage Splices to travel."

I raised an eyebrow and shot her a mischievous grin. "You're giving me keys to the family Buick? Are you sure I'm ready for this? What if I head straight to a frat party or something?"

"Then you will be the creepy old guy that makes everyone uncomfortable."

I winked. "I stick to what I'm good at."

Alex sighed. "Try to pay attention. You need a visual point of reference for where you're going, either through personal experience or a photograph. Then you hold that image in your mind when you're in the Agency elevator and throw the lever. Simple as long as you don't lose your concentration and start thinking about your sorority girl back at the shop or something."

"Wait, what happens if I think about sorority girls?" My grin grew wider.

"To return," Alex said, ignoring the childish comment, "all you do is go back to the Splice you arrived through, and it will pull you back in and return you to the Agency. Wanna try?"

"Wait, that means we have to go back through the turkey farm again."

An evil grin grew on Alex's face. "Yup, and I hear it's singles night."

I ran my hands across my face and up over my head. "I should have never told you about that."

"No, you shouldn't have." Alex's smile grew larger, and she headed off toward turkey hell. "I've already thought of half a dozen gift ideas."

I groaned and followed. "Everyone has a weakness, you know."

"Yeah, but everyone's weakness isn't turkey-phobia."

"That's not what it's called." I tried not to laugh, but even I recognized the absurdity. "It is called meleagrisphobia. It's a condition."

Alex laughed. "Mellon-ass-phobia. Right, my mistake. You can put it in the report to Sabnack when we return."

CHAPTER TWENTY-FIVE

"And what about his family?" Alex and I glanced at each other as Sabnack showed his huge feline teeth in a smile. "Did the doctor's family show any signs of being ill?"

"We didn't think to ask," I said, jumping in to take the hit before Alex.

We had returned to the Agency to report our visit to the doctor's office, thinking Sabnack would berate Alex for another failed mission and start my tally at one, but instead, he seemed happy about our news.

"You could have done better with the children, but you came back with a successful mission, Alex." Sabnack nodded at me. "Seems like a partner was just the thing you needed. Perhaps next time, we'll send you out on something a little more challenging."

Alex smiled, but I recognized the mix of emotion in her eyes. Confusion, frustration, and maybe a little anger. "Thank you, Sabnack. I'm glad everything worked out."

I showed a smile too, and the three of us stood there, staring at each other like a trio of bobble-headed idiots.

Sabnack's eyes flicked out the side window to his office. I

followed his gaze and recognized the two men entering the main hall. My stomach flopped.

"Max ... Jake, get in here." Sabnack's smile disappeared, replaced by a tight-lipped snarl. "Some sort of bug video in Salt Lake City has surfaced on YouTube. You wouldn't know anything about that, would you?"

All of a sudden, my legs wanted to run whether the rest of my body went with them or not. "We should let you go back to work, Sabnack ... Sir ... Mr. Sabnack."

Alex grabbed my arm and jerked me toward the door. Sabnack never gave me a second glance. We managed to escape before Max and Jake had spotted us in his office, thanks to a well-placed corner near his door.

"We should let you go back to work, Sabnack ... Sir ... Mr. Sabnack." Alex mimicked my stuttering exit a little too well.

"We're out, aren't we?" I said.

"No thanks to your graceful exit."

We made our way down the cavernous hall toward the elevator that would take us back to the main level. The glass-walled office reflected flashes of my likeness, along with Alex's and all the other Woebegone rushing through the area.

"So, I think we're free for a while?" Alex cast her eyes to the floor and kept walking, but the statement sounded like a question.

I nodded, acutely aware of the odd tension that had exploded like a gas grenade into the middle of the hallway. I didn't have time for this. I needed to talk to Judas and tell him about Sabnack's reaction to our report. Something gnawed at me, and I couldn't figure out what it was.

Alex let out a sigh and looked at me. "Do you want to abuse our authority and go Topside for a little fun? I need a break."

I stared at her, pretending I hadn't noticed the awkward invitation to a real date. It was like trying to ignore an elephant dressed as a mime.

"No, I think I'm going to head home," I said. "I'm beat and need to check on a few things."

"I'll bet you do," Alex said under her breath.

"Sorry?" I raised an eyebrow, feeling like the biggest idiot loser on the face of the earth.

"I said, I have stuff to do," Alex made an abrupt turn to head back the way we had come. "I need take care of some work before I head back to my apartment. Have a great ride through the slums."

Alex waved over her shoulder and marched away like an Olympic supermodel sprinter.

I ... have ... lost ... my ... MIND! Maybe my meeting with Judas could wait.

I watched Alex a moment longer, all but biting my knuckles with frustration, then turned to rush toward the elevators. The doors slid open with a rattled groan and a snake-faced demon got off. It actually hissed at me on the way by, so I gave him a thumbs-up and the cheesiest grin I could muster.

Once I got to Judas's office, I gave him a rundown of the situation. I hoped he would make that wrinkled, you're a childish idiot face he always made when ... well, pretty much any time I opened my mouth, but this time he seemed as stumped as I was.

"And Sabnack appeared to be satisfied the sample was not viable?" Judas scratched his beard and leaned back in his chair. I grasped the arms of my own bone chair and sat back as well. Seeing him confused and off balance was more disheartening than watching him try to resist the urge to strangle me.

"Alex said they initiate these kinds of dry run missions all the time." I shrugged. "Is it possible he didn't care whether the virus took or not? Maybe he was just happy we didn't screw up the mission."

Judas paused, waiting for me to answer my own question. After a moment, I shook my head. "No way. He seemed much too happy about it. I could see him being satisfied or a little surprised, but not happy. Not if the mission were a total failure."

Judas considered and nodded in agreement. "I can't help but think there is something we're missing."

Judas turned to Procel, who stood at his usual post like a giant gargoyle opposite Mastema. "Do a quiet inquiry through your sources and see what you can discover. Perhaps there is someone out there who can shed a little more light on this situation."

Procel answered with a single deep nod of his head, and Judas faced me. "Have they given you access to the Splice points yet?"

I fumbled in my pocket and pulled out the lapel pin Alex had given me and ran my thumb over the shiny black J. "I haven't tried it on my own yet. My partner gave me the pin today."

"Be careful when you use the Envisage Splice transporter. You could be watched when you come and go, but if someone takes an interest in what you're doing, your destinations can be tracked as well. Make sure you don't do anything that would raise suspicion."

"Not me." I smiled. "I'm a picture of stealth and shadow."

Judas paused and narrowed his eyes, giving me his *be serious* look.

"As I said, wait a few days for things to settle, then go back to that town. What was the place called?"

"Briarsville. I noticed it on a sign last time we were there."

"Fine," Judas looked irritated, probably because he couldn't figure out what the Agency was up to any better than me. "Go back to Briarsville in a few days. See if you can turn over a few new stones. Perhaps you were distracted last time."

I got lost for a moment trying to decide if there were any distractions during our original missions. It was only me and Alex. Alex and her tattoos, her milky white skin, that blue hair, and her lips ...

Shut ... up...

Judas stared at me, waiting for an answer to a question I hadn't heard. I nodded, hoping it was the correct response. "I'll head back as soon as I can."

In the meantime, I wondered if I might be able to turn over a few stones here at the Agency about Stray and that lurker Scarecrow.

Judas nodded. "Let me know what you find out. I will pass word to you if Procel turns anything up that you need to know about."

CHAPTER TWENTY-SIX

A half hour had passed before I tracked Alex down again. When she wasn't in her office, I asked about her apartment, but she wasn't there either. I went from tower three to tower four and to the top floor of tower six before someone told me she had gone to an event in the gym.

A loud cheer rose from a room I couldn't see and then calmed to a low murmur, but the rumble of voices never died away. I walked past several vacant training rooms, walled in glass for outside spectators, full of equipment that looked both familiar and completely alien. They contained everything from baseball bats and katanas to Whip-Cracks and some strange weapon that looked like a three-piece nun-chuck with retractable blades on the ends.

I resisted an urge to examine the new toys and followed the rising roar coming from the main room ahead of me. When I opened one of the big orange double doors, I realized why Alex was there. Pretty much everyone in the building had come to see the show—whatever the show was. Seemed I was the only one who didn't know about it. I excused myself and pushed through the shoulder to shoulder crowd. The bright room, about the size of a couple of basketball courts, held a decent turnout, only without the baskets or the overpaid athletes. I started to wonder if I could spot Alex among the throng of shouting spectators, even with her distinctive blue hair. That's when I realized I had been looking in the wrong place.

One of the Woebegone fans shouted in excitement and grabbed my shoulder. When he pointed toward the center of the room, I saw her. Alex wasn't there to watch the event, she was the event. I had become so preoccupied with the crowd, I hadn't bothered to check out the show.

Alex stood in a floor level fighting ring, and by ring, I mean a maze of wooden pathways lined with rows of spiked poisonous-looking plants, kettles of boiling liquids, and posts with sharpened blades, jutting out at a million odd angles.

Alex wore nothing but a tight pair of shorts and a sports bra. Her tattoos knew no bounds, covering her thighs, back, and even her feet. She had her long blue hair bound in a high ponytail with a hot pink ribbon, completing the punk rock warrior look. My mouth fell open in awe, and I had to force my lips closed with a snap of my teeth. I couldn't stop my eyes from taking in her supple skin and hard muscle. I wanted to look away or at least avoid acting like a midnight stalker at an adult theater. A trench coat and dark glasses would be less obvious.

I was glad she hadn't noticed me. I couldn't tear my eyes away, despite my embarrassment. I didn't want to know how she would react if she caught me ogling her picture-perfect body. From the looks of her fighting gloves, they had already done a fair share of damage that evening. They didn't need to add any of my blood and humiliation.

Her opponent, a scared looking man wearing bright orange sparing armor from head to toe, leapt a hedge of spiked death cactus and tried to reset his defensive stance. Alex anticipated this maneuver and jumped before he did. She met his awkward landing with a hard roundhouse kick to the chest, sending him flying toward a post full of jagged blades.

Alex smirked, leaped forward like a cat, and diverted his fall with a quick jerk of his arm. The man flailed. His head whipped to the side like a toddler saved at the last second from falling down a flight of stairs. Alex let go, and he slid across the wood floor, stopping before he hit another of the death cactus hedges. The crowd went wild again. The stunned Woebegone opponent got up, bowed, and sprinted out of the ring.

Alex held her arms out, and the crowd went quiet. "Any other lessons today?" Everyone found something fascinating to study on the ceiling, on their shoes, on the person standing next to them—anywhere other than a direction that might cause them to make direct eye contact with Alex.

I waited a second, then moved forward through the crowd. Volunteering was a bad idea, a very bad idea, but my legs ignored all of the logic being shouted from my brain. I had just stood the Terminator up for a date and had determined that I wanted to keep my blood and my dignity, or what's left of it, safe within my body. Now I was going to invite Alex to kick my ass in front of all these nice people. Yeah, I had everything well under control.

I moved to the front of the crowd. Alex's gaze locked on mine. A grin, wider than the Cheshire Cat's, grew on her face, and my legs finally got the message. Too late to turn back now. I opened my mouth to announce voluntary suicide, but a voice from the other side of the ring called out to Alex first.

"I have time for a lesson—if you are willing to learn."

Her roguish smile transformed into something more wary and welcoming. She turned toward the Woebegone man emerging on the other side of the room. The crowd began to murmur, and I felt the tension rise. Whoever this Woebegone was, he had just earned a Twinkie from an anonymous fan.

"Sensei Mitsu." Alex bowed. "This is an unexpected honor, though a true master knows a teacher can learn as much from his student as the student can learn from her teacher."

Sensei Mitsu bowed his head. "Learn, yes. As much?" Sensei

Mitsu shrugged a shoulder and leapt a spiky planter, clearing one of the wide paths to bound off the edge of a boiling cauldron. His feet made contact for less than a millisecond, but the strike was enough to tip the cauldron over in Alex's direction. The slick, boiling liquid rolled toward her like a wave.

Alex back-flipped to another path and managed to stay clear of the hot oil, but her landing looked off balance. This was the first time I had ever seen Alex seem unsure of herself.

That wasn't quite right. She had the same unbalanced expression earlier; when we were talking, and she had asked me out on a ...

All at once I realized how hard it must have been for her to open up and offer that invitation, and how bad it had hurt when I pretended nothing happened. My face fell as I realized I may have done more damage to her than she could have ever done to me in that ring.

I stared at Alex's smooth powerful movements and thought that might be stretching things a bit, but I had hurt her, nonetheless.

Sensei Mitsu took advantage of Alex's momentary misstep and flipped over behind her, attempting to catch her in the kidney with a reverse donkey kick.

Alex may have been off balance, but she was able to shift enough to make him miss and then spin to face him. They traded punch after punch, kick after kick, designed to trap joints, break bones, or crush throats; each masterfully blocked and countered with precision.

The mood of the crowd changed. They went from rough and rowdy to watching in shocked awe.

Alex broke the rapid stalemate with a feint to her left and a side flip to an adjacent path. She touched down and reversed directions as Sensei Mitsu took the bait. He leapt toward her with a flying kick meant to hit her in the back and drive her to the ground, but Alex was already in the air, her fist cocked out to the side of her body as she leapt past him with an ugly WWF-style clothesline.

Sensei Mitsu had just enough time to register the fact that he was screwed before Alex's fist hit him in the face.

The blow wasn't enough to do any real damage, but the strike slowed his forward momentum, sending him straight down toward the spiked death plants at his back.

The crowd took a collective gasp. Sensei Mitsu flipped over like a cat in midair and landed in a bridge position across the plants on his fingers and toes.

He stayed that way for a second, then Alex strolled over and put one of her bare tattooed feet right in the middle of his shoulder blades.

Sensei Mitsu laughed. "For a moment, I thought you might help me up."

Alex smiled and shook her head, "That is one lesson I will never forget. I'll never make that mistake again—at least not until you say the magic words."

Sensei Mitsi's arms began to shake. Alex's smile faltered.

The room was silent enough to hear a flea fart, then Sensei sighed. "I yield."

The crowd went the kind of wild you would see if the Cubs won the world series, like that would ever happen.

Alex pulled her foot back and helped Mitsu up. This time he bowed as deep as she did. They both smiled and turned to go their separate ways.

I worked my way through the smiling throng, already rehashing the fight with flailing fists and wild exaggerations. I pulled up beside Alex and shot her my most irresistible smile.

She resisted.

"I thought you had to go home to the wife and kids." Alex kept walking, not bothering to slow down.

"I heard about some sort of hot chick death match going on up here, so I decided to stick around."

I realized that I called Alex a hot chick and prepared myself to be flung into one of the spiked death plants or have my face scalded off with oil. Alex stopped and smiled instead. "I hope you enjoyed the show. About time you headed back to the little woman though, don't you think?"

I paused for a second, realizing the pile of dog crap I could be sinking my foot into.

"Look, I need to explain something about Stray."

Alex started walking again. "No explanation needed—or wanted."

"She's a fresh born I saved before that last firestorm," I stepped to keep up with her. "I put her up until she can figure things out, but I think she has been used as a Disposable for a very long time. When she gets her memories back, things might not be so good for her."

That stopped Alex in her tracks. "How do you know she's a Disposable?"

"I have local sources. I hoped you might be interested in abusing a few of your professional powers to help her out. Find out what she's into and how to keep her safe. Someone known as the Scarecrow was her handler. Ever heard of him?"

Alex stared at me for a minute, looking like she might be considering something, then she shook her head. "This is none of my business. And it's not yours either."

She started to walk away again, but I grabbed her arm. I heard the collective gasp of the crowd play through my mind, but it was too late to do anything about it. Alex looked down at my hand and up at me.

"Stray is one of the good ones." My life was literally in the palm of my hand, but my voice stayed steady, and I stared Alex dead in the eyes. "You know as well as I do, the good ones are pretty rare down here. No one deserves to be used up and thrown away like a Disposable. She needs a break."

A long moment passed where our breathing seemed to be the only thing that existed in the world, then Alex clenched her eyes shut. "I can't believe I'm doing this."

I smiled. "Thank you."

"Let go of my arm."

"Right," I said. "Sorry about that."

"Grab me like that again, and you will be. And don't thank me for helping you yet. Scarecrow works for some real bad people. You cross him, you are buying into serious trouble. The kind of trouble your back-alley friends won't be able to help you out of."

"I guess it's a good thing the midnight ninja's on my side."

"Not funny," Alex said, but she smiled.

"I understand the trouble I'll be getting into, but I think Stray deserves the hand. We all need one now and then."

Alex groaned. "Fine. I know where Scarecrow and his boys like to hang out, but there isn't much you can do about it. You aren't going to spook those guys into leaving her alone. As long as she knows what's going on and how to protect herself, that's about all you can do for her."

I twisted my face into an expression you might make when you stubbed a toe. "Does it count if she's halfway there?"

"I'm sure she can take care of herself, but I can teach her a few self-defense ..."

Alex slowed down and stopped talking when I began to shake my head.

"Wait, you mean she doesn't know?" Alex threw a quick jab into my gut. I pretended like the effortless blow did not feel like a rocket propelled cinder block.

"I figured she spent so much time in misery, I wanted her to enjoy what time she had before all those memories came flooding back. That sort of thing can change a person, screw them up for good. Years of abuse and death and torture with no memory of it, then everything in your past hits you at the same time? That kind of thing's a little tough to bounce back from."

"That's why you should have warned her," Alex growled at me. "I know exactly what being flooded by all those memories feels like because I was just like her. I didn't always survive on the streets. I did time as a Disposable too, but someone got me out." Alex's eyes flicked toward the ring and back to me. "I guess it's time I return the favor."

Alex started walking again, and I followed. "Those memories are going to hit that girl harder than you can imagine, and she doesn't even know they're coming. You didn't do her any favors. You gave her a little taste of normal, so when the shit hits her in the face, the experience will be that much worse. I'm going to get dressed, and we're going back to your shop to warn that poor girl. Both about her memories and about Scarecrow. Jeez, you might as well strap a welcome sign to your roof with her picture on top."

I followed Alex through a door, and she turned around and shoved me back out. "You stay here, cowboy. I'll be out in a minute. You go down and warm up your little smoking bike or whatever you call that scooter monstrosity. We'll leave as soon as I get changed."

I nodded and tried not to panic. Alex was right. I'd wanted to help Stray, but I'd made things worse by not facing the inevitable. She needed to know, and I should have been the one to tell her.

I headed for the elevator, thankful I had Alex to help me. The least I could do was warm up The Rocket. When she was ready to ride, I would speed us back to the shop as fast as its knobby little tires would turn. I thought about what Alex said, about being a Disposable too. The realization explained a lot about her. Why she was so angry. Why her walls were built so high. I only hoped Stray would come out of her ordeal half as well as Alex had.

CHAPTER TWENTY-SEVEN

S tray was in trouble. I knew it before I parked The Rusty Rocket in the street. The door to my shop was open. Not just open, the armored metal had been torn off the hinges and laid in a mangled mess ten yards from the bent frame.

I all but dropped The Rocket and ran up to the shop. Alex stuck close behind. The inside hadn't fared much better than the outside. Everything had been ransacked. The hidden door to the bus storage stood uncovered and open. They had taken everything down to the last root beer. Stray was nowhere to be seen.

Alex peered into the bus over my shoulder and tried to say something, but I turned and pushed her to the side so I could head toward the front counter. My secret compartment appeared untouched. Whoever attacked had hit fast and hard. Stray hadn't even had time to defend herself.

I smacked the false panel and pulled the access open to peer at the contents. Everything was there. I felt both relieved to find my familiar weapons and upset knowing Stray had been caught so off guard she couldn't try for them.

"I don't know what you're thinking, but going after these guys with a couple of pistols ..."

Alex stopped speaking when I pulled out the Whip-Crack and pocketed the Knuckle Stunner.

"Okay, so you stashed away something better than pistols. That doesn't mean you're equipped to use them."

I ignored the comment and moved forward until I stood a few inches from her. "You said you knew where these guys hang out." It was both a statement and a question I would have the answer to.

Alex narrowed her eyes in a look of controlled anger and chuckled as she took a step back. "I understand how you feel, but I don't think you're equipped to deal with the sort of people you're going to meet in a place like that. Trust me, I've been there—more times than I would like to admit—and not as a paying client."

I took another step forward, closing the gap between us again. "I know precisely the type of people who are in there. I was one."

I let that sink in for a moment, then the anger on Alex's face began to look as if it might come to a boil. "You need to explain what you mean by that statement."

"We all have skeletons, Alex. You want to hear about mine? When I was alive, I worked with my cousins trafficking humans in the slave trade. They pulled me in to work the books for them, telling me they owned an import export business. By the time I realized what they imported and exported, I was in as deep as they were."

I spun around and reached deep into the hidden compartment, jerking out another little toy I had saved for a rainy day. At the moment, it poured.

"I could have turned them in and made a deal for a reduced sentence, or maybe no sentence at all, but I was scared. My cousins kept me out of the mud, as they called it, so I just dealt with the books—until they got drunk one night and thought it would be funny to lock me in for a little trip with the cargo."

Tears threatened to well into my eyes, but I willed them back. I didn't deserve even that much release. I clenched my fists and met Alex's eyes, red and full of fury. Her fists had clenched into tight balls as well. I understood why. She had been one of them. No different from the human cargo we had traded in that truck, and I was no better that the low life Disposable dealer who had ruined her.

"That's when I was forced to face what I was doing. When I couldn't ignore the kind of monster I'd become. There were maybe a hundred illegals crammed into that truck. Too many to allow anyone to sit down. The trailer was dark and smelled like sweat and blood and shit, but I didn't care. I deserved every minute. I wanted to be there. To face the thing my self-imposed ignorance had twisted me into. I crouched next to a little girl who'd lost her mother. The ship's crew threw her overboard when she got too mouthy. Another woman lost her son. A different set of smugglers shot him in the head to show others what happens when a slave takes an extra sip of water without asking. Most of the people in that truck were destined for the sex trade, then the drug trade, and then they'd be dead before thirty. I had helped deliver thousands just like them. I couldn't fix the past, but I was determined to change those people's future."

"So, what did you do?" Alex's voice came out as a dark whisper. I wasn't sure if her fury was aimed at me or the heartless cruelty of my story, but the words I said next held more weight than I could imagine.

"Once my cousins had their fun, they let me out at one of their out-of-the-way rest houses. A smelly, old mobile-home tucked deep in the woods. They even locked me into a room with a sixteen-year-old girl as some sort of an apology. It made me sick. I wanted to go after them right there, but I waited. I couldn't take them alone, but later ...

"They spent the night drinking, and I watched and listened. When they passed out, I jimmied the door and stole the keys to the truck. I told the sixteen-year-old that she, her family, and the rest of them were not headed for a better life. I told her what would to become of them if they stayed. I opened the back, found a driver for the truck, and had her enlighten the rest of the passengers. Stray reminds me a lot of that girl. Strong, but kind—overly innocent. I gave the driver directions to the nearest city, all the cash in my pocket along with my credit cards, and I sent them on their way. It was the best I could do—almost the best I could do."

"And your cousins got off scot free?"

I stared down at my feet. I wasn't sure why I couldn't meet Alex's eyes anymore. Whether it was for what I was or the cowardly thing I was about to do.

"My cousins still slept in the mobile-home. I went in ready to make sure their business was closed for good. I didn't have a gun, so I settled for a full gas can and a match. The trailer went up like dry tinder. Unfortunately, my cousins did have a gun. They shot me through a window because I was stupid enough to hang around for the show."

Alex relaxed her hands, but anger still lurked in her eyes. When I stepped back, she glanced away as if she could not bear to look at me any longer.

"I don't expect you to forgive me for the things I did. No one should. But this shop has been my way of making up for a few of those mistakes, and I'll be damned if I let Stray become one of their Disposables again. I don't care if you come with me or not. I'll sleep in the bed I've made, but I need to find Stray. So, I am asking you one ... last ... time. Where is Scarecrow and his crew?"

Alex took a breath and then looked up at me. To my surprise, she had an evil grin plastered on her face. "If you think I'm going to miss fun like this, you're crazy."

CHAPTER TWENTY-EIGHT

The club was called the Wax Worx and, unlike the shanties most Woebegone had to suffer in, places like this enjoyed the full backing of The Nine and all the Hellion management. The outside resembled a multi-angular circus tent built out of black and purple silk, except the place was much larger than physics would allow a normal tent to be. The structure stood several stories tall with large spires jutting up at random angles and looked as if it might cover the better part of a city block. A huge circus-style bill-board flashed the club's name in bright white bulbs that chased themselves in rapid waves and circles. It was like Vegas, only less audacious and in your face. Let's be real, no one can beat Vegas. Not even Hell has that much money.

Alex hopped off the back of The Rocket and I pulled the trusty 98 up onto its stand. "I know we've been over this but listen." Alex grabbed my arm and pulled me around to look at her. I tried to keep myself from shaking apart. I felt as if standing in one place too long might cause my anger and adrenaline to ignite and blow my head off.

"I know what you said, but if you've never been in a place like this ... Well, this is like nothing you've ever seen ... like nothing no one should ever have to see."

"We're wasting time," I said, cutting her off.

"Fine." Alex's face went cold. I hadn't made her angry. She just flipped the switch. I needed the agent I saw in the ring. The one with ice in her veins and vengeance in her eyes. She had triggered that part of her personality and locked everything else away. I knew it, because I did the same thing. I became cold, fearless, and ready to do anything to get Stray back. Alex gestured toward the flap marking the entrance to the club. I marched toward the door and met the eyes of a tall bouncer. I never broke contact once he spotted me. He was about my height, but he looked like he ground oak trees into mulch with his bare hands when he wanted a little light exercise.

He put a hand on my chest and glanced over at Alex. "Do you two have an invitation? I'm sure I can get you in, but your boyfriend will have to stay out here and keep me company."

I twisted my face in disgust. In this place, that statement could mean about anything. "We don't need an appointment. We're with the Judas Agency."

I reached into my pocket and palmed my rainy-day toy so Mulch Machine wouldn't spot it and patted him on the arm. He winced when the device took its sample and jerked away.

"What was that?" Mulch Machine made a grab for my hand, but Alex threw a quick jab and knocked his arm to the side.

I rounded on him and stepped right up to his face. "Do we have a problem here? If we do, I can call half a dozen Hellions here to discuss the reason you are denying two Judas agents entry to your club."

Mulch Machine rubbed his arm and considered this for a moment, then he stepped to the side. "Don't cause any trouble in there."

"If I want to burn the whole place down and plant your ugly corpse in the middle, I will." Alex waited for me to march in through the dark opening and then she followed. Mulch Machine must have run out of witty retorts because he didn't say anything else.

We emerged from a long, draped hall into a huge circus-style arena. The entrance was elevated and allowed spectators to walk the entire perimeter of the entertainment floor on a wide catwalk for a view of everything going on below. And below ... Well, Alex was right. I had spent so much time in my little corner of Scrapyard City that I had forgotten that this was Hell, and in Hell, places like the Wax Worx were as common as a neighborhood bar and grill.

The floor of this particular club housed a multitude of circus rings. Each one featured an atrocity being played out for the grotesque entertainment of Hellion and Woebegone spectators. One had a man strapped to a table with multiple torture instruments hanging over his head. Next to him a woman dressed in an evening gown spun a wheel that picked the particular torture the victim would endure. The little red clicker clacked down and landed on disembowelment. The crowd went wild. The woman walked over, selected a rusty looking bail hook from the array of instruments, and handed it to a smiling man in a tuxedo standing next to the table. The crowd chanted something like Rex or Tex. I assume this was the torture master's name. His arm went up in the air. I turned my head, unwilling to witness the rest.

I lead Alex down the stairs, not bothering to excuse myself as I pushed through the screaming throng of people. None of them seemed to notice. I stopped once to allow a naked woman, blindfolded and bound in rough ropes, to be paraded past me. Behind her, a child followed close behind. My stomach churned, and I wanted to throw up. These people weren't even cattle. Cattle were treated with mercy. These Woebegone were treated like trash. Useless pieces of rotted meat fit for nothing but the gutter.

Burning the place down began to feel like a very real possibility, even if I had to go down with it.

Alex hit me in the arm, and I realized I stood in the middle of the room glaring at ... pretty much everyone. The main bar was a few feet to our left, so I figured that would be as good a place to start as anywhere. I made my way over to a vacant spot, and the bartender made a beeline toward me. He was a fat man with a bald head and a bad complexion. He wore a butcher's apron covered in blood and cleaned a glass with a towel made of black terry cloth.

"We don't serve the entertainment here." His voice sounded like he had swallowed half a dozen beer mugs and burped out glass gravel. "Beat it."

Alex walked up behind me a millisecond later, and Gravel Voice changed his tune. "Ms. Alex. I didn't realize he was with you. I'm sorry. What can I get you?"

I lifted an eyebrow and glanced over at her. She didn't bat an eyelash. "You can get me some information. I'm looking for Scarecrow. Have you seen him?"

Gravel Voice flicked his eyes in my direction. Alex reached out with a finger and touched Gravel Voice's cheek. He jerked so hard he dropped the glass in his hand.

"Please." His voice became all twisted and pleading. "I don't want any trouble. You know I can't tell you that. If word got around that I'm handing out information to the Agency ..."

"I understand," I interrupted. "I run a little side business myself. Reputation is everything."

I smiled and put a hand on Alex's shoulder, backing her off a step.

Gravel Voice nodded and smiled like an idiot. "See, your partner gets it. He understands."

"Right," I continued. "If word got out that you gave up information, or if some of your high paying clients wound up as part of the entertainment, your business would be ruined."

I reached into my pocket and fastened my new gadget around my neck. Gravel Voice began to register that this conversation might not be going the way he had thought it was.

The device, called a Skin Shroud, was an out of this world expensive, one time use product that sampled the DNA of a Woebegone, and temporarily restructured the user's face and body to match the DNA in the device, as long as the general mass of the two subjects were similar. Not a common or comfortable piece of equipment to use, but right now, it was just the tool for the job.

I hit the button to activate the Skin Shroud. Fatty tissue, bone, and muscle began to shift under my skin. The pain brought me to my knees, and Gravel Voice grinned as he watched me go down. I'm sure he thought something had gone wrong. I held in a scream, huddled on the filthy floor, trapped on all fours. My insides felt like they had been sucked into an industrial toffee pull and cranked up to 11. Things cracked and tore and twisted for what felt like an eternity. When the torture machine stopped, the pain subsided as fast as it had started. I staggered to my feet. Gravel Voice's face went pock mark white. My reflection in the bar mirror told me the Skin Shroud had done its job. I was now Mulch Monster, the door man. When Gravel Voice noticed the Whip-Crack in my hand, he fell back against the bar and fumbled for something under the counter.

Alex leapt over the bar and shoved him back as I uncoiled the Whip-Crack. Alex simultaneously held Gravel Voice against the back wall with one forearm while retrieving a sawed-off pump style shotgun from under the counter. She racked the hand cannon, planted the barrel under his chin, and gave me a wink.

I winked back and turned toward the crowd. Before me stood the elite. The worst Hell had to offer. Hitler, Stalin, Mussolini; they had nothing on the people in this arena. The Woebegone here were masters of torture and ruthless death. Saying they were responsible for the tormented recycling of millions would not even scratch the surface, and those who they didn't kill—they liked to watch. Time for me to give them a show.

I swung the Whip-Crack around, spinning the blades into a frenzy, then snapped the whip through the crowd before me. A million whirring teeth chewed waist high through a dozen Woebe-gone and never slowed. I stepped forward, helicoptering the weapon over my head as I surrounded myself with the dredges of the underworld and lowered the Whip-Crack in a perfect arc around my position. This time two dozen Woebegone dressed in the finest Hell had to offer went down, and others began to take notice. I walked forward, spinning the Whip-Crack to increase the momentum. I thought the crowd would run screaming, but they didn't. Instead, the twisted Woebegone turned toward me and began to cheer. A staff member came at me. I flicked the blades in his direction, removing an arm and most of his shoulder. Two more charged from the rear. A quick flip of my wrist sent the whip careening toward their ankles. They went down in a cacophony of screams. The crowd cheered more. They moved in my direction, careful to give me a wide enough berth to remain spectators, but eager to see who I would mow down next.

I made for the closest stage and cut through the main entertain-ment. The torture master stood in his tux, looking stunned and confused. The Whip-Crack bisected him, his lovely assistant, and all of the tools along with the rack that held them. It was too late for the Woebegone on the table. The gruesome wheel had already claimed his life.

The crowd went wild, and more high-class losers were drawn to my show. I jumped to the next ring. The woman I had seen in the audience had been strapped to a board but looked otherwise unharmed. There were six men standing on stage with her, all dressed in gas masks that covered their faces and nothing else. The head entertainer approached me with his arms out as if to say, what are you doing? I removed his arms with a flick of my wrist and ended the show by removing the masks of the six men, along with their heads.

Rage spun the world around me. Bloodlust and hate filled my head like a hot viscous liquid, penetrating my every thought and action. Some of the other stages had not yet caught on to what was happening behind them. I prepared to cut a path through the crowd and interrupt the festivities there as well. Something grabbed hold of my arm, and I turned, ready to remove the hand that dared to hold me back. When I recognized the face connected to it, the realization hit me like a physical blow, real enough to stagger me backward.

"Garlin," he shouted. "What the hell are you doing?"

My cousin, Franco, stood there, looking exactly the way he had when I burned him to death in that mobile home. The day I had killed them all, and I had died.

CHAPTER TWENTY-NINE

I jerked my arm out of Franco's hand and teetered back several steps, ready to run. Even with the Whip-Crack in my hand, panic overran all logic. Only the look of utter confusion on Franco's face stopped me. I set my feet and forced a crooked smile. I had almost blown everything. Franco didn't know me. To him, I was just the Mulch Monster gone wild, which was precisely what he was supposed to think.

I glanced toward Alex and caught a glimpse of her engaged in a close up and personal conversation with the bartender. I hoped she was explaining what would happen if he divulged our little secret.

"I asked you a question," Franco said.

I wrestled my nerves into submission and steadied my legs. "Just thought I'd spice up the show, Boss."

I raised my arms into a victory V and let the Whip-Crack play out at my side. The crowd roared to life, and I pointed to another ring full of performers. Their arms went limp and their faces became white as they shook their heads in an emphatic no. My blood thirsty fans redoubled their cheers, urging me forward, but Franco grabbed my arm and forced it down.

Alex backed away from the bartender at the same time. At first, he seemed compliant, then he rolled away and made a sloppy dive over the bar. For a fat man, he did pretty well. He managed to wind up on his feet and start a short stride sprint in my direction. Alex didn't bother to catch him. She gestured in his direction, and I brought the Whip-Crack around to meet him half-way. It was a surgical strike that took off his head, fast and clean. The crowd responded in kind, cheering and shouting anew. I also noticed the performers had conspicuously disappeared. I could not imagine a more satisfying night on the town.

"Knock that off." Franco grabbed my arm again and pulled it down. "That was my best bartender."

I nodded. "You're right. Here let me help."

I jumped up on a table and cupped my hands around my mouth, ready to kick the satisfaction meter up another notch. "The bartender's dead, folks. You know what that means."

An uneasy hush came over the crowd and everyone stared up at me, even Franco.

"Free Ta-Kill-Ya shots for everyone."

Cheers erupted like thunder, and Franco kicked the table out from under me. I leapt into the air and managed a graceful landing on my feet. Alex met me at my side, and I thought I glimpsed a gleam of pride in her eye. Franco's expression burned with fury. That made me happy too. "What has gotten into you?"

I glanced around at the floor. Woebegone workers were hauling away body parts and mopping up the mess while spectators rushed the bar for their free drinks. "Maybe I overdid it with the free drink bit."

Franco let out a long breath and smacked me on the shoulder. "Naw. The drinks were a nice touch. I'll make four times as much after they're loaded. I like the new weapon, and the hot little girl, too." Franco nodded toward Alex. I developed a sudden urge to spin my whip around and give him a permanent grin.

Alex smiled, winked, and then sneered at him in disgust.

"Where'd you get that scarf? Your granny's closet or did Big Bird throw up all over your neck?"

I glanced down and noticed Franco had added a ridiculous looking yellow scarf to his usual silk shirt and slacks ensemble. Big Bird would have been insulted.

Franco laughed. "Yeah. I like her a lot. You should work her into the act a little more. Maybe with less clothes, but you can't be killing my ring masters like that. What am I going to do until they respawn and regain their memories?"

I shrugged and tried to seem like I cared.

"I'll tell you what you're going to do. You're going to polish up this act of yours, and your little girlfriend is going to pitch in, running the sex stage. When Scarecrow gets back, he can run one too." Franco lifted his head and scanned the thinned-out arena. "He should have been back by now."

"You want me to go check on him?" I said it too quickly. I knew I did, but I couldn't stop myself.

Franco didn't catch on. He seemed too preoccupied working out staffing for the rest of the evening.

"Yeah. I sent him to the warehouse we built after the last firestorm. Have you been there yet?"

I shook my head and tried to hide the nervous anticipation threatening to shake me apart inside.

"The place is two blocks behind the club. You can't miss it." Franco turned to walk off. "Tell him to get his ass back here quick and don't worry about that other job I gave him. He can deal with that guy later. We need him here right now."

The club settled back into its horrific routine, and Franco headed off to deal with a couple fighting at the bar. The empty rings had been abandoned for those that still contained some sort of entertainment, and the booze flowed faster than ever.

I surveyed the crowd and twisted my wrist, making the Whip-Crack rustle and rattle with excitement. "Why don't you head out and find Stray," I said to Alex, without looking at her. "I'm going to stay here and finish up a few things."

I felt the rage building up inside me again, screaming for release, insisting I unchain my weapon and finish the job I had started.

"Don't be stupid." Alex shook my arm and forced me to look at her. "You might be able to take half the place out, maybe more, but they would get to you sooner or later. What would that accomplish? You just wiped out three rings, all of the ring masters, almost a hundred of their best clientele, and it slowed them down for what, fifteen minutes? You try to take this place down, you will wind up dead, and this place will keep on going."

I clenched my teeth and let out a breath through my nose. "It would sure feel good until they got me."

"We're not here for you. We're here for Stray. You want to take down the biggest skin game in The Nine, you'll have to do a little more planning. Now let's go get who we came for."

I groaned my submission, recoiled the Whip-Crack, and fastened it under my coat. "This isn't over. That was my cousin, Franco, and if he's here, so is Charlie. If they're the ones running this place ... This isn't over. I'm coming back to finish this."

"I got that, stud." Alex grinned. "Now let's get out of here before your doppelgänger wanders in here and ruins your little charade."

I had forgotten about Mulch Monster, or even that I didn't look like myself. If he came in and saw me, explanations might be tough. Every second we stayed was another second we risked getting caught. I followed Alex to a dark corner near the exit and shed my disguise, then we went out the same way we came in.

"Thanks, Mulch, my man." I gave the real bouncer a thumbs-up on the way by. "I think Franco's looking for you in there. Said something about you getting the night off."

CHAPTER THIRTY

"How are we supposed to find this place?" Alex threw her arms out and spun, gesturing at the endless rust-colored shanties. The area was more packed with catwalks, hidey-holes, and ramshackle dwellings than my part of town. I couldn't believe Woebegone would be willing to live this close to the Wax Worx. They were like a bunch of chickens waiting around to hand a starving farmer his axe.

I put my hands on top my head as if that would hold down a little of my edgy frustration. "I don't know. Franco told me Scarecrow was two blocks back in the new warehouse. He said the place would be obvious."

"Well, it's not, and now we have about a thousand shanties to go through."

"It's not that bad." I peered around, studying the construction. Everything in The Nine was re-purposed, but that didn't mean you couldn't tell when something had been rebuilt. I searched for dirt, rust, and wear lines in the metal. Places that didn't seem to match the patterns of the surrounding material. I narrowed our possibilities down to a few buildings within seconds.

"Over there." I pointed toward a structure that looked more

disjointed than the others. It had few openings for windows or doors and could be a large open structure on the inside. "Let's try that one first."

Alex shrugged. "We're going to run out of time pretty quick. As soon as that door goon wanders back into the club, your cousin is going to send some friends to see what's going on. Your little comment on the way out made sure he would do just that about ten seconds after we left."

"Not one of my best moves." I shrugged. "But I would love to be in the room for the conversation."

We made our way over to the building and were about to poke our heads inside when a scream broke through the bustling crowd of Woebegone behind us. We turned to see smoke billow out of a third-floor window. A dark-skinned Woebegone burst out the door at ground level. Squat and fat, with a three-strand comb over. I recognized him. He was the Woebegone who had stalked Stray at the shop. He looked right at us, then took off running.

"Scarecrow." Alex and I spoke in unison.

We tore after him as fast as we could, but a second scream pulled me up short. I recognized that voice. Stray.

Alex skidded to a stop a few feet in front of me, crouched like a cat ready to leap in any direction. "That's her, isn't it?"

I nodded.

"Scarecrow is yours. I've got Stray."

"You sure?"

Alex didn't answer; she just sprinted through the open door of the tall burning shanty and disappeared into the darkness.

I ran in the direction Scarecrow had gone. The man was portly and short, so it didn't take long to eat up the distance between us, but being out of shape didn't make him stupid. He was in a dangerous line of work. The kind where a quick getaway could save his skin. He must have anticipated this sort of scenario and had a few surprises waiting for me.

He kicked a brace out from under a large set of spiked barrels as he rounded a corner. Their platform, about fifteen feet above my head, collapsed, and the barrels came crashing down in a deadly landslide of sharpened spikes and jagged steel. I jumped to my left and managed to dodge into a small alcove opened by the destruction of the last storm. Had that opening not been there, I would have been a very ugly pin-cushion.

I clenched my fists and thought about how many ways I would return the favor. The barrels crashed against the hollow metal walls with ear-shattering screeches and booms. When the racket subsided, I clambered over them to escape my crude bunker. Scarecrow had lengthened his lead, but every muscle in my body tensed, wanting him more than ever, and I lit out after him again. I reached for the Whip-Crack, then thought better of it. We needed him alive in case Stray wasn't in that building. The Knuckle Stunner would have to do—for now. I wondered how hard I would need to hit someone to kill them with the Stunner, or even if it were possible. I would have to be careful.

Scarecrow streaked around a labyrinth of catwalks and shot through one shanty after another. He flipped over tables, tore down anything he could put his hands on, and even tossed an unsuspecting Woebegone or two into my path. Desperation drove him, but I ran on vengeance. Nothing would stop me now. Another corner, and he got a head start up a long steel ladder. Big mistake. I overtook him within a few seconds, and he had no way off until he got to the top. I grabbed his foot before he made the catwalk. Unfortunately, he managed to grab the leg of a Woebegone woman on the landing above him. It was enough to knock her off balance and over the short rail. She latched onto the lower bar with one hand as she tumbled, but her grip wouldn't last long. Her feet dangled over four stories of open air. The woman screamed for help as she tried, and failed, to reach up and get a grip with her other hand.

"What are you going to do now, hero?" Scarecrow tried to

shake his leg out of my grasp. "Is it going to be me or the pretty lady?"

I looked at the woman again, and she shrieked in fear. "Please help me. I can't go back to the Fields."

Her fingers began to roll off the rail, and I glared up at Scarecrow. He smiled down at me, already knowing what I would choose.

"I'll be back to retrieve my property later. You can count on that. And I'll make sure I pick you and your pretty little whore up with her, if my little surprise didn't take care of her back at the warehouse."

Panic twisted my stomach. A trap had never occurred to me. It probably hadn't occurred to Alex either. I swung my Knuckle Stunner at Scarecrow's calf in a last-ditch effort to get a shot in.

The hit was so low I had no idea what it would do, but the blow hit him like a dump truck. The shock didn't knock him unconscious, but I saw his calf quiver and flex into a ball of torn muscle beneath his shredded pant leg. Scarecrow howled out a noise I didn't know a man could make, and the Woebegone woman began to fall.

I pushed out hard and swung around like an old shutter, using my right arm and leg as a hinge. My body twisted backward into the air, allowing me enough reach to snatch the woman's wrist. I managed to hold onto her arm when everything jerked tight, but my fingers' tenuous grip on the ladder did not fare as well. The two of us tumbled several more feet until my leg yanked us to a stop again. I had wrapped it through one of the rungs and around the side rail. I tried to slow my breathing and keep a series of high-pitched whimpers from escaping my lips. I was unsuccessful at the latter. I now hung upside down, holding the woman with both hands. She covered my puppy noises with a shriek of her own, then seemed to realize she would survive if she reached out to grab the ladder in front of her face. Her free hand shot out and seized the nearest crossbeam as if it were made of solid gold.

As soon as she stood safe on the ladder, I wriggled around and got myself upright as well. My eyes went back to the catwalk, knowing what I would see. Scarecrow was gone. At least I gave him something to remember me by. I doubted that leg would ever be the same.

The woman lowered herself to the bottom of the ladder, and I descended above her, wanting to kiss the dirt as soon as my feet touched the ground.

"Thank you." The woman reached out and threw her arms around me, sobbing like a child. She was small, thin, and not very tall. If she had been bigger, we'd still be on the ground, but we would resemble a mangled pile of meat spaghetti.

"What can I do for you? Name it, and it's yours."

I raised my eyebrow, and she looked away. She had a thick Russian accent I didn't expect.

"You don't owe me anything," I said.

Her eyes flicked back up to mine. "You saved my life."

"I saved you from the Gnashing Fields," I interrupted. "It's no big deal."

I started to leave, but the woman grabbed my arm. "That man you were chasing. He is bad man, isn't he?"

I tried to smile, but I had a feeling it resembled more of a snarl. "Yes, he is very bad."

"And I kept you from catching him. I'm sorry."

"Don't be," I said. "You had nothing to do with it. The fault was all his."

"I will find this man for you." The woman nodded. "That is what I will do. I cannot bring him to you, but I will find him, and I will tell you where he lives so you may catch him."

I peered at the woman and smiled, this time for real. "Thank you, but he's a dangerous guy. You should stay away from him. I'll find him again."

"No! I will find him for you. Tell me where I may contact you when it is done."

I thought about it for a minute and shook my head. "My name is Gabriel, and you can contact me at the Judas Agency."

Her eyes widened a bit, but she nodded and turned to walk away without another word.

I watched her go and then trotted back in the opposite direction, praying Scarecrow had lied about his trap at the burning shanty. If Alex had gotten hurt or hadn't gotten to Stray in time ... My feet moved faster. And now my cousins would be on our tail.

CHAPTER THIRTY-ONE

The path that brought me back to the warehouse area was more twisted and meandering than I remembered. I met with several curses and dirty looks as I retraced our route of destruction, but I kept my eyes firm and my legs moving. I needed to make my way back before my cousins sent reinforcements.

I still couldn't believe I had left Alex to run into a burning building where an indeterminate number of no-neck goons could have been hiding. We didn't even know if Stray was in the rusty inferno. She might have been twenty steps or twenty miles from our location. The place could have been full of traps, bombs, or those little toy dogs they sell at gift shops that never stop barking. The more my brain unraveled, the faster my feet moved.

When Alex and Stray came into view, I paused and took a moment to close my eyes and thank the Big Man upstairs—way upstairs. I caught my breath and headed toward them. We still needed to move. Safe or no, Scarecrow could double back and spring another surprise or bring backup. He knew the area a lot better than I did. He probably had shortcuts scoped out all over the place.

As I got close, relief chilled back to concern. Alex and Stray sat side by side on an old immovable hunk of machinery. Alex cradled an arm close to her body, and both shoulders were hunched with stress and pain. But that wasn't what worried me. Stray sat next to her, still and silent. Alex, despite her obvious distress, faced her, speaking in soft, comforting tones. Stray stared at nothing in particular. Her face was an ashen mask of pain, the care and sunshine extinguished from her eyes. Her memories had returned. Stray wasn't Stray any more.

"What happened?" I gestured toward Alex's arm, avoiding the gigantic Stray-shaped dinosaur in the room.

Alex managed a pained smile. "Our friend was a little more resourceful than we thought. He rigged up a rain water bomb in the hall outside Stray's room. I avoided most of the spray, but his little surprise misted my arm and back before I got away completely."

"Water?" Even I couldn't talk someone into smuggling in water. It was like asking someone to carry an armed nuclear warhead around in their back pocket. I made a slow attempt to pull away Alex's sleeve and examine her injuries.

The moment my fingers touched her skin, Alex clenched her teeth and flicked her eyes to Stray. "I think you may be focusing on the wrong thing here."

I cringed and looked over at my young shopkeeper. "How are you doing? Are you hurt?"

Stray's head jerked toward me, and she stared flaming daggers into my eyes. "I remember. I know what I am. You can stop pretending."

"What you were," I corrected. "You aren't any more. As long as I'm around, you never will be again."

"That makes two of us." Alex met Stray's intense gaze. "I know what you're going through, and you will pull through this. The first thing you have to understand is that it's over. The cycle ends here, and all the memories you have in your head fall one minute further behind you for every minute you spend with us."

They scrutinized each other in silence so long I began to feel like a third wheel. I tried to break the stalemate by waving my hand between them, but my spazzy little grabber had no effect.

"We should move." I said, trying to talk to them instead. "These guys know where Stray is."

"My name is Zoe."

I glanced over at Stray. "Pardon?"

She looked down to the ground and relaxed again. "I said my name is Zoe."

I smiled a little bit and moved to sit next to her, forgetting about my cousins and their goons for the moment. "It is good to meet you, Zoe. I know you remember a lot of horrible things, but what do you remember about you? Where are you from? When did you get here?"

Alex gave me an approving nod and a smile.

"Everything's still fuzzy. I keep getting flashes of stuff. I feel so angry."

"Try not to focus on that," Alex said. "Focus on the parts you can remember about your past."

"I think I died in the '80s. I don't remember how or anything. This guy took me to a bar after I got here or something ..."

Then Zoe disappeared again, replaced with that ashen-faced ball of hate and anger. Her eyes narrowed, her mouth drew into a razor-sharp line, and her gaze hardened and drifted to nowhere.

"We have to go." I peered up at Alex. "Are you okay to move?"

"I'll be alright, but the three of us aren't going to fit on your wonder cycle. I doubt she would ride at all." Alex glanced behind me, and I saw realization dawn on her face. "Hey, what happened to your guy. Weren't you supposed to be running someone down?"

Now it was my turn to stare at the ground. "He set me up. It's a long story, but he forced me to make a choice, and I had to let him go. I don't know if it makes you feel any better, but he's going to walk with a limp that rivals those burns."

"It makes me feel a little better." Alex scowled. "You can give me the play-by-play later. For now, let's get going. It's obvious that our friend got a heads up before we arrived, so they must have figured us out at the club."

I winced when Alex used the word club, but Stray ... Zoe didn't seem to notice. She was still withdrawn into her own dark world. I wished I could shine a light bright enough to bring her out, but right now I doubted a light that bright even existed, not here in The Nine anyway.

"Why don't you take Zoe and head back to the shop, and we can ..."

"She's not going back to the shop." Alex's voice sounded final. "Stray is lost. She needs someone to guide her back. You and I can't do that, but I know someone who can."

My brow dove deep with apprehension and worry. I wanted to help Zoe, but I wasn't sure about handing her to a stranger in this state of mind. Alex coaxed Zoe up and put an arm around her waist. Zoe stared at the ground, her mind still years and miles away, like an elderly woman lost in her own tragic dementia. Even if I had a logical argument for keeping her with me, I doubted it would matter. Alex was on a mission, and there was little I could do to stop her.

"The place I know is not far." Alex took Zoe by her elbow and guided her forward. "The people there helped me, but they're a little—funny. They won't like it if I bring a stranger. I'll catch up with you ..."

I fell in step behind her. "Too bad," I interrupted. "Handing Zoe off to someone I don't know is one thing. Having no idea where she is or what they are doing with her is another. Besides, you are in no shape to go anywhere by yourself, much less with her."

"We'll be fine." Alex turned and gave me a genuine smile that shook me more than I wanted to admit. "You have to trust me on this one. Zoe will be in good hands, and they can help me too. But if you tag along or try to follow us—things will become complicated."

Alex lowered her voice and nodded me closer. "These are very good guys, but they are dangerous. Management in The Nine doesn't take kindly to those who work against them, especially in their own realm. Someone starts messing with all the torture and brimstone, and the retribution is rough. These guys have to guard against that, and I have seen them put up a vicious fight to protect their identity."

I could not help but consider the irony of her words, considering the position I had landed in within the Judas Agency.

"Fine," I said. "But how will I know you made it alright?"

Alex let out a little giggle that jellied my legs. I forced them back to solidity. I had no idea what was going on but, this was not the time for teenage body chemistry to stage a comeback tour.

"You're awfully worried all of a sudden. Zoe will be fine."

"I know. I'm worried about you."

What did I just say?

Alex gave me a quick glance, and her smile faltered.

"I mean you're injured. You need medical attention." The weak attempt to backpedal only made it worse. I put on a contemplative face and nodded like an idiot.

"Don't worry," Alex said. "We'll both be fine. Now beat it before I have to knock you out and leave you here in the street."

"I'd like to see you try."

Alex raised an eyebrow.

I stopped walking. "Okay, no I wouldn't. Contact me the second you're out."

Alex nodded and waved me away. Then they disappeared around a corner, and they were gone.

CHAPTER THIRTY-TWO

While Stray and Alex were hidden away in some secret underground Bat Cave psych-ward/hospital for the damned, I figured I could use the time to take my side trip back to Briarsville and visit the doc. I did pretty well for my first time using the waypoint transporter. I chose the dumpster rather than the turkey nightmare because—well … turkeys.

Turns out you can pick the point where you're going to land, but not the condition of the landing spot when you get there. I found myself swimming in a dumpster overflowing with garbage. My body wound up suspended in the center of the giant steel coffin between bags bursting with half eaten burgers, melted milkshakes, and enough leftover french-fries to brick a scale model of the Great Wall of China.

I pushed a cola slurry trash bag off my face, and my hand squished through a pile of sliced tomatoes. I prayed the plastic was more than a single ply. It moved without showering me in brown sticky goo as I pulled my boot out of a pan of refried beans. It came out with a shluck sound and gave me enough freedom to roll out over the side.

I stared down at my refried shoe and thought the turkey farm might not be so bad. My hair felt heavy and matted. I reached up to pluck a slab of greasy wilted lettuce off my scalp. A gag escaped my throat. Of course, this was better than the turkeys. Anything was better than that gobbling roar sucking your soul out through your eyeballs. The thought of being near them made me want to be sick.

I forced the image out of my mind and brushed myself off as best I could before making my way down the alley. Wind rattled a soda can across the asphalt, and a shutter banged against a far-off wall. The scene felt so ominous, I half expected a homeless zombie to leap out of a garbage pile. I gave Hefty-Bag pyramid a wide birth and hurried toward the street. This was the first time I had been alone and Topside in a very long time. It felt wrong, and in a way, I guess it was. I mean, when you head to The Nine, you're not meant to make a return trip.

I forced myself to straighten and step out onto the street like I owned the place. Turned out I could have. Not one of the little shops appeared to be open and several had heavy plywood nailed over the windows. They could have prepped for a hurricane with less lumber and difficulty. The town had been put out of its misery, but I couldn't see a reason why.

I spotted someone in a pair of jeans and a t-shirt jogging across the street a few blocks away. Maybe he knew what happened. I hurried down the main drag, hopping over trash bags and dodging the skeletons of display cases and discarded office furniture. More than half the businesses had been cleaned out too. When I rounded the corner to follow the jean-clad jogger, I found ... Well, it looked like everyone in the town had set up camp outside the doc's house/office.

Running made me feel like a geriatric dog with a bad case of asthma, so I gave up trying to catch the lone jogger. You would think one of the perks of being dead would mean never having to worry about being in shape. I took my time wheezing up the block toward the crowd. When I got closer, I realized it wasn't a crowd so much as an angry mob. People yelled at the house, tromped through bushes, and pushed over the doc's gates and fences. They seemed mere moments from throwing brick-shaped care packages through the front windows.

I approached a woman who stood on the outskirts of the crowd. Her face looked just as pinched and angry as the others, but she did not seem to be participating in the pre-riot party.

"What's happening?"

She looked me up and down, as if I'd just asked why water was wet. I smiled and tried to look friendly, but the woman's expression didn't change. She stared at me long enough to make a mannequin fidget, then she turned her attention back toward the crowd and nodded in the direction of the house. "That man there is a killer. Or at least he made a lot of people real sick and won't do anything to help them. Either way you look at it, he's a killer. The man needs to come out and pay for what he's done. He needs to come out and help these people, not sit in his house and watch cable TV."

I peered at the house. "I don't understand."

The old woman dipped one eyebrow. "Ain't you listening? The doc isn't sick, everyone else is. Everyone who's seen him got sick. My cousin saw him last week. He passed away last night, and he ain't the only one. There's been plenty more."

"How many more?"

The old woman turned and gave me another once over. "Where'd you come from anyway? You don't look like you belong around here, and that fancy outfit looks like the one stolen out of Tom Stullery's store the other night."

All of a sudden, I felt very exposed. I tried to look casual, but I had a feeling my face had taken on the color of a baboon's ... it wasn't important.

"I just came to tell the doc thanks for helping us out the other day."

The woman's eyes got wide, and she took a step back. I really put my foot in this one. I tried to think fast.

"Or at least he would have if he hadn't been so busy. We never got in to see him. We only talked to his secretary."

The woman seemed to relax a bit. "Well, I don't think you'll be doing much thanking today. If these people have their way, there's going to be some big trouble around here."

"Why doesn't someone call the cops?"

"Only had two in town. One is sick in bed, and the other is dead, bless his soul. I called the state law, but it'll take a while for them to get here."

I nodded. "You should get home before this gets ugly," I said.

She shook her head. "I'm staying. The man needs to pay for whatever he did, but he don't deserve to be drug out in the street like a dog. If I can help stop that, I will."

I nodded, admiring the old woman. I didn't doubt she could stop it either.

"I could use some help if you're willing." She didn't look at me, she just stared at the house and the circling crowd of jackals.

I wanted to stay. The doc didn't deserve what was about to come down on him and neither did his family, but there was a bigger game at work here. I just shook my head and said, "I need to get back."

This was not a lie. I needed to get back and tell Judas what had happened, and I needed to do it now.

The woman gave me a side-long glance and let out a little huff. "Well, run along then. Enjoy those fancy clothes."

Guilt weighed on me and made me feel heavy, but I backed away. "I'll call the State patrol again and see if I can move them any faster."

"You do that," she said, never bothering to look at me again, then I turned around and ran.

CHAPTER THIRTY-THREE

"I would have wished for better news." Judas paced back and forth across his office, stroking his thick beard while Mastema followed his movements with that half grinning tilt of her head. "The mortality and infection rate may be as bad as we suspected. Procel managed to purchase a bit of information about that sample you procured. It seems the contagion you released is not only deadly, but also incurable. Less than one percent of the human population is immune to the disease, but a single carrier has the potential to infect thousands without knowing it."

I stood between the two bone chairs facing his desk and wished he would make a trip to Ikea and pick up something a little less murdery to sit in.

"The whole town had pretty much closed up shop. I don't know how many people live in Briarsville, but it has to be a several hundred at least. How are we going to help that many people?"

Mastema let out a little giggle and put a hand over her face. I noticed for the first time that Procel was not present to balance out the Judas tag team and wondered what he might be up to.

"You want to know how to help the residents of your little town?" Judas said, rounding on me. "You act before any of this happens. Those people are already corpses, and you still can't see the bigger picture."

I sat back on my heels and felt my shoulders do their best impression of the ears on a frightened rabbit. My gaze fell to the floor, and I shook my head. He was right.

"I'm so sorry. I should have stopped her. This is all my fault."

Judas sighed and stepped toward me. He put a hand on my shoulder and shook me just enough to draw me out of the pit I wanted to drown myself in.

"There was no way for you to know this would turn out to be so serious."

When I didn't look up, he stood in front of me and clasped both my shoulders in his hands. "Listen to me. Yes, you should have acted when you had the opportunity, but there is nothing to be done about it now. You must deal with the threat as it presents itself today. There is no time for pity, self or otherwise."

I tried to stiffen my spine and stand up straight. Judas grinned at me through his beard. His gleaming teeth made him appear both kind and vicious at the same time. A doting wolf wearing three-thousand-dollar cashmere. I had never seen anything more terrifying in my life.

"I can be a bit hard on my recruits. It's something I have tried to improve over the last three hundred years or so. When my recruit failed to prevent the attack at your American Pearl Harbor, he didn't even bother with ritual suicide. He went directly to the Gnashing Fields and threw himself into the pools of burning sulfur."

I cringed.

A spark of frustrated anger gleamed in Judas's eye. "He witnessed the escalating effect of inaction as well. Japan purchased your country's way into that war with the blood of hundreds of American sailors. In the end, the United Stated repaid that debt with two atomic bombs and more than a quarter-million Japanese deaths."

I swallowed hard and wished I could lie down on something—like broken glass.

Judas dropped his hands and turned away from me. "I've been working on a lighter touch ever since."

"You've made some real improvement." At least I wasn't ready to throw myself into a molten pool of sulfur—yet.

"I think so." Judas turned back to look at me and gave me that wolf's grin again. "You're still here."

I answered with a slow nod and half a smile. Judas took a step toward his desk then stopped to glance back at me again. "You aren't going to do something stupid the moment you leave, are you?" Judas pointed a finger at me. His smile had disappeared. "If you jump off this building, swimming laps in the sulfur pools will seem preferable to what I'll have waiting for you when you re-spawn."

"No, no jumping. I am not going to jump." I got a little chill as I wondered if his Pearl Harbor guy had the same lap pool idea.

"Excellent." Judas went back to pacing. "I will put a team together and contain the threat in Briarsville. You need to find out what Sabnack's next move will be. I will discover what I can, but my resources exist far outside your subversive cell. We must know what they are planning, as well as where and when they intend to carry out their plans."

I shook my head and held up a hand. "If you can contain the threat in the town, then what is the big deal? If you can come up with a cure, the disease is no real threa ..." I trailed off. "Wait, what do you mean by contain?"

Judas pinched the bridge of his nose. "Maybe it would be easier to throw you out the window after all." Mastema straightened on her perch and jerked her head in my direction, her grin growing wider.

"Imagine a disease carried by tens, hundreds, or even thousands of people who don't know they have it. The disease would spread to countless masses in a matter of weeks, to include more of the immune carriers. Anyone who was not sick would be seen as suspect and unwittingly turned into a target. Carriers in hiding with the healthy, hoping to avoid the infected, would only infect more people. Animosity would grow. Blame would pass to the innocent few who resisted the disease. They would be hunted down like dogs. Accused of causing every death, like your good doctor. But that's not the worst part. Killing the immune would eliminate the only possible antigen to the plague as well."

Judas let the scenario play out in my head and nodded. "Imagine if there weren't enough of these carriers to go around. They would be sold and harvested like cattle. Luxuries for the rich. Tainted black market hope for the poor. This is worse than a simple disease. If this plays out the way I perceive, this will be the black plague and every world war rolled into one."

I half sat, half collapsed onto the floor and put my head in my hands.

"Judas, sir," I said. "No offense, but you really need to work on your suicide prevention program."

CHAPTER THIRTY-FOUR

I wandered the courtyard area between the towers trying to decide on a course of action—any action—that could improve the situation. The huge circular buildings surrounded me like a spiraling crown. Intricately patterned stone pathways connected each of the towers and led to a large patio and statue in the center. The first time I saw it, the image shocked me into silence. Even now I found the depiction difficult to look at. The figures seemed so lifelike, I almost expected them to start moving, save the fact that they were about twenty feet tall. One figure represented Judas, the other Jesus. There was no mistaking either. Judas leaned in for the infamous kiss while Jesus held his hand to the betrayer's face in a gesture so tender, understanding, and forgiving, it made me want to weep.

I stared at that statue now. We all had a job to do. No matter how difficult, unfair, or unpleasant, the job had to be done. I'm sure that was not the intended meaning of the figure. It was meant to celebrate betrayal and deceit. Precisely what the Judas Agency was all about. But I saw something very different. A man serving his master in the most difficult way anyone could imagine. He served Him by sending Jesus to His last and most important destination. His Crucifixion.

"I could use an idea here," I said to the huge effigy before me. The last thing I expected was an answer.

"Who are you talking to?" Alex wandered up next to me, her hands tucked in the back pockets of her jeans. She tilted her head to the side and leaned in like she was straining to eavesdrop on a private conversation.

I glanced at Alex, then back at the statue. I gave it an awkward wave, feeling a little uneasy.

"Are you waving at a statue?" Alex looked up at the figures and back at me.

I opened my mouth to explain, decided I couldn't, and moved on.

"Why did your first mission fail?"

Alex's eyebrows went up. "Why yes, I'm fine, and Zoe is okay too. Thanks for asking."

I nodded. "I'm serious. What happened?"

"Why do you care?"

Alex crossed her arms. I could almost see her begin construction on one of her walls.

"Call it a hunch. Professional curiosity. Whatever."

Alex stared me down for a second, then her shoulders dropped, and she looked around as if she wanted to be sure no one else heard us.

"I had to get stuck with a partner who's all about sharing," she grumbled.

I smiled, but I didn't say anything. I didn't want to give her an opening to change the subject.

"It was no big deal. The mission, I mean. I was supposed to break into an office and replace a few files. Easy. I was a courier after all. Dealing with paperwork and packages Topside was my thing."

Alex put her back to the statue, leaning against the eight-foot circular base.

"Anyway, everything went fine. I got into the building, went to the prescribed office, and was in the middle of refiling the new paperwork when the lights went on. I drew my gun, ready to shoot, but standing there was the one friend I had in the world."

"You had a friend?"

I took half a step back and raised a hand, realizing what I'd just blurted out.

"I didn't mean that the way it sounded."

"Don't act so surprised. I can be likable if I try. She worked the front desk at a building I frequented Topside. We hit it off for some reason and became friends. Turned out she had gotten a new job. A promotion. Lucky her."

Alex's eyes fell, and her voice got low and angry.

"Turns out her boss called and needed something from the office in the middle of the night. Unusual, but it was an emergency, after all. What a coincidence she happened to arrive just in time to catch me."

"What did you do?"

"I stood there at first. She had no clue about my real identity, of course. What could I say? Oh, don't worry, I'm just a dead secret agent making a quick house call from Hell?"

I shrugged.

"Right, So, I told her I was a dead secret agent out of Hell, and I was there on a job."

I laughed. "How did that go over?"

"Not as good as you might expect. I had to point my gun at her, or she would have run off to call the cops. It took some convincing and a little show of my fire trick, but she calmed down and believed me after a while. She swore never to reveal my secret and even offered to help me when and where she could."

"She got caught up in the whole James Bond thing." I nodded.

"I'll bet she wouldn't be so eager to join up if she knew about the turkeys."

Alex blinked. "Anyway—the conversation went well, but that's when Max and Jake showed up on the scene."

"What?"

"Turns out they had gotten wind of the mission and had set up the chance meeting between my friend and me. They tisked and told me how disappointed they were in my behavior—revealing the secrets of our organization and all. They pulled out a gun and shot my friend in the head."

I clenched my fists and felt my face twist with disgust and anger.

"They couldn't wait to get back and rat me out to Sabnack. They had set the whole thing up just because they thought it would be fun to make me look like an idiot."

"I'm sorry."

Alex gave a non-committal shrug, but hurt and fury were written all over her face.

I, on the other hand, could not be happier the story turned out the way it had. Not that her friend got killed or that the two stooges set her up. I was happy to hear that she didn't pull that trigger. It meant she cared and might just be the ally I needed in this pit of vipers.

I looked around and stepped in close to Alex. "I need to tell you something. But it's a secret, and you have to swear never to tell anyone else."

CHAPTER THIRTY-FIVE

"What do you mean, 'Stop them?'" I had told Alex about my trip back to Briarsville, the doctor, and the sick people. I had even speculated about the destructive possibilities of the disease, but that was it. I told her nothing about Judas and my double agent status with the Agency. Even still, I might have pushed too far. The expression of utter bafflement on Alex's face made a crop of sweat bead on my lip. Not a common occurrence in the freezing temperatures of The Nine. I curled my fingers over my mouth, trying to look attentive, and cover my erupting panic attack.

"I'm not sure if you're aware of this," Alex said. "But we work for an Agency that causes this sort of thing, not one that stops it. We're on the wrong side of the tracks for that gig."

"I know." I dropped my hand and shifted my eyes back and forth to make sure no one approached within earshot. "But this is different. This is the World Series, Super Bowl, and The Daytona 500 of diseases all rolled into one. If this gets a foothold, it could wipe everything out."

Alex let out a snicker. "Everyone always thinks the next disease, flood, or terrorist attack is going to be the one to wipe everything out. This will be like everything else. You aren't going to survive here if you analyze every little mission. Just do your job and go home."

"You don't mean that. I know you, Alex. You're not just another Agency psychopath. I get why you're here, but don't try to tell me you don't care."

Alex narrowed her eyes and turned to walk away, but I wasn't going to let her off that easy. I grabbed her arm and pulled her around to face me—or at least that's what I had planned to do. Alex had other ideas. She put my wrist into some sort of Mohican death lock and drove me to my knees with one hand. I figure I still won because she stopped either way.

"Okay … alright," I panted. "You certainly have a right to your opinion." I tried to look up and flash her a smile, but she just tightened her hold, drawing a little squeak for mercy instead.

"I can mean that, because without this job, I don't have a place to live. I can mean that, because if I screw things up here, I am nothing more than another Disposable like Zoe."

The pressure on her hold loosened, and I dared a glance upward. Her eyes softened, and she threw my arm to the side with a grunt. "You could never understand."

I rubbed my sore hand and rose to step in closer to her. "You are not disposable."

I let the unyielding words hang, wanting them to sink in. "We might be stuck here, but it doesn't mean we can't fight to rise above it. I get that you don't want to risk what you've worked for, but don't ever tell me you're disposable."

Alex stared at me. Something inside her cracked. Not all the way, just enough to let a moment of pure vulnerability escape her brilliant brown eyes, then the moment was gone, and she went to leave again. I reached for her a second time, but my aching hand seemed to develop a mind of its own and jerked itself back to my side before I touched her.

"You have to have family up there," I pleaded.

A pair of Woebegone agents rounded the corner and walked toward us in the courtyard. Alex spun and plastered her hand across my mouth, driving me back into the base of the statue again.

"Will you shut up?" she hissed. "Just talking about this is enough to get us sent to the fields for a long time. No, I have no family up there. And if you will recall, the only friend I had is dead, thanks to Jake and his fat-boy sidekick."

Alex lowered her hand, smiling as if we were having a pleasant conversation as the two agents got close. When the interlopers passed, her face twisted with anger again.

"Even if I did have family up there, they never did anything for me. If they want to plant a disease to thin the herd, good for them. Maybe it will pull out some of the weeds up there too."

She narrowed her eyes, daring me to refute her.

I stiffened my chin and leaned in close, until my face was inches from hers. "How long does it take for you to get your hair that color?"

Alex's face went slack, then the rest of her body relaxed, and she took a step back. "You are ridiculous. Leave me alone." She turned for the third time and started walking away. Instead of stopping her, I trotted to keep up.

"I'm serious. That has to be a lot of work, right? And where do you get time to dye it?" I reached out and touched a lock of her billowing blue hair. "So shiny."

Alex knocked my hand away. "I'm going to break your wrist if you touch my hair again." Her voice sounded serious, but she was smiling.

"Listen, I was only trying to say you're better than most of the lowlifes down here. If you didn't care about anything, you would have canoed your friend's skull when she caught you rummaging through her files."

"They weren't her files, she just worked there."

"Whatever. The point is, there's a difference between doing what we have to and doing what's right. There is a line. And we didn't just cross it, we sprinted past and gave it the finger on the way by."

Alex stopped. We were almost to the building, and I was pretty sure she didn't want to risk someone overhearing our conversation. Her face shifted from frustration to sadness, and maybe a little shame. "Fine. You're right. This disease crosses the line. It's horrible, and I wish we had never found it, or brought it back, or infected that poor family. I never want to hurt people who don't deserve it. But that changes nothing. I'd like to help, but this is eternity, and it's just not worth the risk. I'm sorry."

Alex let her gaze fall to the ground, and she resumed her path toward the building. "I won't tell anyone what you're up to. Just don't get yourself killed. I've gotten sort of used to you."

She pulled the handle to open the huge door, and my mind went wild. I had appealed to every good virtue she had, and nothing had worked. Then it hit me.

"Max and Jake are heading up the end operation."

Alex stopped.

I held my breath. I wasn't one-hundred percent sure, but everything pointed to them. And right now I needed a Hail Mary the way a snowball longed for an unsuspecting face.

The door swung closed, and Alex sauntered toward me, eyes narrow and suspicious.

"How do you know this?"

"Think about it," I said. "Sabnack called them in as soon as we reported what we knew in the town. We saw them in Salt Lake City. They've been in our business ever since we started this thing. It's them. I know it."

Alex stared at the ground, running a hand through her hair. "I don't know."

"How do you think it would go over if they failed to carry off this little project? I'll bet they'd be in some pretty hot water, ruining a chance like this."

Alex looked up at me. Her eyes were still narrowed, but she

wore a wicked grin on her face. "You are pure evil, you know that?"

"I know," I said. "That's why chicks dig me." I did a double arm bicep pose. Alex answered with a Siamese Jiujutsu jab to a pressure point in each arm. It made me want to urinate.

I put my arms down, refusing to show the excruciating pain— or breathe. "So, you in or what?"

"If it means sticking it to those goons, I'm in."

I pumped my fist, sending a wave of new agony through my arm, but I grinned and whimpered on the inside.

Alex smiled one of the biggest smiles I'd ever seen. "Hurts, doesn't it?"

"So bad." I grinned back. "Now let's go get revenge on some bad guys."

CHAPTER THIRTY-SIX

"What are we doing here, Gabe? We don't have time for this." Alex beat on the inside of an outhouse door, trying to force the thing open. I had already stepped out of mine without incident, like the last time we'd been here to tour the tech expo, but the storage center must have shifted around since then. Somewhere in this ocean of sea green poop monoliths, Alex was trapped with her door pressed against another outhouse.

I tilted my head into the air and yelled in no particular direction "Keep talking. I can't find you."

A machine gun rap came from somewhere behind me as Alex punched the plastic sidewall of her prison about a thousand times. "You better find me quick. This isn't funny. I think they repossessed this thing from a monkey cage. They didn't even bother to clean it."

I tried not to laugh, which forced a loud snort out of my nose.

"Are you laughing?" More bangs, this time slower and much louder.

"I am most certainly not laughing." My voice cracked. I couldn't help it.

Sounds of Alex's assault led me to a fresh group of plastic

outhouses all strapped together in a neat square. One of them moved with short jerks that coincided with each bang. "There's nothing to laugh at here. What if I can't find you? I mean, you might be anywhere. There has to be close to a thousand twin outhouses in this yard. Most of them are stacked right next to each other. If you're in the middle. I might never get you out."

I waited a second and watched the little green water closet stop moving, then go crazy with vibration. "Get me out of here, Gabe. Get me out, or I am going to get myself out and stuff you in." The outhouse began to rock back and forth, and I noticed it hung off the edge of its pallet. Alex must have taken a swinging start from the back, because she hit the wall, and the whole thing started to go over.

Images of outhouse swirlies danced in my head as I dove for the tumbling stink bomb. Alex let out a scream, and I threw my weight against the teetering wall before it gained enough momentum to tumble.

"Gabe? Is that you?"

"Yeah. Don't worry. I've got you."

"Oh, thank God. I'm getting out to kill you now."

I heard the door rattle. "It's still stuck."

A groan of frustration escaped my lips. I tried to push the outhouse back onto the pallet, but something blocked me from pushing it all the way in. Now it fell over every time I let go.

"I have an idea," I said. "But you're not going to like it."

"Whatever it is, think of something else." Alex rattled the door again, but it was still jammed against something on the other side.

"Too late. I'm already moving." I shoved one corner of the outhouse, then the other, shimmying the thing back and forth until it began to walk its way free, then I let the whole thing tilt even farther in my direction.

Alex screamed, "Gabe, what are you doing?" Her voice went up an octave with each word.

"Try to open the door." I grunted with the weight, thinking my calculations may not have taken being smushed into a plastic poop pancake into account.

The door crashed once, and Alex bounded out. The momentary pressure of her launch was enough to buckle my knees, but I managed to hold on and spin out of the way in time to escape the falling crap hammer.

A multicolored fluid traced its way down hill in my direction like a monster from a horror flick, poising for attack. Alex smacked me in the arm hard enough to make my fingers curl while I danced away from the ooze.

"You knew where I was the whole time."

"Not the whole time."

Alex reached back to take another swing at me.

"Hey, I kept you from falling. And I got you out without being glazed like a doughnut, so give me a little credit."

She let her hand hover for a moment and dropped it to her side. I took in a deep breath and realized breathing through my nose was a mistake. The ooze had a bite.

Alex crossed her arms and shook her head as I choked and tried to smother the odor with my hand.

"We can't stand here," Alex said. "This isn't Grand Central Station, but it is midday, and someone could wander through. You want to tell me why you stuck me in that stink coffin?"

I pulled my hands away from my face and gave her a nod. "We're going to the games."

Alex's eyebrows went up, and I headed toward the road. "The Olympic games? Please don't tell me we're here because you want to watch beach volleyball."

"Yes," I said. "We landed in a steamy outhouse graveyard to score box seats to the beach volleyball games. Of course not— well, maybe the Brazilians ..."

Alex backhanded me in the arm.

"Kidding, sheesh." I made a show of rubbing the spot where

she'd hit me. "We're here because this is my best guess as to where Max and Jake are going to spread their super sniffles."

Alex got to the street and stopped next to an old mailbox overgrown by tall dry weeds. "Your best guess?" She turned around and headed back toward the outhouses.

I grabbed her arm and stopped her. "Think about it. They'll want to spread this thing worldwide, right? What better place than the Olympics? This is a one stop shop. There are people and athletes from all over the world. All they have to do is release the virus and let them all bring the super bug home to mommy and daddy."

Alex considered this, and she shook her head. "They wouldn't release it like a bug bomb. The effect wouldn't be immediate, but people would get sick too fast. The CDC would have enough warning to react before it spread and took hold. They need to target people who possess a natural immunity to the disease."

My hopes deflated along with my theory, but I couldn't shake the feeling that I was still right somehow. Then it hit me. "What better place to find their perfect subjects than a worldwide pool of healthy athletes with recent blood tests on file? Does the Judas Agency have resources to tap into confidential medical records?"

Alex nodded. "Easy. The Judas Agency excels at gathering information and secrets. They make big brother look like a closet loving hermit."

"If they accessed the athlete's records, it would be easy to find the ones who possess immunity as long as they knew what to search for."

Alex blinked. "That's a pretty good theory."

"Try not to look so shocked."

I let go of Alex's arm and waved at an old truck heading toward us up the road.

"It gives them a target and exposing only the immune would allow the disease time to spread before it's discovered. Plus, infecting an athlete guarantees maximum delivery because they'll be shaking hands, making public appearances, signing autographs, you name it. They'll spread the disease world-wide in a matter of weeks."

The truck slowed down, and the driver, an ancient hard-faced farmer wearing a plaid shirt with rolled up sleeves, eyed Alex and then looked at me. "You folks got trouble?"

I leaned into his passenger window and nodded. "My cousin left us stranded out here."

He eyed Alex again. "You folks get into an argument or something."

I flashed him a sad smile and lowered my voice. "He's never liked my wife. Can't look past the outside to see what matters in the middle, you know?"

I waited for a second while the farmer considered this. He nodded and turned his gaze toward the road. "I know the type. Have a brother like that. Haven't talked to him in years. Called my wife a whore because she wore a skirt above her knees to the school dance."

The farmer looked back at me and winked. "Always liked those knees."

I laughed. Alex tilted her head to the side, looking impatient.

"Your cousin didn't call her a whore, did he?" The farmer's eyes narrowed a bit when he asked the question.

"Let's just say we found ourselves in need of a different direction."

"Well, hop in," the farmer said. "I can take you into town. From there you can catch a bus or make a call. Whatever you need to do."

I stepped away from the window and motioned for Alex to jump into the cab of the old Chevy. She slipped past me, an expression of pure astonishment on her face. I got in behind her and slammed the door.

"You kids need any cash?" The farmer lifted his left hand from the side of his seat and revealed an old thirty-eight service revolver. Adrenaline lit every nerve in my body for a moment, but the farmer tucked the gun under his seat as if he had stowed an old rag. Alex never flinched, and it reminded me that regular weapons couldn't hurt us up here. Had he been holding a rainwater squirt gun, however ...

Alex stared as the old farmer moved with a sort of ancient grace that betrayed a wisdom and strength only a lifetime of hard labor could teach. He produced a twenty from his front pocket and offered it to Alex.

"Here ya go, young lady."

Alex held a hand up in protest, but the farmer insisted.

"You and your husband remind me of my wife and me when we were young."

I tried to imagine the conservative farmer standing at the altar with his tattooed, blue-haired bride-to-be and had to smile.

Alex took the twenty. "Thank you." She gave me a cynical wink. "If your wife is half as lucky as I am, she has had a wonderful life."

The farmer nodded and put the truck in gear, without looking at us. "I do my best, ma'am." He smiled. "Matter fact, why don't you tell me where you're headed. I need to give the old truck a stretch. If you don't mind a stranger's company, I'd be glad to run you folks wherever you want to go."

CHAPTER THIRTY-SEVEN

I waved at the farmer as he pulled out of the parking lot of the Salt Lake City Olympic Center. Cars lined the parking lot like endless crops of glass and steel, surrounded by a sea of strollers, sunglasses, and lunch coolers. The tide of people flowing into the huge stadium complex reminded me of an hourglass, sifting its infinite sand through the tiny opening in the middle. I couldn't even imagine how many people the center was capable of holding if this represented a small fraction of the day's attendants.

"This is a stupid idea." Alex motioned toward the pulsating crowd. "We're never going to find them."

I squinted and pretended to scan a few of the faces. "Yeah, this might take a few more minutes than I thought."

"A few minutes? We could be here for a year and never run into them. I don't even know how we're going to stay close enough to the athletes to watch them. For that matter, those two idiots could hit them somewhere else; their hotels or a restaurant. What if they pose as a driver? They would have them all to themselves for several minutes." Alex threw up her arms. "This is hopeless. I can't believe I signed on for this. I don't know why I'm calling them idiots. We're the ones trying to catch water in a butterfly net."

I blinked. "Nice one."

"Shut up."

"Don't worry. We'll figure everything out." I waved my hand and fanned the air, trying to clear a rancid emission someone was kind enough to leave on their way by. "You're good at carrying out carefully planned missions. Me? I am better at playing things by ear."

Alex stared at me. "This is not playing things by ear. Playing things by ear is figuring out what to say to a snitch when you get there. This is ... what are you doing?"

I fanned my face with a little more enthusiasm, trying to evade the assault on my olfactory senses. I surveyed the people up wind, ready to do a little overreacting. The bean burrito fart grenades were getting downright foul.

When my scan of the area produced no obvious suspects, I glanced at Alex. "Please tell me that's not you."

"What are you talking about?" Alex smacked my hand. "Stop fanning your face like an old church lady. You look like you're going to have a stroke."

"It is you." My eyes went wide. "What did you eat?"

"Stop screwing around, Gabe."

"Are we really going to pretend that smell isn't here? I can almost see it. If someone walks through your death fog, we're going to be blamed for releasing mustard gas into the crowd." I gave up on fanning and slapped my palm over my nose. "At least you didn't let go in the truck. We'd all be dead if you gassed us in there."

Alex stared at me, her eyes a mix of confusion and aggravation.

"I'm just kidding ... Wait, are you serious? You can't smell that?" I dropped my hand and let a trickle of air enter my nose. The odor hit me like a physical slap in the face.

Alex's shoulders sagged in resignation, and she proceeded to circle me, sniffing the air like a dog greeting a new friend.

"I don't smell anything. What does it smell like?"

My eyebrows shot up. "Oh, I don't know. Something subtle. A mix of turpentine and onions garnished with a bag of sweaty gym socks. My eyes are starting to water. You seriously can't smell that?"

I put my head up. The odor seemed familiar somehow. I smelled it once before when ... My eyes flicked through the bustling crowd, scanning their belongings rather than their faces. A faint breeze came from the south, so I put my nose into the wind and started walking.

"Where are you going?" Alex held her ground, refusing to move.

"Come on. I have a hunch. You got something better to do?"

Alex threw her hands up and followed me toward the main building. I sniffed the air here and there when I had to, keeping us on track. The rest of the time I breathed through my mouth and tried not to taste the horrible greasy smell assaulting my senses.

The crowd became even more dense inside the arena. People ambled along the displays and billboards showcasing the athletes competing in this year's games. Shops and vendors occupied every available space, making it impossible for visitors to walk in a straight line without running into someone peddling beer, food, or some sort of Olympic memorabilia.

I pushed through a crowd of people holding miniature German flags. They cursed me in a short choppy language until Alex brought up the rear, bumping and staring each of the big Germans into silence.

My nose led me around a corner, through a corridor, and out into an open courtyard where more people sat at tables and enjoyed the Utah heat while they ate volumes of the aforementioned food items from all over the world. I paused a moment and let my nose zone in on the stink swirling among the other smells. When I had it, I moved to follow, but a hand grabbed the back of my coat, bringing me to a halt again.

Alex stared at a crowd of children celebrating a birthday party. They all wore bathing suits and assaulted each other with giant squirt guns and water balloons.

I grinned. "Relax. You said regular water can't hurt us. Only rain water or holy water."

Alex reached up and pushed my head toward the kids re-arming station. An old outdoor water spigot with a sign labeled, Non-Potable Rain Water, Do Not Drink. Irrigation only.

"How environmentally responsible of them." A chill ran up my spine. I'd almost walked right through the middle of that minefield. "What do they water in here, concrete and asphalt?"

Alex shrugged, and we backed away slow and easy. "Don't know, don't care. Let's just go around. Way around."

I nodded. I could use the exercise.

We rounded the aqua death party, and my nostrils reacquired the trail near a day use rental area. A clerk stood behind a counter where rows of strollers and wagons remained corralled inside a blue chain link fence. He looked positively suicidal with enthusiasm. Past that were the lockers. Huge red metal boxes covered an Olympic mural that formed the bulk of the open rear wall. The onion turpentine odor became so strong we almost swam in it. Nothing stopped the pervasive odor from seeping in. It was like diving underwater and trying not to drown by plugging my nose and breathing through my mouth. Then I discovered why. Durian fruit.

The aromatic dumpster rot wafted off the rind as Jake dropped it onto the floor. Max shoved his face into another huge piece and took a bite as if he held a ripe red watermelon. I gagged and had to slap a hand over my mouth to keep from throwing up.

The fingers of Max's free hand worked the combination on one of the big red lockers.

"You have got to be kidding me." Alex stared at the two stooges. "How did you do that?"

I shrugged. "I guess I have a nose for stupid." I gagged again and turned my head to the side.

"Are you alright?" Alex seemed to realize how exposed we were. She grabbed my arm and hauled me back, forcing me to duck low and blend with the crowd. Max and Jake stood less than twenty yards away. Hundreds of people roamed the area, but a single wayward glance in the wrong direction would blow our cover.

We made our way around to a kiosk selling hats and t-shirts, where we had a clear view of what Max and Jake were up to without casting a spotlight on ourselves. Max finished his fruit and dropped his rind on the floor, then he reached into the locker to pull out a heavy-duty briefcase.

"Your luck astounds me." Alex pretended to try on a hat covered in pink rhinestones and peered across the crowd.

"This is just how I planned it." I didn't bother acting like I was browsing. I was too busy plastering my hand against my face, then it hit me. The smell was gone.

I pulled my hand away and gave the air a tentative sniff. When my sinuses didn't revolt and try to escape through my eyes, I took a deep breath and almost laughed with relief.

"The contagion has to be in that briefcase," Alex said, inter- rupting my celebration. "They haven't deployed it yet."

I nodded and glanced at a very suspicious cashier who had taken a sudden and keen interest in our conversation. I smiled, took the hat off of Alex's head and set it back on the rack. There was a beer stand closer to the lockers, and I got ready to sprint in that direction. "Stay here, and when I give you a signal, find a way to distract them."

Alex looked at me. "And what are you going to do?"

"I'm not really sure," I admitted. "But we have to steal that briefcase."

CHAPTER THIRTY-EIGHT

"I'm not really the distraction type." Alex crossed her arms and shifted her gaze to the crowd behind us.

I rounded on her. "Not the distraction type? You are a tattooed supermodel with blue hair. The Las Vegas strip is less distracting."

I tensed everything from my toes to my eyeballs and spread my feet, ready to run toward the nearby beer stand. "We don't have time to argue. If we lose them again, we might not get another chance. We need to separate them from that—package," I said, still aware of the kiosk merchant straining to hear our hushed conversation.

Alex didn't move. Her gaze drifted off, and she cocked her head, grinning as if she had settled into some sort of amusing daydream. I began to wonder if she had heard a word I said, then she reached into her pocket, pulled out the twenty the farmer gave her on the way here, and shrugged. "I'll be back."

I was stunned to momentary stillness as Alex hurried into the crowd behind us. I took a breath to shout her name and held it. She would hear me. I was so angry half the stadium would hear me, but Jake and Max would too. I let the breath out with a deep growl of frustration. What was I supposed to do now? Sit here and wait for something to happen? Hope she came back to explain her plan? The one that involved parts that were more comfortable and convenient to her?

I trained my eyes on the two stooges. She had sixty seconds. After that, I would head over with or without her.

Max lugged the industrial briefcase to a tall bar table nearby, and they both sat down to stare at their phones. Jake looked like a toddler in a highchair while Max enveloped his stool like bread dough dropped on a sixteen-penny nail.

Neither of them spoke, but each rested an arm on that briefcase. The Stooges may have their faults—lots of faults—but they weren't stupid. Now that they had the case, it would to take a miracle to wrench the contagion out of their hands.

I considered the feasibility of a smash and grab ... Well, more of just a grab, when a small yellow sphere hurled past my head, pelting me with something that felt like a million staples dipped in battery acid. I winced and jerked away, a millennium too late to do any good. My heel caught the edge of a curb, forcing me to perform an arm-flailing clown yoga stunt to keep from landing flat on my back. I still ended up on my butt.

The owner of the hat kiosk fired off an impressive international cursing stream I didn't understand. I was thankful the chopped profanity wasn't aimed at me. She passed my seated position with several shuffling steps, almost knocking off her rhinestone Olympic sun-visor as she waved her arms.

I got to my feet and dared a peek over the sparkling display to search for the attackers, but the assault had already passed. A dozen swimsuit clad children, screaming like berserker banshees. Several of them held colorful water balloon grenades, much like the one that had threatened to crater my head, and each had some sort of insane looking water gun. They packed everything from lime green sub-compact machine water guns to huge orange water bazookas. Beauties I couldn't have conceived of in my wildest adolescent wet dreams.

Jake and Max considered the oncoming horde with dispassion at first, then the first balloon grenade hit the concrete at their feet. Max must have had some exposed skin, because he stood up, spit the bar chair out of his butt cheeks, and tumbled over backward. Jake took a second or two longer to catch on. But when he saw Max scrambling along the french-fry encrusted floor, his tiny brain made the circuit, and he jumped down to help his friend.

"You kids beat it." Jake tried to sound menacing, but his voice came out so high, he sounded more like an elderly grandmother scolding her cats. The kids cackled and advanced with relentless abandon. They were within firing range now, and Jake had to know it.

Max managed to right his massive bulk, so Jake went for the briefcase. His hand touched the handle as a purple water grenade exploded on top of the table. Jake screamed. This time he sounded more like the cats than the old lady, and the kids took aim with their water cannons and opened fire. Jake and Max abandoned their package and ran through the crowd, knocking people down as they went. The kids pursued like a band of giggling mercenary maniacs. I couldn't blame them. Grownups didn't offer that kind of reaction every day.

A kid bringing up the rear swung his dripping cannon around to be sure no one flanked their position, then he waved a twenty-dollar bill and flashed a thumbs up. I thought he was looking at me, so I returned the gesture with an awkward thumbs up of my own, then I turned around to see Alex standing behind me, arms crossed over her chest.

"So, are you just going to stand there with your thumb up in the air, or are you going to get over there?"

I gave her an awestruck nod. "You almost killed me. That was amazing." I let out a manic stream of laughter.

Alex dropped her arms and lost her composure as well. "If I could replay that for the rest of eternity, I would be happy."

We ran for the briefcase, skipping through the reformed chaos of the crowd, and got to the table at the same time. I reached for the handle and jerked back with a hiss of frustration. The briefcase, the table, the chairs, even the floor was soaking wet with rain water.

"I wish they'd been a little more accurate," I said.

"Picky, picky. Just grab a few napkins."

I snatched a chrome dispenser off an adjoining table and proceeded to tear out the little brown napkins like a kitten on a toilet paper roll rampage. When I had enough, I reached for the latch and pushed the little metal squares to the side. We both held our breath. Nothing happened.

"It's locked." My gaze shot over to Alex.

"I'll go find a knife or something. Maybe we can break the case open." Alex started to leave, but I stopped her.

"We can't break the case." I lowered my voice so only Alex could hear me. "If they think someone tampered with their cargo, they might not carry on with the mission. This is too important to chance a simple screw-up like that. We have to make them think everything is just as they left it, or they might request fresh samples of the contagion."

Alex threw out her hands. "We have to do something."

I peered at the case. The locks seemed solid. At least solid for a high-end travel suitcase. We could open it, but the latches would look like we went at them with a crowbar. I spun the case around and studied the bottom. The hinges were exposed—bare metal to accent the brushed aluminum finish of the case. I dried them as best I could, set an index finger on the end of each one and closed my eyes.

"What are you doing?" Alex said. "They could be back any second."

I moved my fingers in tiny little circles, feeling the rounded end of the hinge pins become pitted, then rough. I concentrated harder, focusing all my anger and frustration into the metal.

"Gabe, if you don't open your eyes and tell me what you're doing, I'm going to pry them open with a spork."

I pulled my hands away from the briefcase to reveal two off-colored circles to the right of each hinge.

"What did you do?"

I shrugged. "I rusted off the end of the hinge pins. We should be able to slip them out and open the case without breaking the locks on the other side, if we're careful. We'll need a couple of toothpicks to push them through."

Alex grabbed my face and kissed me on the lips. "You are a genius."

I cleared my throat and tried not to act like she hit me with a stun-gun. "Uh, you're welcome."

We worked the pins out with relative ease and got the top open far enough to see the interior. The case held two innocuous looking aerosol spray cans cradled in foam padding. White with a strange tip on the end. I glanced up and realized how many people would die if one of those cans ruptured or even spritzed a few drops into the air. All of a sudden, those innocent containers seemed more like atom bombs than aerosol cans.

"I take it back," I said. "We have to get this out of here. We can't chance them getting away with these things. They'll think someone snatched their briefcase and head back to the Agency, but at least we'll have more time to come up with a plan."

Alex held up a finger and searched the large shopping areas around us. She seemed to spot something, and for the second time, she ran into the crowd without any explanation. We really needed to work on our communication skills. "If she comes back with more water-guns ..."

I didn't have time to finish my sentence. Alex held two aerosol cans in her hands. The tips on top resembled the ones in the briefcase. The labels read Nasamist Isotonic Saline Spray. "For the natural relief of dry stuffy nose," Alex recited with a cheesy car-sales grin.

The cans were a little smaller and shaped a bit different, but if Jake and Max hadn't seen them, they wouldn't know the difference. Alex tore the plastic labels off the saline spray, and I reached into the case to retrieve the contagion bombs.

"Be careful with those," Alex said.

I wanted to throw her a comeback, but sweat ran down my head like Niagara Falls and my palms felt as though they had been slathered in butter. Witty retorts didn't seem prudent.

Alex slipped the decoy cans into their cradled slots in the briefcase and let the lid fall back into place, spraying little droplets of water all over the back of my hands.

I hissed through my teeth, and Alex glanced up at the sound. "Pull yourself together. You look like you're about to hyperventilate. Put those things in your pocket before something happens to make you drop them."

I let out a grumbling laugh and slid a can into each of my outside pockets while Alex pushed the hinge pins back in place. It had only been a few minutes, and other than a couple of inconspicuous looking ovals etched into chrome accent band encircling the case, everything looked exactly the same as the stooges left it. The bustling crowd never gave us a second glance, and the kids kept Max and Jake busy long enough for us to do our business. I felt a smile tug the edge of my lips as we turned to make our clean getaway, then my face fell. "I just had a terrible thought."

Alex stared at me. "What?"

"Those kids. We sent them running after some of the most ruthless agents in The Nine. What if Max and Jake do something horrible to them?"

Alex laughed. "They won't. Something like that would draw too much attention. If those two idiots lay one hand on those kids, a thousand cameras are going to record their faces from every angle. Their days as Judas agents will be over. Every law enforcement Agency in the country would be looking for the two men who attacked a group of innocent children at the Olympic games."

My smile returned, and I stopped next to a door marked, Break Room—Employees Only. "Let's wait in here until our buddies get back. We can keep an eye on the case and make sure they take the bait before we leave."

Alex nodded. "Good idea. I wouldn't mind seeing them walk away with it."

I reached for the door, but it shot open before I could touch the handle.

"Oh, don't you worry, princess." Max said, his huge bulk all but blocking the entire opening. "You'll see us walk away with everything we need."

CHAPTER THIRTY-NINE

M ax reached out and wrapped my jacket, and about a thousand chest hairs, into his meaty fist. I sailed through the air amidst a sea of vending machines and countertop microwaves to enter the break room head first. Confusion, disbelief, and panic twisted my tongue and prevented me from uttering more than a shocked little peep. My hands went to my pockets out of instinct, protecting my volatile cargo, leaving my face to lead the way through an array of cheap chairs, condiment holders, and one surprisingly sturdy wood table.

My vision blurred, and I went down like a sack of doorknobs.

"Leave him alone."

I blinked a dozen time in rapid succession and managed to clear my head enough to see Alex throw a high kick at Max's face. He ducked, but the move allowed Alex enough room to skirt past and squeeze into the room. Max let out a chuckle and slammed the door, locking it as Alex took up a protective position in front of me.

"Are you okay?" She chanced a quick glance down and grimaced. "Might want to fix your shoulder and stand up."

I staggered to my feet and reached toward a burning sensation in my shoulder. Something sharp bit at my fingers. A large piece of glass from a broken serving tray. It must have been on the table that used my face to slow my body's forward momentum. It was jammed back to the counter now, and the rest of the tray was nowhere to be seen. The wound wasn't as painful as it looked, so I pulled the glass out with a quick jerk. The foolish move escalated the previously tolerable pain to black out levels and garnished it with a teaspoon of lemon and rock salt. I staggered back a couple of steps, trying to steady myself, and peered down to see my skin already mending. The sight of my exposed tissue melding together like slimy goo did not improve my queasy unease, but I was all at once thankful that we were Topside instead of down under in The Nine.

"I'll be taking the canisters you have stored in your pretty little raincoat." Max stood in front of the door, one hand at his side, the other behind his back. "Don't bother pretending you don't have them. I watched you and your girlfriend make the switch."

I shrugged. "Yeah, but unless I've forgotten something, you have a problem."

"What's that?"

I took a step forward and stood next to Alex again. "Correct me if I'm wrong, but you told me the only two ways for us to die up here are to run through a rain water slushy or be attacked by another agent's manifested power."

"Well, those aren't the only ways," Alex said. "But I think they're the only ones that matter right now."

"Good enough for me." I turned my eyes back to Max. "Seems to me the only thing you have to fight with is your overdeveloped sense of meal portions. You rung my bell pretty good, but you caught us by surprise. If memory serves, the last time you tangled with my girlfriend here, you wound up face down, wheezing in the dirt."

Alex glanced over at me. "Girlfriend?"

I leaned toward her and whispered, "Dramatic effect." I made sure my voice was loud enough to benefit Big Max as well.

Max never lost his smile. I pretended it didn't bother me, but the fact that nothing I said seemed to faze him had me a little worried. Since Alex shifted into a fighting stance, I could only assume she had that same crawly sensation inching up the back of her neck.

Max took a step in our direction, still holding that foreboding hand behind his back. "I'll give you credit. That thing with the kids. That was a cute trick, but Jake and I have been doing this awhile. Long enough to get the drop on a couple of pups like you."

Max shifted his gaze to Alex. "I am a little disappointed that you didn't notice my new outfit. I wore this just for you."

"Greasy chic? You always wear that stupid jumpsuit."

Max made a show of smoothing the front of his mechanic unitard. "Look close. I made a little change after our last dance. This one is made out of Nomex. It's fireproof."

The crawly feeling on my neck crept down my back and took hold of my spine.

"Plus, I think the lighter color brings out my eyes. They're aqua blue."

Dread became realization as Max drew one of the kid's huge bazooka water-guns out from behind his back. "I want you to know that when this is all over, I'm going to make sure the Gnashing Fields are only the first stop you'll enjoy in a long treasonous eternity of pain."

Max drew back a long plastic handle at the back of the gun and aimed the nozzle toward Alex. "Give me the cans, and I will make this fast. Make me dig them out of your wet coat, and I'll paint my name a thousand times across her face before I let her die."

Alex had her face set in an expression of pure hate, but I could see the sweat beginning to mat her perfect blue hair. "Don't make it easy for him, Gabe. He's going to do it anyway."

I peered at Alex and then back at Max. Die easy or die slow. I didn't want to die at all. Choice C, none of the above, sounded like the best option to me. I reached into my pockets with both hands and drew out the aerosol cans. They felt smooth and cold and deadly. I just felt helpless.

Max smiled and motioned toward the counter to the right. "Set them down there, and we can get this over with."

I gave Alex a worried look, but she never took her eyes off Max. I moved away from her and headed for the counter. I stopped near the breakroom sink and set the aerosol cans down. Before I turned around again, something caught my eye. The rest of the broken serving platter. The pieces must have been in the sink before we got into the room—all but the one that had ended up in my shoulder. Someone must have broken it before we got there. Almost half of the platter was still intact, a semi-circle blade of razor-sharp glass. I let my hand rest on the counter next to the sink and faced Alex. "I can't believe you talked me into this."

Alex broke her stare down death-match with Max for half a second. Just enough to glance at me and say, "Excuse me?"

"This whole thing was her idea." I gestured toward Alex. "I told her this was stupid. Risking a mission like this to get revenge for a prank you pulled on her."

Max's grin widened. "All this for me? What was it? Our little trick with your Topside bestie? That really got to you, huh? I'm flattered you went to this much trouble getting even."

"What? This was not my idea ..."

"What if I promise to help you guys." That stopped Alex in her tracks. "What if I promised to help you carry out this mission. It's not like she's been much of a mentor. I could use some real guidance out here. We can finish her off, take the cans, and complete the job."

Max looked down, seeming to consider. Alex stared searing acid in my direction. I lifted the broken platter far enough out of the sink for her to see.

Her expression never changed. She didn't even glance at it

before she turned her head back to Max. "He's just trying to save his worthless skin. He has been about as useful as a leadless pencil. Trust me, he won't be any help to you."

"Look," I said. "I don't mean to be indelicate, but if Jake met the business end of a water balloon, you might need a partner to finish the job here. I'm your best bet for a successful mission. And the party attack idea ..." I pointed at Alex again.

I watched the gears creak around in Max's head at a painfully slow pace, then his pudgy eyes crinkled to a scowl, and he waddled in my direction, keeping his water cannon trained on Alex.

"Why don't you wiggle your way over there, sweetheart? The kid here's right. I need at least two people to carry out this mission. I owe it to Jake to make a mess out of you before we go."

Max moved across the room like a force of nature, plowing through overturned chairs and tables until he had his back to me, ready to blast Alex straight to the Gnashing Fields.

"Any last words?"

"Yes. You should have waited for Jake."

I drew out the broken platter and axed the sharpened edge onto Max's exposed wrist. I put everything I had into the blow, maybe a little too much. The glass bit into Max's skin and stayed there, lodged into bone like a forearm windshield. The water gun went streaking to the floor and cracked on the hard tiles, materializing a Slip and Slide of death on the speckled linoleum.

I jumped back. Max dove forward, launching his incredible girth a solid three inches off the ground before he toppled in Alex's direction. Just enough to avoid a rain water acid bath. A floor drain drew off most of the deadly liquid, allowing his stellar long dive to work in avoiding the stream.

Alex caught Max on his way down and managed to wrap him in a triple swizzle sideways neck hold that made me wonder if she was part snake. I had a hunch Max would never be able to turn his head in a forward direction again. In the end, it didn't matter.

"Let me give you a little piece of advice," Alex growled

through clenched teeth. "Next time you try to protect yourself with something, use the whole thing. A fireproof suit doesn't do any good without the hood."

Alex pressed her hands to either side of Max's head. I reached out to stop her, but it was too late. Blazing red light came out of Max's eyes, nose, and ears. He opened his mouth as if to scream, but bright orange light showed there as well. A second later the light went out, and smoke erupted from the spaces instead, looking like windows in a dwindling house fire, spreading the sharp odors of burnt hair and charred flesh.

Alex closed her eyes and let Max's body loll to the side as she unwrapped her hold on him. She shook and tried to stand but couldn't quite make it on the first try. It took me a second to wake up and hurry over to help her.

"Are you okay?"

"Fine." She glanced down at Max and then jerked her head away, tears in her eyes. "Can we get out of here?"

I nodded and led her to the door. She faced the wall as I unlocked the deadbolt to peek outside. Nothing but the usual hustle and bustle that had been there before. "Coast is clear."

I opened the door and stepped out, leading Alex by the hand behind me.

"Wait!" I turned and steadied Alex for a second and went back into the breakroom. When I came out, I had two aerosol cans tucked into the pockets of my coat. I reached around and locked the doorknob before I let the door swing closed, then grabbed an out of order sign off of a soda machine and stuck it to the door.

"Good enough for a getaway, I hope."

Alex managed a weak smile. "There won't be anything to find in an hour anyway. His body will dry into dust. All anyone will find is a pile of sand and an oversized pair of coveralls."

"Really?" I led her around a crowd of excited French nationals watching a soccer match on one of those huge flat screen televisions. They all screamed, "Goooooooaaaaal," in unison.

"Wouldn't do us much good to leave corpses all over the place up here," Alex said. "Imagine the confusion it would cause at the census bureau."

I laughed, and Alex gained more of her composure back. "Did you notice that the suitcase was gone when we left?"

Alex glanced up at me. "Gone?"

I nodded. "Doesn't mean anything. Someone may have snatched it or turned it into lost and found, but ..."

"If Jake came back and got it, we're going to have some explaining to do at the Agency."

"If Jake has that case, we won't be the ones doing the explaining." I smiled, and we wandered toward the exit.

"You know, we have a little time ..." I nodded toward the arena.

Alex rolled her eyes. "We're not going to see if the Brazilians are playing volleyball."

CHAPTER FORTY

"Y ou ready for this?" I glanced over at Zoe, and she nodded her head. The three of us were back in The Nine, standing at the door of a well-built shanty. The place was huge. Big enough to house dozens of Woebegone. Many visited this place, but only one man called it his home.

I glanced up and down the street. Eyes watched us from every direction. Sad, used, and pathetic eyes. The eyes of the lost and wandering. Eyes of horror and doubt. I knew those eyes. They were the same ones Zoe used to look at me when I first met her. Full of terror and fear.

She didn't have those eyes any more. When I looked at her now, I saw years of sadness and anger lurking under her innocent beauty. Her appearance hadn't changed since she had regained her memory. She was still the same petite, little blonde who could charm any lowlife creep in The Nine, but her smile—her smile had changed. The innocence had been stolen away, replaced with hard wariness. Seeds of suspicion and cynicism had been planted deep and would never be rooted out completely. We were here to pay a visit to the one who had cultivated those vile weeds.

I tightened my grip on the Knuckle Stunner and let the Whip-

Crack unfurl and fall. Zoe stood to the side, and I set the blades buzzing with a flick of my wrist. The thick, whizzing cable shot forward, and the shanty door all but exploded into a shower of thin metal shards. I didn't waste any time in making my way through. Zoe followed, carrying an unassuming-looking metal box in her hands.

I took control of the large center room inside, keeping the Whip-Crack writhing and hissing at my side. I had no fear. Anger and shame had erased all that away. Anger for Zoe and Alex. The way they had been used, and the memories they would have to bear. Shame for the life I once led as one of these people, forever trying to atone for my past sins.

Doors led to rooms on the outside walls, and a metal staircase stood to our right, leading to a catwalk and more rooms on a second floor. The layout reminded me of an old west saloon and brothel—if brothels had been made out of corrugated steel and old tin.

Standing in the rear of the large room, shirtless in all his beer-gutted glory, was Scarecrow. There were a few dirty couches scattered between us. The one he scrambled over to escape was still occupied by two young women. They watched, in various stages of undress, and seemed a little too happy to be slaves in The Nine. They were unashamed, as likely to invite us in as throw us out. Scarecrow, on the other hand, wore a familiar rabbit-caught-in-a-corner expression I had come to know and love.

He turned and sprinted toward the back of the room. More of a one-legged drag really, but he did the best he could. I was happy to see our last meeting had left such an impression. The women on the couch giggled as they watched him scurry away, still not bothering to cover their naked bodies. His bare feet made a slap swish sound with every step. Somehow, he managed to kick the empty liquor bottles and drug paraphernalia out of the way as he went. There were enough bongs, mirrors, and needles in the place to supply the Hollywood elite for the next three centuries.

I swept an empty wine bottle to the side with my foot and followed Scarecrow at a casual pace. The girls on the couch smiled and winked. One stared at me, while the other studied Zoe, licking her lips like a hungry jackal.

I glanced back and saw Zoe's expression. Not angry or flirty, but knowing and sad. Scarecrow disappeared through a door at the rear of the room. Zoe and I made our way in that direction. A screech came out of the darkness where Scarecrow had gone, like a mouse caught in a trap. Several meaty thumps vibrated the floor, then a crash. Scarecrow said something about please and sorry, more thumps and more crashes.

Zoe and I waited outside the door. I pretended to check the time, and Zoe adjusted her gloves and stared at the ceiling. A few seconds later, Scarecrow came tumbling back through the door. We watched him roll by and put his hands out, simultaneously trying to defend himself and figure out which way was up.

"Please. I never did anything to you."

Alex came bounding out of the darkness behind him like a cat. She was on him before his butt stopped sliding across the floor. "Be glad you haven't. But were not here to talk about me."

Alex managed some sort of crazy roll and locked Scarecrow's neck between her thighs. His hands went up to stop her, but she threw her weight over and flipped him forward, tossing his body into the corner next to his would-be escape. He landed with a grunt, upside down and struggling to right himself, as the three of us advanced on him.

"Remember me?" Zoe said.

Scarecrow rolled over, and his nose crinkled in disgust. "This is about her? Take her. I have plenty more."

Alex balled a fist, ready to pound out the national anthem on his face, but I grabbed her arm.

"Before your mouth gets you beat into paste, we need you to understand something. You aren't giving Zoe to us. She's leaving, and there is nothing you can do about it. She's under the protection of the Judas Agency now. You will leave her alone, or face what we can bring to bear on your whole organization."

Scarecrow's gaze shot from me to Alex and then to Zoe. "Bull shit."

Zoe stepped forward and pressed her boot heel into Scarecrows splayed fingers. A scream reminiscent of a baby pig spewed from his thin lips, and he took a swing at her leg. Alex blocked his arm, reached out and wrenched his nose between her forefinger and thumb.

"I don't like that sort of language," Zoe said. "Apologize."

"Okay, okay. I'm sorry. I'm sorry."

Alex let go of his nose, and Zoe released some of the pressure from his fingers, but she did not let him pull his hand away. "As my friend was saying, I'm leaving. And if I were you, I would find another line of work. I know I'll never stop people like you, but I'm going to make it my mission to find your kind and make their lives a living Hell within Hell."

I smiled and pulled an envelope out of my pocket. The wide manila had been labeled with my cousins' names, Franco and Charlie. "In case you have trouble remembering our conversation later, this note goes over the particulars. It's important your bosses know what we talked about."

"Trust me." Scarecrow glared at us. "I won't forget any of you."

Alex and I straightened and took a step back.

"I'm not sure," I said. "You know how it is when things get —stressful."

Zoe popped the latch on the metal box she had been cradling throughout the ordeal.

"Details are lost, names get confused," I continued. "We just want to make sure everyone gets what's coming to them."

Zoe reached into her box and let it clatter to the floor at her feet. In her gloved hand, she held a pink water-balloon the size of a ripe cantaloupe. Scarecrow's eyes narrowed with confusion for a moment, then they shot wide with terror. I wedged the letter in the door frame. Someone would make sure my cousins got it. Alex and I headed toward the exit. First, a shout, then a splash followed by lots of screams, then Scarecrow didn't scream anymore. The two girls on the couch watched us go, still grinning with oblivious fascination. Zoe caught up, grabbed them by the hair and pulled them up. "Time for a little tough love, ladies. If I am going to start somewhere, I may as well start with the two of you."

She passed us, dragging the giggling half-naked women in her wake. Alex and I looked at each other as she disappeared out the door.

"All of a sudden, you don't look so tough," I said.

Alex cracked a smile on one side of her mouth. "Anytime you want to try me, just let me know."

CHAPTER FORTY-ONE

I opened the front window to the shop for the first time in what felt like an eternity. The foul air had an almost visceral feel, and the cold hovered somewhere near sub-testicle freezing. I watched a Woebegone with no pants stride down the street and another on the upper catwalk, trying on a pair of shiny, new rag-slacks. It felt good to be home.

A movement caught my eye just below the level of the window. When I leaned forward to see what it was, my heart turned to stone. Mastema crouched just out of sight, poised like a cat ready to strike. Her clawed hands were stained in blood, and more of the crimson gore streaked her face and lips just under her ever-present blindfold. She moved her non-seeing gaze in my direction, showing her jagged teeth. She had been hunting.

I couldn't even force myself to react. My hands locked onto the cold steel countertop, and I clenched my teeth so hard my head began to vibrate. If Judas wanted me dead, fine, but he didn't have to send Mastema to my home. To Zoe and Alex. This had nothing to do with them.

I managed to open my mouth, ready to say something, but

Mastema put a gory finger to her lips to shush me. She reached back to slip something out of her spiked bikini armor. Maybe if I died quietly, she would forget about Zoe and Alex back in the bus behind me. She revealed the item with a flourish. I braced myself for some sort of blow, then let out a breath and stared in confusion.

Mastema didn't have a weapon, not that she needed one. She held a cloth, a scarf—not just any scarf. Mastema had my cousin's ridiculous yellow scarf in her clawed hand.

She ran the fabric across her cheek, throwing her head back as if in ecstasy, then I noticed the blood soaking the second half of the bright yellow fabric. It looked as if her hunt had been a success.

Mastema snapped her head back toward me and then tossed the ruined cloth to the ground, revealing an even wider grin as the realization of my cousin's death washed over my face. Then without another word, she spun and loped away. She stayed low, moving with the grace of a jungle ape, then spread her wings to take flight. I hadn't noticed, but Woebegone in the area were conspicuously absent around my shop. Now that Mastema had moved on, I heard terror filled screams fill the air as she streaked above the shanty rooftops and disappeared.

"Those bastards wiped us out." Zoe hopped out of the old bus, crinkling an empty Twinkie wrapper in her hand. "They even took your locket."

I let out a screech and spun around to face her.

Zoe stopped in her tracks. "What's wrong with you? Your face is whiter than Casper's ass."

"Nothing's wrong." I tried to regain my composure, but my brain still seemed to be rebooting. "I just can't believe they took my locket. What are they going to do with something like that?"

"Nothing." Alex stepped off the bus behind Zoe and leaned against the battered door jamb. "They took it because they could, and because the locket belonged to you."

"I'm sure I'll get lots of chances to pay them back." I turned around and propped the other window open, taking an opportunity to calm my nerves and make sure Mastema had left the building. That was one encore I did not want to see.

"How are our guests doing in the bus?" I eyed the open door and tried to regain a little of my home-happy smile. Zoe had brought the two girls from Scarecrow's pleasure palace and insisted we keep them until they recovered from whatever ordeal they had been through.

"They're coming down hard," Zoe said. "Scarecrow had them so doped up they forgot they were in The Nine—literally. They thought this was all a dream, and Scarecrow was some kind of billionaire gigolo."

"Wonder where they got that idea." I sneered. "At least they have room to crash now that the bus is empty." The words came out more venomous than I had intended. None of this was Zoe's fault, but when it came to my shop, sometimes it was tough to resist lashing out at any available target. "Have you come up with something to do with the girls once you scare them straight? We can't house the entire Woebegone population in my broken-down bus."

Zoe curled her upper lip and looked like she was about to say something more than a little nasty—which I probably deserved. But she took a breath and relaxed. "No, but I will. Don't worry."

She started to turn away, but she paused and faced me again. "I'm sorry. I still have trouble sorting through things sometimes."

I nodded. "Take all the time and space you need. You all deserve it."

Zoe gave me a weak smile and stepped through the opening to go outside.

"You better be careful." Alex reached over to help Zoe lift the door off the ground and break my sad stare. "Threatening your cousins' organization, even with the Judas Agency behind us on this, will only slow them down for a while. Sooner or later, they'll figure out you're on your own out here. When they do, they'll be looking for payback."

"Let 'em come." Zoe slammed the door against the wall, jerking it out of Alex's fingers. "I'm an old hand at the Gnashing Fields. If they think they're going to take me without a fight, I'll serve them up a Whip-Crack course in severed limb anatomy. This girl doesn't take any shit, especially from some lowlife Disposable dealers who think they can pick me up and smoke me like a carton of old Marlboros."

Alex and I blinked. Neither of us had gotten used to Zoe's new persona. She still looked like Stray, and even held onto many of her kind and caring traits, but when her darker side peeked through, Zoe was a whole different person.

I couldn't help but glance out my window at the bloodied scarf again. "Something tells me we won't see them again, at least not anytime soon."

"It doesn't matter," Zoe said. "They can bring an army, but they aren't running me out of my home."

"Your home?" I grinned. "I don't remember signing over a mortgage. Did we get married when I wasn't looking?"

I felt Alex's eyes on me and wished I hadn't said that last part.

"You wish," Zoe said. "And I think I've earned a corner in this little hole of yours. Besides what are you going to do, close the place up while you're out on your top-secret missions? Find someone else to run it? I don't think so."

"Maybe I'll just close the shop down."

"Go ahead. That'll just mean less competition for me when I open up my own shop. The Woebegone around here like me better than you anyway."

Alex smiled. "I really like her."

I narrowed my eyes and glared at Zoe. "Yeah. I guess I like her too. It's worthless, but you can have half the shop."

Zoe tried to contain her smile, but I saw a bit of Stray struggling to escape around the edges. "Gee thanks. Half of an empty shop. I should be charging you for getting this place off the ground again."

"You know," Alex walked over to the fallen heat curtain and gathered the heavy fabric in a long strip over her hand. "Some of the apartments at the Judas Agency are pretty big. It wouldn't be unheard of to have two people staying in one place. I could put a good word in for you and see if they would let Zoe stay."

I turned and stared at Alex. "You would try to get Zoe and me into an apartment at the Judas Agency—to live together—in the same place?"

Alex glared back at me. "What difference does it make if you're here or there? At least in an apartment you don't have to worry about the fire storms or Disposable dealers sneaking up on you."

Zoe answered before I could open my mouth. "Thanks, but I think I'm going to stay here. I like running the shop, and I'm not afraid of handling those dealers. Besides, what would I do with my groupies back there?" Zoe gestured toward the rear door in the shop.

"You sure?" I looked at her. "There could be a lot of heat around the corner."

"We'll have to deal with that when it happens."

I shrugged. "I guess we're holding the fort down here."

The Woebegone didn't have much. For some of them, this shop was all they had to look forward to. I didn't want to abandon it, either. Besides, I got the feeling Judas might be coming to appreciate my unorthodox methods. Sending Mastema to pluck my cousin out of the population was his way of saying I had done a good job. Or maybe he had the gore princess bloody her hands as a warning not to screw up again. Either way, Franco was off our tail, for now, and we had time to rebuild and reset. Zoe was right. We would deal with the rest when it came. In the meantime, I would keep doing my job with Alex at the Judas Agency.

"I thought you might turn me down, but I figured I'd offer," Alex said. "You did a decent job out there. You earned it."

"Thanks, boss." I smirked. "You didn't do so bad yourself."

"Don't push your luck," Alex said, but she had a smile on her face.

"Seriously. Thank you for all you did. You didn't have to help me get Zoe or stop Max and Jake."

Alex snorted. "It was worth it just to see them bolt when those kids showed up."

All three of us laughed, even Zoe.

Our laughter eventually died, replaced by an awkward silence, then Alex shrugged and broke the spell. "I'm glad we helped Zoe." She winked over at her. "Turns out she's a pretty cool chick. And I would do anything to get one over on those two stooges. All you have to do is ask."

I nodded, deciding not to challenge her motivations. I knew she was happy to stick it to the stooges whenever she could, but I suspected there was a beating heart that cared about the people Topside as well.

"I have a little time." Alex finished gathering the heat blanket and fastened it into its spot on the ceiling. "I'll help you two piece this shack together before I head back. We can at least make sure the door will lock." She patted the door, and it slid down to the ground with a crash.

"Maybe you should let me handle the door," I said. "You're better at breaking than fixing."

"Fine," She raised her hands and stepped back from the door. "You play handyman and I'll stick to breaking faces."

I laughed. "Deal."

"Speaking of broken faces," Alex punched my arm. "I got a message that Sabnack has our next assignment. I guess there's no rest for wreaking havoc on the wicked."

"Already?" I hefted the door off the ground and tested the lock. "Maybe we'll get to do something good on this job."

Alex laughed. "Like that would ever happen. We work for the Disaster Factory not the Girl Scouts."

"Yeah." I shoved the door back into its frame and replaced the heavy pins. "But a guy can dream."

Not ready to leave The Nine?
Read New Dominion Now

FIND OUT JUDAS' TOPSIDE POWER
IN THIS FREE SHORT STORY

Download EXILED now

When Judas finds out one of his agents has gone rogue, he must go Topside to personally deal with him; even if that means wielding his own power and facing the past that haunts him.

Exiled, a short story in the world of The Judas Files, follows Judas on a Topside mission where he must face his own demons.

Download EXILED now (https://BookHip.com/JZLRATN)

THANKS FOR READING!

Did you love *The Nine?* Join the C.G. Harris Legion to stay up to date on upcoming books, receive book intel, useless trivia, special giveaways, plus you'll learn about Hula Harry and get his Drink of the Week. https://www.cgharris.net/legion-sign-up-page

Let other readers know what you thought of, The Nine, by Leaving a Review

Find out what Gabe and Alex are up to next. Read chapter one of *New Dominion*, book 2 in The Judas Files.

Buy Book 2 Now:
NEW DOMINION

NEW DOMINION

Chapter One

"Errand boys." I tugged at the collar of my shirt, trying to loosen the noose-tight tie around my neck. "We work for the most terrifying agency in the world ... underworld ... and now we're Topside playing the part of overdressed mailmen."

"Speak for yourself." Alex smoothed her tailored black jacket and sleek pants then shifted her briefcase from one hand to the other. "I make this look good."

I couldn't argue, but I wouldn't let her know that. "Even without the hair?" I pointed to the auburn wig she used to camouflage her Ty-D-Bol blue-colored locks.

She narrowed her eyes at me and glanced at the suit I had chosen for the occasion. "At least I didn't come dressed as a pallbearer at a gangster's funeral."

"What's wrong with what I have on?" I peered down at my ensemble, brushing off the collar.

"Double breasted pinstripes went out in the 1920s. All you're missing is the fedora."

"The classics never go out of style."

"A 67' Camaro is a classic. You look like a pimp for a geriatric home."

I shot her a glare in place of a witty comeback. A sure sign I didn't have one. The awkward silence stretched as we scrutinized the tiny, boring office we waited in. Desk, filing cabinet, drooping ficus in the corner that hadn't seen a drop of water since the last ice age.

"So, what's in that fancy briefcase?" I couldn't take it anymore. If I had to endure one more moment of silence, I would dive out the seven-story window and take the ficus with me.

"I have no idea." She held the case up and looked it over.

"You didn't even check it out?" I asked. "It could be anything. A bomb, an envelope full of money, or puppies."

"Puppies?" She rolled her eyes. "Nothing is ticking—or barking. And it's locked. I already tried."

I started to suggest a more aggressive investigative tactic, but I was cut short when the office door opened. A man walked in wearing a bright smile and casual dress, making our monkey suits appear even more out of place.

He seemed to be in his mid-forties with salt and pepper hair. Clean, but not slicked back and spit shined like your typical CEO executive. This guy looked like your buddy next door. He had his sleeves rolled up and collar loose, ready to lend a hand to whatever job needed doing. I adjusted my tie again, suddenly feeling suffocated.

"Nicholas Powel." He reached out to shake our hands, meeting our gaze with infectious enthusiasm.

"I'm Gabe Gantry, and this is my associate, Alexandrea Neveu."

Alex's sudden glare made me grin. She hated it when I used her full name.

"Please, call me Alex."

"Alex, it is." Nick hurried around to the other side of a desk littered with papers, files, and coffee mugs. "Please forgive my mess. I was here pretty late last night working on some last-minute requests from the DEA."

I raised an eyebrow. Alex and I had been briefed about some sort of medical tech Nick had in the works, but that's all we knew. Considering we were sent up to play the part of an advanced, ultra-secure research firm, vague details didn't feel like enough to sell it. Then again, when you took your marching orders from a lion-headed demon, you didn't ask too many questions either.

The Nine, a name we locals crafted in an attempt to warm up Hell's PR problems, wasn't at the end of any rainbow, but after forty years, I still managed to carve out a cozy armpit to exist in. That was, until Judas Iscariot recruited me into his agency. He was in the business of delivering disasters, death, and destruction to those living Topside. Imagine my surprise when he also informed me that I would be moonlighting as a wrench in the operation. He wanted me to work as a double agent, to find and stop the worst disasters from ever happening.

I couldn't tell anyone about my gold star position, of course. That would be too easy. I reached into my pocket and fingered the single denarius that bonded me to Judas and his calling. Betray the secret, and it would suck my soul into an abyss that made Hell seem like a preschool with extra finger paints. It made the daily grind a challenge, and not knowing what my grubby little hands were into was never a good start.

"The DEA, they can be real sticklers, can't they?" My ridiculous ploy to tease out more information drew a sideways glare from Alex. Her eyes practically screamed the adage about ignorance and bliss.

Nick let out a cynical laugh and nodded as he shuffled through his papers and stacked them in messy piles all over his desk. He glanced up at us again, and the manic smile on his face was so big I had to fight taking a step back.

"I suppose there's no harm in telling you. Everyone will know soon enough." He straightened and looked around the room as if eavesdroppers hid inside the tiny office somewhere. "They approved our treatments this morning, on a preliminary basis anyway. They are still awaiting the clinical trials from your firm, of course."

He glanced down at the briefcase Alex held in her hand. She had her hand clutched around the handle, leaning into Nick's every word. So much for the whole ignorance and bliss thing. She stared at him, her brows knitted in concentration and confusion.

After an awkward pause, she snapped out of it. "Yes. Of course. I'm sorry." She handed him the case. "I think this should be everything. Why don't you check while we're still here?"

I grinned at her, and she shot me a quick glare, all but daring me to say something. I knew she was just as curious.

Nick flopped the case over onto the smallest stack of papers on his desk. After fumbling with the code, the top popped open. With a single hand, Nick retrieved a fat envelope full of paperwork as though it were a priceless Fabergé egg. He turned it over in his hands, his smile never losing an ounce of its feverish delight.

"I can't tell you how much I appreciate you delivering this data in person. When you're dealing with something this ground-break-ing, security is so important. Allowing any of this to leak onto the internet could be catastrophic."

"We understand completely." Alex shot him a rueful smile. "Our firm is all about discretion, and we will always do our best to meet your needs." She pointed at the case. "We also backed up the data to a portable drive, per your request. Everything was done on isolated servers of cour—"

Alex cut off as Nick pulled something else from the briefcase. An odd-looking little doll about the size of a Christmas tree orna-ment. It seemed to be made of wrapped twine with old nails stuck in for arms and legs. The weird little thing had a rough face drawn onto its round head, two dots for eyes, and a curved line for a smile. It looked so creepy. I was glad Nick had the mini monster in his hand rather than mine.

"I can't believe you remembered." He let out a chuckle.

This time Alex's eyebrows shot up, but Nick didn't notice. He already had the phone in his hand, dialing a four-digit extension.

"Ryan, would you mind coming in here for a moment?"

"This is perfect." Nick caressed the strange, little figure.

Alex stared at him as if she was watching someone chew glass. I almost snorted with laughter.

The door to Nick's office opened without a knock, and in stepped a young Japanese looking man with short, black hair. A thin beard highlighted his chin, and he wore a red polo shirt with beige slacks. Despite being neat, everything seemed a little off somehow.

"Gabe, Alex, I would like you to meet Ryan. He is the true hero behind everything here."

Ryan did not move from the doorway. He just stood there, hands clasped, his gaze diverted to the ground, rocking back and forth. He glanced up, never really meeting our eyes, offered a smile, then peered at the floor again.

"Have you seen my glasses?" Ryan squinted without ever looking around. "I can't find my glasses. I need my glasses to see."

Nick let out a little chuckle. "I'll help you find your glasses in a few minutes. Look at what these nice people brought for you."

Ryan's eyes shot up to the figure in Nick's hand, and a grin grew across his face. He walked over, plucked the doll out of Nick's palm, then stepped back to examine every inch, as if the little doll were the most complex item he had ever seen.

Ryan rushed over to Alex, quick as a cat, pinning her arms to her sides in a hug, then he hurried over to do the same to me. I went to hug him back, but Ryan managed to duck my embrace and scurried back to the door.

"Thank you, both. This is nice. I need to find my glasses."

Ryan disappeared into the hall, leaving Alex and me to gape at the open doorway in bewilderment.

Nick let us rest in our incomprehension for a moment before he answered the obvious question. "Ryan is autistic. He is also a mathematical savant in the areas of robotics and bioengineering. Out here, he has trouble with the simplest of tasks—like finding his glasses." Nick chuckled. "But put him in a lab, and that young man can work miracles the likes this world has never seen."

"You have got to be kidding," I said, then caught myself. "I mean, no disrespect intended, I just ..."

"It's all right." Nick chuckled again. "Savants like him sometimes attain an ability to hyper focus on specific things. We've been lucky enough to employ him here where he was needed most. Without Ryan, we would have never achieved the feat that will change our world."

"And what feat is that?" The words escaped my lips before I realized I had asked the question.

Alex shot me another of her trademark glares before turning a smile to Nick. She opened her mouth to cover my blunder, but before she could get anything out, Nick blurted, "Developing the cure for cancer, of course."

Keep Reading Book 2 now:
NEW DOMINION

Haven't read the other books in The Judas File series? Get them now:

The Judas Files Completed Series:

Book 1-THE NINE

Book 2-NEW DOMINION

Book 3-ARTFUL EVIL

Book 4 - WAR ORIGIN

Book 5 - FINAL RUIN

NOW ON AUDIO!
AVAILABLE ON ALL AUDIOBOOK PLATFORMS

The Judas Files are also available on audio read by award-winning narrator, MacLeod Andrews.

LISTEN TO THE AUDIOBOOKS NOW

Here's what listeners are saying:

"The book is a perfect blend of gritty thriller, heartwarming hidden hero, and dry humor. The narrator Andrews does an amazing job of bringing the characters and story to life."

"Well worth the purchase! Fantastic story by C.G. Harris, stellar narration by MacLeod Andrews."

"If you are a fan of the Dresden Files type of hero who is equal parts sassy, lovable, and punchable, then you will love Gabe. I was utterly enthralled by this envisioning of hell and the creatures who reside there. I had never imagined the underworld in this way, but it makes perfect sense. The side characters show growth and charm throughout the story, and left me wanting more. The audiobook narrator did a fantastic job with the voices and emotion throughout the story. I highly recommend this!"

A NEW SERIES BY C.G. HARRIS
THE RAX: A YA APOCALYPTIC ALIEN SCIENCE FICTION TRILOGY

When the earth becomes a base for alien drug lords, humanity's fate rests on the shoulders of a blind teen and his small band of rebels.

Book 1-OUT OF DARKNESS

Book 2-INTO THE LIGHT

Book 3-DANCE IN SHADOWS

ABOUT THE AUTHOR

C.G. Harris is an award winning science-fiction and fantasy author from Colorado who draws inspiration from favorites, Jim Butcher, Richard Kadrey and Brandson Sanderson. For nearly a decade, Harris has escaped the humdrum of the real world by creating fictional characters and made-up realities. When not writing, Harris spends time collecting the illusive arcade token, from the golden age when Dig Dug and Frogger were king. Harris knows the value of such a collection will only be seen in the confused faces of those family members left behind long after C.G. Harris is gone.

Do you have questions, comments or ideas for future plots? Contact C.G. at: CGharrisAuthor@gmail.com

Follow Me on:

Made in United States
Orlando, FL
17 August 2022

21200701R00143